THE
MALEFACTOR

E. Phillips Oppenheim

1st WORLD
LIBRARY
Literary Society

The Malefactor

E. Phillips Oppenheim

© 1st World Library – Literary Society, 2004
PO Box 2211
Fairfield, IA 52556
www.1stworldlibrary.org
First Edition

LCCN: 2005906462

Softcover ISBN: 1-4218-1520-6
Hardcover ISBN: 1-4218-1420-X
eBook ISBN: 1-4218-1620-2

Purchase *"The Malefactor"*
as a traditional bound book at:
www.1stWorldLibrary.org/purchase.asp?ISBN=1-4218-1520-6

1st World Library Literary Society is a nonprofit
organization dedicated to promoting literacy by:

- Creating a free internet library accessible from any
computer worldwide.
- Hosting writing competitions and offering book
publishing scholarships.

**Readers interested in supporting literacy
through sponsorship, donations or
membership please contact:
literacy@1stworldlibrary.org
Check us out at: www.1stworldlibrary.ORG
and start downloading free ebooks today.**

The Malefactor
contributed by Tim, Ed & Rodney
in support of
1st World Library Literary Society

CONTENTS

BOOK I

BOOK II

BOOK I

A SOCIETY SCANDAL

Tall and burly, with features and skin hardened by exposure to the sun and winds of many climates, he looked like a man ready to face all hardships, equal to any emergency. Already one seemed to see the clothes and habits of civilization falling away from him, the former to be replaced by the stern, unlovely outfit of the war correspondent who plays the game. They crowded round him in the club smoking room, for these were his last few minutes. They had dined him, toasted him, and the club loving cup had been drained to his success and his safe return. For Lovell was a popular member of this very Bohemian gathering, and he was going to the Far East, at a few hours' notice, to represent one of the greatest of English dailies.

A pale, slight young man, who stood at this right hand, was speaking. His name was Walter Aynesworth, and he was a writer of short stories - a novelist in embryo.

"What I envy you most, Lovell," he declared, "is your escape from the deadly routine of our day by day life. Here in London it seems to me that we live the life of automatons. We lunch, we dine, we amuse or we bore ourselves, and we sleep - and all the rest of the world does the same. Passion we have outgrown, emotion we have destroyed by analysis. The storms which shake humanity break over other countries. What is there left to us of life? Civilization ministers too easily to our needs, existence has become a habit. No wonder that we are a tired race."

"Life is the same, the world over," another man remarked. "With every forward step in civilization, life must become more mechanical. London is no worse than Paris, or Paris than Tokyo."

Aynesworth shook his head. "I don't agree with you," he replied. "It is the same, more or less, with all European countries, but the Saxon temperament, with its mixture of philosophy and philistinism, more than any other, gravitates towards the life mechanical. Existence here has become fossilized. We wear a mask upon our faces; we carry a gauge for our emotions. Lovell is going where the one great force of primitive life remains. He is going to see war. He is going to breathe an atmosphere hot with naked passion; he is going to rub shoulders with men who walk hand in hand with death. That's the sort of tonic we all want, to remind us that we are human beings with blood in our veins, and not sawdust-stuffed dolls."

Then Lovell broke silence. He took his pipe from his mouth, and he addressed Aynesworth.

"Walter," he said, "you are talking rot. There is nothing very complex or stimulating about the passion of war, when men kill one another unseen; where you feel the sting in your heart which comes from God knows where, and you crumple up, with never a chance to have a go at the chap who has potted you from the trenches, or behind a rock, a thousand yards off. Mine is going to be, except from a spectacular point of view, a very barren sort of year, compared with what yours might be if the fire once touched your eyes. I go where life is cruder and fiercer, perhaps, but you remain in the very city of tragedies."

Aynesworth laughed, as he lit a fresh cigarette.

"City of tragedies!" he exclaimed. "It sounds all right, but it's bunkum all the same. Show me where they lie, Lovell, old chap. Tell me where to stir the waters."

Several of those who were watching him noticed a sudden change in Lovell's face. The good humor and bonhomie called up by this last evening amongst his old friends had disappeared. His face had fallen into graver lines, his eyes seemed fixed with a curious introspective steadiness on a huge calendar which hung from the wall. When at last he turned towards Aynesworth, his tone was almost solemn.

"Some of them don't lie so very far from the surface, Walter , " he said. "There is one" - he took out his watch - "there is one which, if you like, I will tell you about. I have just ten minutes."

"Good!"

"Go ahead, Lovell, old chap!"

"Have a drink first!"

He held out his hand. They were all silent. He stood up amongst them, by far the tallest man there, with his back to the chimney piece, and his eyes still lingering about that calendar.

"Thirteen years ago ," he said, "two young men - call

them by their Christian names, Wingrave and Lumley - shared a somewhat extensive hunting box in Leicestershire. They were both of good family, well off, and fairly popular, Lumley the more so perhaps. He represented the ordinary type of young Englishman, with a stronger dash than usual of selfishness. Wingrave stood for other things. He was reticent and impenetrable. People called him mysterious."

Lovell paused for a moment to refill his pipe. The sudden light upon his face, as he struck a match, seemed to bring into vivid prominence something there, indescribable in words, yet which affected his hearers equally with the low gravity of his speech. The man himself was feeling the tragedy of the story he told.

"They seemed," he continued, "always to get on well together, until they fell in love with the same woman. Her name we will say was Ruth. She was the wife of the Master of Hounds with whom they hunted. If I had the story-writing gifts of Aynesworth here, I would try to describe her. As I haven't, I will simply give you a crude idea of what she seemed like to me.

"She was neither dark nor fair, short nor tall; amongst a crowd of other women, she seemed undistinguishable by any special gifts; yet when you had realized her there was no other woman in the room. She had the eyes of an angel, only they were generally veiled; she had the figure of a miniature Venus, soft and with delicate curves, which seemed somehow to be always subtly asserting themselves, although she affected in her dress an almost puritanical simplicity. Her presence in a room was always felt at once. There are some women, beautiful or plain, whose sex one scarcely recognizes. She was not one of these! She seemed to carry with her the concentrated essence of femininity. Her quiet movements, the almost noiseless rustling of her clothes, the quaint, undistinguishable perfumes which she used, her soft, even voice, were all things which seemed individual to her. She was like a study in undernotes, and yet" - Lovell paused a moment - "and yet no Spanish dancing woman, whose dark eyes and voluptuous figure have won her the crown of the demi-monde, ever possessed that innate and mystic gift of kindling passion like that woman. I told you I couldn't describe her! I can't! I can only speak of effects. If my story interests you, you must build up your own idea of her."

"Becky Sharpe!" Aynesworth murmured.

Lovell nodded.

"Perhaps," he admitted, "only Ruth was a lady. To go on with my story. A hunting coterie, as you fellows know, means lots of liberty, and a general free-and-easiness amongst the sexes, which naturally leads to flirtations more or less serious. Ruth's little affairs were either too cleverly arranged, or too harmless for gossip. Amongst the other women of the hunt, she seemed outwardly almost demure. But one day - there was a row!"

Lovell paused, and took a drink from a glass by his side.

"I hope you fellows won't think that I'm spinning this out," he said. "It is, after all, in itself only a commonplace story, but I've carried it locked up in my memory for years, and now that I've let it loose, it unwinds itself slowly. This is how the row came about. Lumley one afternoon missed Wingrave and Ruth from the hunting field. Someone most unfortunately happened to tell him that they had left the run together, and had been seen riding together towards White Lodge, which was the name of the house where these two young men lived. Lumley followed them. He rode into the stable yard, and found there Ruth's mare and Wingrave's covert hack, from which he had not changed when they had left the field. Both animals had evidently been ridden hard, and there was something ominous in the smile with which the head groom told him that Lady Ruth and Wingrave were in the house.

"The two men had separate dens. Wingrave's was much the better furnished, as he was a young man of considerable taste, and he had also fitted it with sporting trophies collected from many countries. This room was at the back of the house, and Lumley deliberately crossed the lawn and looked in at the window."

Lovell paused for a moment or two to relight his pipe.

"Remember," he continued, "that I have to put this story together, partly from facts which came to my knowledge afterwards, and partly from reasonable deductions. I may say at once that I do not know what Lumley saw when he played the spy. The housekeeper had just taken tea in, and it is possible that Wingrave may have been holding his guest's hand, or that something in their faces or attitude convinced him that his jealousy was well founded. Anyhow, it is certain that Lumley was half beside himself with rage when he strode away from that window. Then in the avenue he must have heard the soft patter of hounds coming along the lane, or perhaps seen the pink coats of the huntsmen through the hedge. This much is certain. He hurried down the drive, and returned with Ruth's husband."

Lovell took another drink. No one spoke. No one even made a remark. The little circle of listeners had caught something of his own gravity. The story was an ordinary one enough, but something in Lovell's manner of telling it seemed somehow to bring into their consciousness the apprehension of the tangled web of passions which burned underneath its sordid details.

"Ruth's husband - Sir William I will call him - stood side by side with Lumley before the window. What they saw I cannot tell you. They entered the room. The true story of what happened there I doubt if anyone will ever know. The evidence of servants spoke of raised voices and the sound of a heavy fall. When they were summoned, Sir William lay on the floor unconscious. Lady Ruth had fainted; Lumley and Wingrave were both bending over the former. On the floor were fragments of paper, which were afterwards put together, and found to be the remains of a check for a large amount, payable to Lady Ruth, and signed by Wingrave.

"The sequel is very soon told. Sir William died in a few days, and Wingrave, on the evidence of Lumley and Ruth, was committed for manslaughter, and sent to prison for fifteen years!"

Lovell paused. A murmur went round the little group of listeners. The story, after all, except for Lovell's manner of telling it, was an ordinary one. Everyone felt that there was something else behind.

So they asked no questions whilst Lovell drank his whisky and soda, and refilled his pipe. Again his eyes seemed to wander to the calendar.

"According to Lady Ruth's evidence," he said thoughtfully, "her husband entered the room at the exact moment when she was rejecting Wingrave's advances, and indignantly refusing a check which he was endeavoring to persuade her to accept. A struggle followed between the two men, with fatal results for Sir William. That," he added slowly, "is the story which the whole world read, and which most of it believes. Here, however, are a few corrections of my own, and a suggestion or two for you, Aynesworth, and those of you who like to consider yourselves truth seekers. First, then, Lady Ruth was a self-invited guest at White Lodge. She had asked Wingrave to return with her, and as they sat together in his room, she confessed that she was worried, and asked for his advice. She was in some money trouble, ingeniously explained, no doubt. Wingrave, with the utmost delicacy, offered his assistance, which was of course accepted. It was exactly what she was there for. She was in the act of taking the check, when she saw her husband and Lumley. Her reputation was at stake. Her subsequent course of action and evidence becomes obvious. The check unexplained was ruin. She explained it!

"Of the struggle, and of the exact means by which Sir William received his injuries, I know nothing. There is the evidence! It may or may not be true. The most serious part of the case, so far as Lady Ruth was concerned, lay in the facts as to her husband's removal from the White Lodge. In an unconscious state he was driven almost twelve miles at a walking pace. No

E. Phillips Oppenheim

stimulants were administered, and though they passed two doctors' houses no stop was made. A doctor was not sent for until half an hour after they reached home, and even then they seemed to have chosen the one who lived furthest away. The conclusion is obvious enough to anyone who knows the facts of the case. Sir William was not meant to live!

"Wingrave's trial was a famous one. He had no friends and few sympathizers, and he insisted upon defending himself. His cross examination of the man who had been his friend created something like a sensation. Amongst other things, he elicited the fact that Lumley, after first seeing the two together, had gone and fetched Sir William. It was a terrible half hour for Lumley, and when he left the box, amongst the averted faces of his friends, the sweat was pouring down his face. I can seem him now, as though it were yesterday. Then Lady Ruth followed. She was quietly dressed; the effect she produced was excellent. She told her story. She hinted at the insult. She spoke of the check. She had imagined no harm in accepting Wingrave's invitation to tea. Men and women of the hunt, who were on friendly terms, treated one another as comrades. She spoke of the blow. She had seen it delivered, and so on. And all the time, I sat within a few feet of Wingrave, and I knew that in the black box before him were burning love letters from this woman, to the man whose code of honor would ever have protected her husband from disgrace; and I knew that I was listening to the thing which you, Aynesworth, and many of your fellow story writers, have so wisely and so ignorantly dilated upon - the vengeance of a woman denied. Only I heard the words themselves, cold, earnest words, fall one by one from her lips like a sentence of doom - and there was life in the thing, life and death! When she had finished, the whole court was in a state of tension. Everyone was leaning forward. It would be the most piquant, the most wonderful cross examination every heard - the woman lying to save her honor and to achieve her vengeance; the man on trial for his life. Wingrave stood up. Lady Ruth raised her veil, and looked at him from the witness box. There was the most intense silence I ever realized. Who could tell the things which flashed from one to the other across the dark well of the court; who could measure the fierce, silent scorn which seemed to blaze from his eyes, as he held her there - his slave until he chose to give the signal for release? At last he looked away towards the judge, and the woman fell forward in the box gasping, a crumpled up, nerveless heap of humanity.

"'My lord,' he said, 'I have no questions to ask this witness!'

"Everyone staggered. Wingrave's few friends were horrified. After that there was, of course, no hope for him. He got fifteen years' penal servitude."

Like an echo from that pent-up murmur of feeling which had rippled through the crowded court many years ago, his little group of auditors almost gasped as Lovell left his place and strolled down the room. Aynesworth laid his hand upon his shoulder.

"All the time," he said, "you were looking at that calendar! Why?"

Lovell once more faced them. He was standing with his back to a round table, strewn with papers and magazines.

"It was the date," he said, "and the fact that I must leave England within a few hours, which forced this story from me. Tomorrow Wingrave will be free! Listen, Aynesworth," he continued, turning towards him, "and the rest of you who fancy that it is I who am leaving a humdrum city for the world of tragedies! I leave you the legacy of a greater one than all Asia will yield to me! Lady Ruth is married to Lumley, and they hold today in London a very distinguished social position. Tomorrow Wingrave takes a hand in the game. He was once my friend; I was in court when he was tried; I was intimately acquainted with the lawyer's clerk who had the arrangement of his papers. I know what no one else breathing knows. He is a man who never forgives; a man who was brutally deceived, and who for years has had no other occupation than to brood upon his wrongs. He is very wealthy indeed, still young, he has marvelous tenacity of purpose, and he has brains. Tomorrow he will be free!"

Aynesworth drew a little breath.

"I wonder," he murmured, "if anything will happen."

Lovell shrugged his shoulders.

"Where I go," he said, "the cruder passions may rage, and life and death be reckoned things of little account. But you who remain - who can tell? - you may look into the face of mightier things."

OUTSIDE THE PALE

Three men were together in a large and handsomely furnished sitting room of the Clarence Hotel, in Piccadilly. One, pale, quiet, and unobtrusive, dressed in sober black, the typical lawyer's clerk, was busy gathering up a collection of papers and documents from the table, over which they had been strewn. His employer, who had more the appearance of a country gentleman than the junior partner in the well-known firm of Rocke and Son, solicitors, had risen to his feet, and was drawing on his gloves. At the head of the table was the client.

"I trust, Sir Wingrave, that you are satisfied with this account of our stewardship," the solicitor said, as his clerk left the room. "We have felt it a great responsibility at times, but everything seems to have turned out very well. The investments, of course, are all above suspicion."

"Perfectly satisfied, I thank you," was the quiet reply. "You seem to have studied my interests in a very satisfactory manner."

Mr. Rocke had other things to say, but his client's manner seemed designed to create a barrier of formality between them. He hesitated, unwilling to leave, yet finding it exceedingly difficult to say the

E. Phillips Oppenheim

things which were in his mind. He temporized by referring back to matters already discussed, solely for the purpose of prolonging the interview.

"You have quite made up your mind, then, to put the Tredowen property on the market," he remarked. "You will excuse my reminding you of the fact that you have large accumulated funds in hand, and nearly a hundred thousand pounds worth of easily realizable securities. Tredowen has been in your mother's family for a good many years, and I should doubt whether it will be easily disposed of."

The man at the head of the table raised his head. He looked steadily at the lawyer, who began to wish that he had left the room with his clerk. Decidedly, Sir Wingrave Seton was not an easy man to get on with.

"My mind is quite made up, thank you, on this and all other matters concerning which I have given you instructions," was the calm reply. "I have had plenty of time for consideration," he added drily.

The lawyer had his opening at last, and he plunged.

"Sir Wingrave," he said, "we were at college together, and our connection is an old one. You must forgive me if I say how glad I am to see you here, and to know that your bad time is over. I can assure you that you have had my deepest sympathy. Nothing ever upset me so much as that unfortunate affair. I sincerely trust that you will do your best now to make up for lost time. You are still young, and you are rich. Let us leave business alone now, for the moment. What can I do for you as a friend, if you will allow me to call you so?"

Wingrave turned slightly in his chair. In his altered position, a ray of sunshine fell for the first time upon his gaunt but striking face. Lined and hardened, as though by exposure and want of personal care, there was also a lack of sensibility, an almost animal callousness, on the coldly lit eyes and unflinching mouth, which readily suggested some terrible and recent experience - something potent enough to have dried up the human nature out of the man and left him soulless. His clothes had the impress of the ready-made, although he wore them with a distinction which was obviously inherent; and notwithstanding the fact that he seemed to have been writing, he wore gloves.

"I am much obliged to you, Rocke," he said. "Let me repeat your question. What is there that you can do for me?"

Mr. Rocke was apparently a little nonplussed. The absolute imperturbability of the man who had once been his friend was disconcerting.

"Well," he said, "the governor sent me instead of coming himself, because he thought that I might be more useful to you. London changes so quickly - you would hardly know your way about now. I should like you to come and dine with me tonight, and I'll take you round anywhere you care to go; and then if you don't want to go back to your old tradespeople, I could take you to my tailor and bookmaker."

"Is that all?" Wingrave asked calmly.

Rocke was again taken aback.

"Certainly not," he answered. "There must be many

E. Phillips Oppenheim

ways in which I could be useful to you, but I can't think of them all at once. I am here to serve you professionally or as a friend, to the best of my ability. Can you suggest anything yourself? What do you want?"

"That is the question," Wingrave said, "which I have been asking myself. Unfortunately, up to now, I have not been able to answer it. Regarding myself, however, from the point of view of a third party, I should say that the thing I was most in need of was the society of my fellow creatures."

"Exactly," Rocke declared. "That is what I thought you would say! It won't take us long to arrange something of the sort for you."

"Can you put me up," Wingrave asked, "at your club, and introduce me to your friends there?"

Rocke flinched before the steady gaze of those cold enquiring eyes, in which he fancied, too, that a gleam of malice shone. The color mounted to his cheeks. It was a most embarrassing situation.

"I can introduce you to some decent fellows, of course, and to some very charming ladies," he said hesitatingly, "but as to the club - I - well, don't you think yourself that it would scarcely be wise to -"

"Exactly," Wingrave interrupted. "And these ladies that you spoke of -"

"Oh! There's no difficulty about that," Rocke declared with an air of relief. "I can make up a little dinner party for tonight, if you like. There's an awfully smart

American woman over here, with the Fanciful Fan Company - I'm sure you'd like her, and she'd come like a shot. Then I'd get Daisy Vane - she's all right. They don't know anything, and wouldn't care if they did. Besides, you could call yourself what you liked."

"Thank you," Wingrave said. "I am afraid I did not make myself quite clear. I was not thinking of play fellows. I was thinking of the men and women of my own order. Shall I put the matter quite clearly? Can I take my place in society under my own name, renew my old friendships and build up new ones? Can I do this even at the risk of a few difficulties at first? I am not a sensitive man. I am prepared for the usual number of disagreeable incidents. But can I win my way through?"

With his back against the wall, Rocke displayed more courage. Besides, what was the use of mincing matters with a man who had all the appearance of a human automaton, who never flinched or changed color, and whose passions seemed dried up and withered things?

"I am afraid not, Sir Wingrave," he said. "I should not recommend you to try, at any rate for the present."

"Give me your reasons," was the cool response.

"I will do so with pleasure," Rocke answered. "About the time of the trial and immediately afterwards, there was a certain amount of sympathy for you. People felt that you must have received a good deal of provocation, and there were several unexplained incidents which told in your favor. Today, I should think that the feeling amongst those who remember the affair at all is rather the other way. You heard, I

E. Phillips Oppenheim

believe, that Lady Ruth married Lumley Barrington?"

"Yes."

"Barrington has been very successful at the Bar, and they say that he is certain of a judgeship before long. His wife has backed him up well, they have entertained lavishly, and today I should think that she is one of the most popular hostesses in London. In her earlier days, I used to hear that she was one of the very fast hunting set - that was the time when you knew her. I can assure you that if ever that was true, she is a completely altered woman today. She is patroness of half a dozen great charitable schemes, she writes very clever articles in the Reviews on the Betterment of the Poor Question, and royalty itself visits at her house."

"I see," Wingrave said drily. "I was not aware of these changes."

"If ever," Mr. Rocke continued, "people were inclined to look a little askance at her, that has all gone by. Today she is one of the last women in the world of whom people would be likely to believe ill."

Wingrave nodded slowly.

"I am very much obliged to you," he said, "for this information. You seem to have come here today, Mr. Rocke, with good intentions towards me. Let me ask you to put yourself in my place. I am barely forty years old, and I am rich. I want to make the most of my life - under the somewhat peculiar circumstances. How and where should you live?"

"It depends a little upon your tastes, of course," Rocke

answered. "You are a sportsman, are you not?"

"I am fond of sport," Wingrave answered. "At least I was. At present I am not conscious of having any positive tastes."

"I think," Rocke continued, "that I should first of all change my name. Then, without making any effort to come into touch with your old friends, I should seek acquaintance amongst the Bohemian world of London and Paris. There I might myself, perhaps, be able to help you. For sport, you might fish in Norway or Iceland, or shoot in Hungary; you could run to a yacht if you cared about it, and if you fancy big game, why, there's all Africa before you."

Wingrave listened, without changing a muscle of his face.

"Your programme," he remarked, "presupposes that I have no ambitions beyond the pursuit of pleasure."

Rocke shrugged his shoulders. He was becoming more at his ease. He felt that his advice was sound, that he was showing a most comprehensive grasp of the situation.

"I am afraid," he said, "that none of what we call the careers are open to you. You could not enter Parliament, and you are too old for the professions. The services, of course, are impossible. You might write, if your tastes ran that way. Nowadays, it seems to be the fashion to record one's experiences in print, if - if they should happen to be in any way exceptional. I can think of nothing else!"

E. Phillips Oppenheim

"I am very much obliged to you," Wingrave said. "Your suggestions are eminently practical. I will think them over. Don't let me keep you any longer!"

"About this evening," Rocke remarked. "Shall I fix up that little dinner party? You have only to say the word!"

"I am very much obliged to you, but I think not," answered Wingrave. "I will dine with you alone some evening, with pleasure! Not just as present!"

Rocke looked, as he felt, puzzled. He honestly wished to be of service to this man, but he was at a loss to know what further suggestion he could make. There was something impenetrable about his client, something which he could not arrive at, behind the hard, grim face and measured words. He could not even guess as to what the man's hopes or intentions were. Eventually, although with some reluctance, he took up his hat.

"Well, Sir Wingrave," he said, "if there is really nothing I can do for you, I will go. If you should change your mind, you have only to telephone. You can command me at any time. I am only anxious to be of service to you."

"You have already been of service to me," Wingrave answered quietly. "You have spoken the truth! You have helped me to realize my position more exactly. Will you give your father my compliments and thanks, and say that I am entirely satisfied with the firm's conduct of affairs during my - absence?"

Rocke nodded.

"Certainly," he said. "That will please the governor! I must be off now. I hope you'll soon be feeling quite yourself again, Sir Wingrave! It must seem a bit odd at first, I suppose, but it will wear off all right. What you want, after all, is society. Much better let me arrange that little dinner for tonight!"

Wingrave shook his head.

"Later on, perhaps," he answered. "Good morning!"

A STUDENT OF CHARACTER

Left alone, Wingrave walked for several minutes up and down the room, his hands behind him, his head bent. He walked, not restlessly, but with measured footsteps. His mind was fixed steadfastly upon the one immediate problem of his own future. His interview with Rocke had unsettled - to a certain extent unnerved - him. Was this freedom for which he had longed so passionately, this return into civilized life, to mean simply the exchange of an iron-barred cell for a palace whose outer gates were as hopelessly locked, even though the key was of gold! Freedom! Was it after all an illusion? Was his to be the hog's paradise of empty delights; were the other worlds indeed forbidden? He moved abruptly to the window and threw it open. Below was Piccadilly, brilliant with May sunshine, surging with life. Motors and carriages, omnibuses and hansoms, were all jostled together in a block; the pavements were thronged with a motley and ever-hurrying crowd. It seemed to him, accustomed to the callous and hopeless appearance of a less happy tribe, that the faces of these people were all aflame with the joy of the springtime. The perfume from the great clusters of yellow daffodils and violets floated up from the flower sellers' baskets below; the fresh, warm air seemed to bring him poignant memories of crocus-starred lawns, of trim beds of hyacinths, of the song of birds, of the perfume of drooping lilac. Grim and motionless, as a figure of fate, Wingrave looked down from his window, with cold, yet discerning eyes. He was still an alien, a denizen in another world from that which flowed so smoothly and pleasantly below. It was something to which he did not belong, which he doubted, indeed, if ever again he could enter. He had no part in it, no share in that vigorous life, whose throbbings he could dimly feel, though his own heart was beating to a slower and a very different tune. They were his fellows in name only. Between him and them stood the judgment of - Rocke!

The evil chances of the world are many! It was whilst his thoughts traveled in this fashion that the electric landaulette of Lady Ruth Barrington glided round the corner from St. James' Street, and joined in the throng of vehicles slowly making their way down Piccadilly. His attention was attracted first by the white and spotless liveries of the servants - the form of locomotion itself was almost new to him. Then he saw the woman who leaned back amongst the cushions. She was elegantly dressed; she wore no veil; she did not look a day more than thirty. She was attractive, from the tips of her patent shoes, to the white bow which floated on the top of her lace parasol; a perfectly dressed, perfectly turned out woman. She had, too, the lazy confident air of a woman sure of herself and her friends. She knew nothing of the look which flashed down upon her from the window overhead.

Wingrave turned away with a little gasp; a half-stifled exclamation had crept out from between his teeth. His cheeks seemed paler than ever, and his eyes unnaturally bright. Nevertheless, he was completely master of himself. On the table was a large deed box of papers, which Rocke had left for his inspection. From

E. Phillips Oppenheim

its recesses he drew out a smaller box, unlocked it with a key from his chain, and emptied its sole contents - a small packet of letters - upon the table. He counted them one by one. They were all there - and on top a photograph. A breath of half-forgotten perfume stole out into the room. He opened one of the letters, and its few passionate words came back to his memory, linked with a hundred other recollections, the desire of her eyes, of her lips raised for his, the caressing touch of her fingers. He found himself wondering, in an impersonal sort of way, that these things should so little affect him. His blood ran no less coldly, nor did his pulses beat the faster, for this backward glance into things finished.

There was a knock at the door. He raised his head.

"Come in!"

A slim, fair young man obeyed the summons, and advanced into the room. Wingrave eyed him with immovable face. Nevertheless, his manner somehow suggested a displeased surprise.

"Sir Wingrave Seton, I believe?" the intruder said cheerfully.

"That is my name," Wingrave admitted; "but my orders below have evidently been disobeyed. I am not disposed to receive visitors today."

The intruder was not in the least abashed. He laid his hat upon the table, and felt in his pocket.

"I am very sorry," he said. "They did try to keep me out, but I told them that my business was urgent. I have been a journalist, you see, and am used to these little maneuvers."

Wingrave looked at him steadily, with close-drawn eyebrows.

"Am I to understand," he said "that you are in here in your journalistic capacity?"

The newcomer shook his head.

"Pray do not think," he said, "that I should be guilty of such an impertinence. My name is Aynesworth. Walter Aynesworth. I have a letter for you from Lovell. You remember him, I daresay. Here it is!"

He produced it from his breast coat pocket, and handed it over.

"Where is Lovell?" Wingrave asked.

"He left for the East early this morning," Aynesworth answered. "He had to go almost at an hour's notice."

Wingrave broke the seal, and read the letter through. Afterwards he tore it into small pieces and threw them into the grate.

"What do you want with me, Mr. Aynesworth?" he asked.

"I want to be your secretary," Aynesworth answered.

"My secretary," Wingrave repeated. "I am much obliged to you, but I am not requiring anyone in that capacity."

"Pardon me," Aynesworth answered, "but I think you are. You may not have realized it yet, but if you will consider the matter carefully, I think you will agree with me that a secretary, or companion of some sort, is exactly what you do need."

"Out of curiosity," Wingrave remarked, "I should be glad to know why you think so."

"Certainly," Aynesworth answered. "In the first place, I know the story of your life, and the unfortunate incident which has kept you out of society for the last ten years."

"From Lovell, I presume," Wingrave interrupted.

"Precisely," Aynesworth admitted. "Ten years' absence from English life today means that you return to it an absolute and complete stranger. You would be like a Cook's tourist abroad, without a guide or a Baedeker, if you attempted to rely upon yourself. Now I am rather a Bohemian sort of person, but I have just the sort of all-round knowledge which would be most useful to you. I have gone a little way into society, and I know something about politics. I can bring you up-to-date on both these matters. I know where to dine well in town, and where to be amused. I can tell you where to get your clothes, and the best place for all the etceteras. If you want to travel, I can speak French and German; and I consider myself a bit of a sportsman."

"I am sure," Wingrave answered, "I congratulate you upon your versatility. I am quite convinced! I shall advertise at once for a secretary!"

"Why advertise?" Aynesworth asked. "I am here!"

Wingrave shook his head.

"You would not suit me at all," he answered.

"Why not?" Aynesworth asked. "I forget whether I mentioned all my accomplishments. I am an Oxford man with a degree, and I can write tolerable English. I've a fair head for figures, and I don't require too large a salary."

"Exactly," Wingrave answered drily. "You are altogether too desirable? I should not require an Admirable Crichton for my purpose."

Aynesworth remained unruffled.

"All right," he said. "You know best, of course! Suppose you tell me what sort of a man would satisfy you!"

"Why should I?" Wingrave asked coldly.

"It would amuse me," Aynesworth answered, "and I've come a mile or so out of my way, and given up a whole morning to come and see you. Go on! It won't take long!"

Wingrave shrugged his shoulders.

"I will not remind you," he said, "that you came on your own initiative. I owe you the idea, however, so I will tell you the sort of person I shall look out for. In the first place, I do not require him to be a gentleman."

"I can be a shocking bounder at times," Aynesworth murmured.

"He must be more a sort of an upper servant," Wingrave continued. "I should require him to obey me implicitly, whatever I told him to do. You have a conscience, I presume?"

"Very little," Aynesworth answered. "I have been a journalist."

"You have the remnants of one, at all events," Wingrave said, "quite sufficient, no doubt, to interfere with your possible usefulness to me. I must have someone who is poor - too poor to question my will, or to dispute my orders, whatever they might be."

"I have never," Aynesworth declared, "possessed a superfluous half-crown in my life."

"You probably possess what is called a sense of honor," Wingrave continued. "You would certainly disapprove of some of my proceedings, and you would probably disobey my orders."

"Sense of honor!" Aynesworth repeated. "You have too flattering an opinion of me. I don't know what it is. I always cheat at cards if I get the chance."

Wingrave turned away.

"You are a fool," he said, "and you won't suit me."

"When can I come?" Aynesworth asked.

"You can stay now," Wingrave answered. "Your salary will be four hundred a year. You will live at my expense. The day you disobey an order of mine, you go! No notice, mind!"

"Agreed," Aynesworth answered. "What should I do first? Send you a tailor, I should think."

Wingrave nodded.

"I will give the afternoon to that sort of people," he said. "Here is a list of the tradesmen I used to deal with. Kindly avoid them."

Aynesworth glanced at the slip of paper, and nodded.

"All out-of-date now," he remarked. "I'll be back to lunch."

E. Phillips Oppenheim

A DELICATE MISSION

Aynesworth was back in less than an hour. He carried under his arm a brown paper parcel, the strings of which he commenced at once to untie. Wingrave, who had been engrossed in the contents of his deed box, watched him with immovable face.

"The tailor will be here at two-thirty," he announced, "and the other fellows will follow on at half an hour's interval. The manicurist and the barber are coming at six o'clock."

Wingrave nodded.

"What have you there?" he asked, pointing to the parcel.

"Cigars and cigarettes, and jolly good ones, too," Aynesworth answered, opening a flat tin box, and smelling the contents appreciatively. "Try one of these! The finest Turkish tobacco grown!"

"I don't smoke," Wingrave answered.

"Oh! You've got out of it, but you must pick it up again," Aynesworth declared. "Best thing out for the nerves - sort of humanizes one, you know!"

"Humanizes one, does it?" Wingrave remarked softly. "Well, I'll try!"

He took a cigarette from the box, curtly inviting Aynesworth to do the same.

"What about lunch?" the latter asked. "Would you care to come round with me to the Cannibal Club? Rather a Bohemian set, but there are always some good fellows there."

"I am much obliged," Wingrave answered. "If you will ask me again in a few days' time, I shall be very pleased. I do not wish to leave the hotel just at present."

"Do you want me?" Aynesworth asked.

"Not until five o'clock," Wingrave answered. "I should be glad if you would leave me now, and return at that hour. In the meantime, I have a commission for you."

"Good!" Aynesworth declared. "What is it?"

"You will go," Wingrave directed, "to No. 13, Cadogan Street, and you will enquire for Lady Ruth Barrington. If she should be out, ascertain the time of her return, and wait for her."

"If she is out of town?"

"She is in London," Wingrave answered. "I have seen her from the window this morning. You will give her a message. Say that you come from me, and that I desire to see her tomorrow. The time and place she can fix, but I should prefer not to go to her house."

Aynesworth stooped down to relight his cigarette. He felt that Wingrave was watching him, and he wished to keep his face hidden.

"I am unknown to Lady Ruth," he remarked. "Supposing she should refuse to see me?"

Wingrave looked at him coldly.

"I have told you what I wish done," he said. "The task does not seem to be a difficult one. Please see to it that I have an answer by five o'clock -"

Aynesworth lunched with a few of his particular friends at the club. They heard of his new adventure with somewhat doubtful approbation.

"You'll never stand the routine, old chap!"

"And what about your own work!"

"What will the Daily Scribbler people say?"

Aynesworth shrugged his shoulders.

"I don't imagine it will last very long," he answered, "and I shall get a fair amount of time to myself. The work I do on the Daily Scribbler doesn't amount to anything. It was a chance I simply couldn't refuse."

The editor of a well-known London paper leaned back in his chair, and pinched a cigar carefully.

"You'll probably find the whole thing a sell," he remarked. "The story, as Lovell told it, sounded dramatic enough, and if the man were to come back to life again, fresh and vigorous, things might happen, provided, of course, that Lovell was right in his suppositions. But ten or twelve years' solitary confinement, although it mayn't sound much on paper, is enough to crush all the life and energy out of a man."

Aynesworth shook his head.

"You haven't seen him," he said. "I have!"

"What's he like, Walter?" another man asked.

"I can't describe him," Aynesworth answered. "I shouldn't like to try. I'll bring him here some day. You fellows shall see him for yourselves. I find him interesting enough."

"The whole thing," the editor declared, "will fizzle out. You see if it doesn't? A man who's just spent ten or twelve years in prison isn't likely to run any risk of going there again. There will be no tragedy; more likely reconciliation."

"Perhaps," Aynesworth said imperturbably. "But it wasn't only the possibility of anything of that sort happening, you know, which attracted me. It was the tragedy of the man himself, with his numbed, helpless life, set down here in the midst of us, with a great, blank chasm between him and his past. What is there left to drive the wheels? The events of one day are simple and monotonous enough to us, because they lean up against the events of yesterday, and the yesterdays before! How do they seem, I wonder, to a man whose yesterday was more than a decade of years ago!"

E. Phillips Oppenheim

The editor nodded.

"It must be a grim sensation," he admitted, "but I am afraid with you, my dear Walter, it is an affair of shop. You wish to cull from your interesting employer the material for that every-becoming novel of yours. Let's go upstairs! I've time for one pool."

"I haven't," Aynesworth answered. "I've a commission to do."

He left the club and walked westwards, humming softly to himself, but thinking all the time intently. His errand disturbed him. He was to be the means of bringing together again these two people who had played the principal parts in Lovell's drama - his new employer and the woman who had ruined his life. What was the object of it? What manner of vengeance did he mean to deal out to her? Lovell's words of premonition returned to him just then with curious insistence - he was so certain that Wingrave's reappearance would lead to tragical happenings. Aynesworth himself never doubted it. His brief interview with the man into whose service he had almost forced himself had impressed him wonderfully. Yet, what weapon was there, save the crude one of physical force, with which Wingrave could strike?

He rang the bell at No. 13, Cadogan Street, and sent in his card by the footman. The man accepted it doubtfully.

"Her ladyship has only just got up from luncheon, sir, and she is not receiving this afternoon," he announced.

Aynesworth took back his card, and scribbled upon it

the name of the newspaper for which he still occasionally worked.

"Her ladyship will perhaps see me," he said, handing the card back to the man. "It is a matter of business. I will not detain her for more than a few minutes."

The man returned presently, and ushered him into a small sitting room.

"Her ladyship will be quite half an hour before she can see you, sir," he said.

"I will wait," Aynesworth answered, taking up a paper.

The time passed slowly. At last, the door was opened. A woman, in a plain but exquisitely fitting black gown, entered. From Lovell's description, Aynesworth recognized her at once, and yet, for a moment, he hesitated to believe that this was the woman whom he had come to see. The years had indeed left her untouched. Her figure was slight, almost girlish; her complexion as smooth, and her coloring, faint though it was, as delicate and natural as a child's. Her eyes were unusually large, and the lashes which shielded them heavy. It was when she looked at him that Aynesworth began to understand.

She carried his card in her hand, and glanced at it as he bowed.

"You are the Daily Scribbler," she said. "You want me to tell you about my bazaar, I suppose."

"I am attached to the Daily Scribbler, Lady Ruth Barrington," Aynesworth answered; "but my business this afternoon has nothing to do with the paper. I have called with a message from - an old friend of yours."

She raised her eyebrows ever so slightly. The graciousness of her manner was perceptibly abated.

"Indeed! I scarcely understand you, Mr. - Aynesworth."

"My message," Aynesworth said, "is from Sir Wingrave Seton."

The look of enquiry, half impatient, half interrogative, faded slowly from her face. She stood quite still; her impassive features seemed like a plaster cast, from which all life and feeling were drawn out. Her eyes began slowly to dilate, and she shivered as though with cold. Then the man who was watching her and wondering, knew that this was fear - fear undiluted and naked.

He stepped forward, and placed a chair for her. She felt for the back of it with trembling fingers and sat down.

"Is - Sir Wingrave Seton - out of prison?" she asked in a strange, dry tone. One would have thought that she had been choking.

"Since yesterday," Aynesworth answered.

"But his time - is not up yet?"

"There is always a reduction," Aynesworth reminded her, "for what is called good conduct."

She was silent for several moments. Then she raised

her head. She was a brave woman, and she was rapidly recovering her self-possession.

"Well," she asked, "what does he want?"

"To see you," Aynesworth answered, "tomorrow afternoon, either here or at his apartments in the Clarence Hotel. He would prefer not to come here!"

"Are you his friend?" she asked.

"I am his secretary," Aynesworth answered.

"You are in his confidence?"

"I only entered his service this morning," he said.

"How much do you know," she persisted, "of the unfortunate affair which led - to his imprisonment?"

"I have been told the whole story," Aynesworth answered.

Her eyes rested thoughtfully upon his. It seemed as though she were trying to read in his face exactly what he meant by "the whole story."

"Then," she said, "do you think that anything but pain and unpleasantness can come of a meeting between us?"

"Lady Ruth," Aynesworth answered, "it is not for me to form an opinion. I am Sir Wingrave Seton's secretary."

"What is he going to do?" she asked.

"I have no idea," he answered.

"Is he going abroad?"

"I know nothing of his plans," Aynesworth declared. "What answer shall I take back to him?"

She looked at him earnestly. Gradually her face was softening. The frozen look was passing away. The expression was coming back to her eyes. She leaned a little towards him. Her voice, although it was raised above a whisper, was full of feeling.

"Mr. Aynesworth," she murmured, "I am afraid of Sir Wingrave Seton!"

Aynesworth said nothing.

"I was always a little afraid of him," she continued, "even in the days when we were friendly. He was so hard and unforgiving. I know he thinks that he has a grievance against me. He will have been brooding about it all these years. I dare not see him! I - I am terrified!"

"If that is your answer," Aynesworth said, "I will convey it to him!"

Her beautiful eyes were full of reproach.

"Mr. Aynesworth," she said, in a low tone, "for a young man you are very unsympathetic."

"My position," Aynesworth answered, "does not allow me the luxury of considering my personal feelings."

She looked hurt.

"I forgot," she said, looking for a moment upon the floor; "you have probably been prejudiced against me. You have heard only one story. Listen" - she raised her eyes suddenly, and leaned a little forward in her chair - "some day, if you will come and see me when I am alone and we have time to spare, I will tell you the whole truth. I will tell you exactly what happened! You shall judge for yourself!"

Aynesworth bowed.

"In the meantime?"

Her eyes filled slowly with tears. Aynesworth looked away. He was miserably uncomfortable.

"You cannot be quite so hard-hearted as you try to seem, Mr. Aynesworth," she said quietly. "I want to ask you a question. You must answer it? You don't know how much it means to me. You are Sir Wingrave Seton's secretary; you have access to all his papers. Have you seen any letters of mine? Do you know if he still has any in his possession?"

"My answer to both questions is 'No!'" Aynesworth said a little stiffly. "I only entered the service of Sir Wingrave Seton this morning, and I know nothing at all, as yet, of his private affairs. And, Lady Ruth, you must forgive my reminding you that, in any case, I could not discuss such matters with you," he added.

She looked at him with a faint, strange smile. Afterwards, when he tried to do so, Aynesworth found it impossible to describe the expression which flitted

E. Phillips Oppenheim

across her face. He only knew that it left him with the impression of having received a challenge.

"Incorruptible!" she murmured. "Sir Wingrave Seton is indeed a fortunate man."

There was a lingering sweetness in her tone which still had a note of mockery in it. Her silence left Aynesworth conscious of a vague sense of uneasiness. He felt that her eyes were raised to his, and for some reason, which he could not translate even into a definite thought, he wished to avoid them. The silence was prolonged. For long afterwards he remembered those few minutes. There was a sort of volcanic intensity in the atmosphere. He was acutely conscious of small extraneous things, of the perfume of a great bowl of hyacinths, the ticking of a tiny French clock, the restless drumming of her finger tips upon the arm of her chair. All the time he seemed actually to feel her eyes, commanding, impelling, beseeching him to turn round. He did so at last, and looked her full in the face.

"Lady Ruth," he said, "will you favor me with an answer to my message?"

"Certainly," she answered, smiling quite naturally. "I will come and see Sir Wingrave Seton at four o'clock tomorrow afternoon. You can tell him that I think it rather an extraordinary request, but under the circumstances I will do as he suggests. He is staying at the Clarence, I presume, under his own name? I shall have no difficulty in finding him?"

"He is staying there under his own name," Aynesworth answered, "and I will see that you have no difficulty."

"So kind of you," she murmured, holding out her hand. And again there was something mysterious in her eyes as she raised them to him, as though there existed between them already some understanding which mocked the conventionality of her words. Aynesworth left the house, and lit a cigarette upon the pavement outside with a little sigh of relief. He felt somehow humiliated. Did she fancy, he wondered, that he was a callow boy to dance to any tune of her piping - that he had never before seen a beautiful woman who wanted her own way?

E. Phillips Oppenheim

THE GOSPEL OF HATE

"And what," Wingrave asked his secretary as they sat at dinner that night, "did you think of Lady Ruth?"

"In plain words, I should not like to tell you," Aynesworth answered. "I only hope that you will not send me to see her again."

"Why not?"

"Lady Ruth," Aynesworth answered deliberately, "is a very beautiful woman, with all the most dangerous gifts of Eve when she wanted her own way. She did me the scanty honor of appraising me as an easy victim, and she asked questions."

"For instance?"

"She wanted me to tell her if you still had in your possession certain letters of hers," Aynesworth said.

"Good! What did you say?"

"I told her, of course," Aynesworth continued, "that having been in your service for a few hours only, I was scarcely in a position to know. I ventured further to remind her that such questions, addressed from her to me, were, to say the least of it, improper."

Wingrave's lips parted in what should have been a smile, but the spirit of mirth was lacking.

"And then?"

"There was nothing else," Aynesworth answered. "She simply dismissed me."

"I can see," Wingrave remarked, "your grievance. You are annoyed because she regarded you as too easy a victim."

"Perhaps," Aynesworth admitted.

"There was some excuse for her, after all," Wingrave continued coolly. "She possesses powers which you yourself have already admitted, and you, I should say, are a fairly impressionable person, so far as her sex is concerned. Confess now, that she did not leave you altogether indifferent."

"Perhaps not," Aynesworth admitted reluctantly. He did not care to say more.

"In case you should feel any curiosity on the subject," Wingrave remarked, "I may tell you that I have those letters which she was so anxious to know about, and I shall keep them safe - even from you! You can amuse yourself with her if you like. You will never be able to tell her more than I care for her to know."

Aynesworth continued his dinner in silence. After all, he was beginning to fear that he had made a mistake. Lovell had somehow contrived to impart a subtly tragic note to his story, but the outcome of it all seemed to assume a more sordid aspect. These two

E. Phillips Oppenheim

would meet, there would be recriminations, a tragic appeal for forgiveness, possibly some melodramatic attempt at vengeance. The glamour of the affair seemed to him to be fading away, now that he had come into actual contact with it. It was not until he began to study his companion during a somewhat prolonged silence that he felt the reaction. It was then that he began to see new things, that he felt the enthusiasm kindled by Lovell's strangely told story begin to revive. It was not the watching for events more or less commonplace which would repay him for the step he had taken; it was the study of this man, placed in so strange a position, - a man come back to life, after years of absolute isolation. He had broken away from the chain which links together men of similar tastes and occupations, and which goes to the creation of type. He was in a unique position! He was in the world, but not of it. He was groping about amongst familiar scenes, over which time had thrown the pall of unfamiliarity. What manner of place would he find - what manner of place did he desire to find? It was here that the real interest of the situation culminated. At least, so Aynesworth thought then.

They were dining at a restaurant in the Strand, which Aynesworth had selected as representing one, the more wealthy, type of Bohemian life. The dinner and wine had been of his choosing. Wingrave had stipulated only for the best. Wingrave himself had eaten very little, the bottle of wine stood half empty between them. The atmosphere of the place, the effect of the wine, the delicate food, and the music, were visible to a greater or less degree, according to temperament, amongst all the other little groups of men and women by whom they were surrounded. Wingrave alone remained unaffected. He was carefully and correctly dressed in clothes borrowed from his new tailor, and he showed not the slightest signs of strangeness or gaucherie amongst his unfamiliar surroundings. He looked about him always, with the cold, easy nonchalance of the man of the world. Of being recognized he had not the slightest fear. His frame and bearing, and the brightness of his deep, strong eyes, still belonged to early middle age, but his face itself, worn and hardened, was the face of an elderly man. The more Aynesworth watched him, the more puzzled he felt.

"I am afraid," he remarked, "that you are disappointed in this place."

"Not at all," Wingrave answered. "It is typical of a class, I suppose. It is the sort of place I wished to visit."

In a corner of the room Aynesworth had recognized a friend and fellow clubman, who was acting at a neighboring theater. He was dining with some young ladies of his company, and beckoned to Aynesworth to come over and join them. He pointed them out to Wingrave.

"Would you care to be introduced?" he asked. "Holiwell is a very good fellow, and the girls might interest you. Two of them are Americans, and they are very popular."

Wingrave shook his head.

"Thank you, no!" he said. "I should be glad to meet your friend some time when he is alone."

It was the first intimation which Aynesworth had received of his companion's sentiments as regards the other sex. Years afterwards, when his attitude towards them was often quoted as being one of the extraordinary features of an extraordinary personality, he remembered his perseverance on this occasion.

"You have not spoken to a woman for so many years," he persisted. "Why not renew the experience? Nothing so humanizing, you know - not even cigarettes."

Wingrave's face fell, if possible into sterner lines. His tone was cold and hard.

"My scheme of life," he said, "may be reconstructed more than once before I am satisfied. But I can assure you of this! There will be no serious place in it for women!"

Aynesworth shrugged his shoulders. He never doubted but that in a month of two his vis-a-vis would talk differently.

"Your scheme of life," he repeated thoughtfully. "That sounds interesting! Have you any objection, I wonder, to telling me what manner of life you propose to lead?"

It was several moments before Wingrave answered him. He was smoking a cigar in a mechanical sort of way, but he obviously derived no pleasure from it. Yet Aynesworth noticed that some instinct had led him to choose the finest brand.

"Perhaps," he said, letting his eyes rest coldly upon his questioner, "if I told you all that was in my mind you would waive your month's salary and get back to your journalism!"

Aynesworth shrugged his shoulders.

"Why should you suppose that?" he asked. "I am not a moralist myself, nor am I the keeper of your conscience. I don't think that you could frighten me off just yet."

"Nevertheless," Wingrave admitted, "there are times when I fear that we shall not get on together. I begin to suspect that you have a conscience."

"You are the first," Aynesworth assured him, "who has ever flattered me to that extent."

"It may be elastic, of course," Wingrave continued, "but I suspect its existence. I warn you that association with me will try it hard."

"I accept the challenge," Aynesworth answered lightly.

"You are rasher than you imagine," Wingrave declared. "For instance, I have admitted to you, have I not, that I am interested in my fellow creatures, that I want to mix with them and watch them at their daily lives. Let me assure you that that interest is not a benevolent one."

"I never fancied that you were a budding philan-thropist," Aynesworth remarked, lighting a fresh cigarette.

"I find myself," Wingrave continued thoughtfully, "in a somewhat unique position. I am one of the ordinary human beings with whom the world is peopled, but I am not conscious of any of the usual weaknesses of sentiment or morality. For instance, if that gentleman with the red face, who has obviously eaten and drunk too much, were to have an apoplectic fit at the moment, and die in his chair, it would not shock or distress me in the least. On the contrary, I should be disposed to welcome his removal from a world which he obviously does nothing to adorn."

Aynesworth glanced at the person in question. He was a theatrical agent and financier of stock companies, whom he knew very well by sight.

"I suppose," Wingrave continued, "that I was born with the usual moral sentiments, and the usual feelings of kinship towards my fellow creatures. Circumstances, however, have wholly destroyed them. To me, men have become the puppets and women the dancing dolls of life. My interest in them, if it exists at all, is malevolent. I should like to see them all suffer exactly as I have suffered. It would interest me exceedingly."

Still Aynesworth remained silent. He was anxious to hear all that was in the other's mind, and he feared lest any interruption might divert him.

"There are men in the world," Wingrave continued, "called philanthropists, amiable, obese creatures as a rule, whose professed aim in life it is to do as much good as possible. I take my stand upon the other pole. It is my desire to encourage and to work as much evil as possible. I wish to bring all the suffering I can upon those who come within the sphere of my influence."

"You are likely," Aynesworth remarked, "to achieve popularity."

Wingrave regarded him steadfastly.

"Your speech," he said, "is flippant, but you yourself do not realize how near it comes to the truth. Human beings are like dogs - they are always ready to lick the hand that flogs them. I mean to use the scourge whenever I can seize the opportunity, but you will find the jackals at my heels, nevertheless, whenever I choose to whistle."

Aynesworth helped himself to a liqueur. He felt that he needed it.

"One weakness alone distresses me," Wingrave continued. "In all ordinary matters of sentiment I am simply a negation. There is one antipathy, however, which I find it hard to overcome. The very sight of a woman, or the sound of her voice, distresses me. This is the more unfortunate," he continued, "because it is upon the shoulders of her sex that the greater portion of my debt to my fellow creatures rests. However, time may help me!"

Aynesworth leaned back in his chair, and contemplated his companion for the next few moments in thoughtful silence. It was hard, he felt, to take a man who talked like this seriously. His manner was convincing, his speech deliberate and assured. There was not the slightest doubt but that he meant what he said, yet it seemed to Aynesworth equally certain that the time would come, and come quickly, when the unnatural hardness of the man would yield to the genial influence of friendship, of pleasure, of the subtle joys of freedom. Those past days of hideous monotony, of profitless, debasing toil, the long, sleepless nights, the very nightmare of life to a man of Wingrave's culture and habits, might well have poisoned his soul, have filled him with ideas such as these. But everything was different now! The history of the world could show no epoch when pleasures so many and various were there for the man who carries the golden key. Today he was a looker-on, and the ice of his years of bitterness had not melted. Tomorrow, at any moment, he might catch a whiff of the fragrance of life, and the blood in his veins would move to a different tune. This was how it seemed to Aynesworth, as he studied his companion through the faint blue mist of tobacco smoke.

"This expression of your sentiments," he remarked at last, "is interesting so far as it goes. I am, however, a practical person, and my connection with you is of a practical order. You don't propose, I presume, to promenade the streets with a cat-o-nine-tails?"

"Your curiosity," Wingrave remarked, "is reasonable. Tomorrow I may gratify some portion of it after my interview with Lady Ruth. In the meantime, I might remark that to the observant person who has wits and money, the opportunities for doing evil present themselves, I think, with reasonable frequency. I do not propose, however, to leave things altogether to chance."

"A definite scheme of ill-doing," Aynesworth ventured to suggest, "would be more satisfactory?"

"Exactly," he admitted.

He called for the bill, and his eyes wandered once more around the room as the waiter counted out the change. The band were playing the "Valse Amoureuse"; the air was grown heavy with the odor of tobacco and the mingled perfumes of flowers and scents. A refrain of soft laughter followed the music. An after-dinner air pervaded the place. Wingrave's lip curled.

"My lack of kinship with my fellows," he remarked, "is exceedingly well defined just now. I agree with the one philosopher who declared that 'eating and drinking are functions which are better performed in private.'"

The two men went on to a theater. The play was a society trifle - a thing of the moment. Wingrave listened gravely, without a smile or any particular sign of interest. At the end of the second act, he turned towards his companion.

"The lady in the box opposite," he remarked, "desires to attract your attention."

Aynesworth looked up and recognized Lady Ruth. She was fanning herself languidly, but her eyes were fixed upon the two men. She leaned a little forward, and her gesture was unmistakable.

Aynesworth rose to his feet a little doubtfully.

"You had better go," Wingrave said. "Present my compliments and excuses. I feel that a meeting now would amount to an anti-climax."

Aynesworth made his way upstairs. Lady Ruth was alone, and he noticed that she had withdrawn to a chair where she was invisible to the house. Even Aynesworth himself could not see her face clearly at first, for she had chosen the darkest corner of the box. He gathered an impression of a gleaming white neck and bosom rising and falling rather more quickly than was natural, eyes which shone softly through the gloom, and the perfume of white roses, a great cluster of which lay upon the box ledge. Her voice was scarcely raised above a whisper.

"That is - Sir Wingrave with you?"

"Yes!" Aynesworth answered. "It was he who saw you first!"

She seemed to catch her breath. Her voice was still tremulous.

"He is changed," she said. "I should not have recognized him."

"They were the best ten years of his life," Aynesworth answered. "Think of how and in what surroundings he has been compelled to live. No wonder that he has had the humanity hammered out of him."

She shivered a little.

"Is he always like this?" she asked. "I have watched him. He never smiles. He looks as hard as fate itself."

"I have known him only a few hours," Aynesworth reminded her.

"I dare not come tomorrow," she whispered; "I am afraid of him."

"Do you wish me to tell him so?" he asked.

"I don't know," she answered. "You are very unfeeling,

Mr. Aynesworth."

"I hope not," he answered, and looked away towards the orchestra. He did not wish to meet her eyes.

"You are!" she murmured. "I have no one to whom I dare speak - of this. I dare not mention his name to my husband. It was my evidence which convicted him, and I can see, I know, that he is vindictive. And he has those letters! Oh! If I could only get them back?"

Her voice trembled with an appeal whispered but passionate. It was wonderful how musical and yet how softly spoken her words were. They were like live things, and the few feet of darkened space through which they had passed seemed charged with magnetic influence.

"Mr. Aynesworth!"

He turned and faced her.

"Can't you help me?"

"I cannot, Lady Ruth."

The electric bell rang softly from outside, and the orchestra commenced to play. Lady Ruth rose and looked at herself in the mirror. Then she turned and smiled at her visitor. The pallor of her face was no longer unnatural. She was a wonderful woman.

"I shall come tomorrow," she said. "Shall I see you?"

"That," he answered, "depends upon Sir Wingrave."

E. Phillips Oppenheim

She made a little grimace as she dismissed him. Wingrave did not speak to his companion for some time after he had resumed his seat. Then he inclined his head towards him.

"Have you come to terms with her ladyship?" he asked drily.

"Not yet!" Aynesworth answered.

"You can name your own price," he continued. "She will pay! Don't be afraid of making her bid up. She has a good deal at stake!"

Aynesworth made no reply. He was thinking how easy it would be to hate this man!

"HAST THOU FOUND ME, O MINE ENEMY?"

Aynesworth was waiting in the hall on the following afternoon when Lady Ruth arrived. He had half expected that she would drive up to the side door in a hansom, would wear a thick veil, and adopt the other appurtenances of a clandestine meeting. But Lady Ruth was much too clever a woman for anything of the sort. She descended at the great front entrance from her own electric coupe, and swept into the hotel followed by her maid. She stopped to speak to the manager of the hotel, who knew her from her visits to the world-famous restaurant, and she asked at once for Sir Wingrave Seton. Then she saw Aynesworth, and crossed the hall with outstretched hand.

"How nice of you to be here," she murmured. "Can you take me to Sir Wingrave at once? I have such a busy afternoon that I was afraid at the last moment that I should be unable to come!"

Aynesworth led her towards the lift.

"Sir Wingrave is in his sitting room," he remarked. "It is only on the first floor."

She directed her maid where to wait, and followed him. On the way down the corridor, he stole a glance at her. She was a little pale, and he could see that she had

E. Phillips Oppenheim

nerved herself to this interview with a great effort. As he knocked at the door, her great eyes were raised for a moment to his, and they were like the eyes of a frightened child.

"I am afraid!" she murmured.

There was no time for more. They were in the room, and Wingrave had risen to meet them. Lady Ruth did not hesitate for a moment. She crossed the room towards him with outstretched hands. Aynesworth, who was standing a little on one side, watched their meeting with intense, though covert interest. She had pushed back her veil, her head was a little upraised in a mute gesture of appeal.

She was pale to the lips, but her eyes were soft with hidden tears. Wingrave stood stonily silent, like a figure of fate. His hands remained by his sides. Her welcome found no response from him. She came to a standstill, and, swaying a little, stretched out her hand and steadied herself by grasping the back of a chair.

"Wingrave," she murmured, and her voice was full of musical reproach.

Aynesworth turned to leave the room, but Wingrave, looking over her head, addressed him.

"You will remain here, Aynesworth," he said. "There are some papers at that desk which require sorting."

Aynesworth hesitated. He had caught the look on Lady Ruth's face.

"If you could excuse me for half an hour, Sir

Wingrave," he began.

"I cannot spare you at present," Wingrave interrupted. "Kindly remain!"

Aynesworth had no alternative but to obey. Wingrave handed a chair to Lady Ruth. He was looking at her steadfastly. There were no signs of any sort of emotion in his face. Whatever their relations in the past might have been, it was hard to believe, from his present demeanor, that he felt any.

"Wingrave," she said softly, "are you going to be unkind to me - you, whom I have always thought of in my dreams as the most generous of men! I have looked forward so much to seeing you again - to knowing that you were free! Don't disappoint me!"

Wingrave laughed shortly, and Aynesworth bent closer over his work, with a gathering frown upon his forehead. A mirthless laugh is never a pleasant sound.

"Disappoint you!" he repeated calmly. "No! I must try and avoid that! You have been looking forward with so much joy to this meeting then? I am flattered."

She shivered a little.

"I have looked forward to it," she answered, and her voice was dull and lifeless with pain. "But you are not glad to see me," she continued. "There is no welcome in your face! You are changed - altogether! Why did you send for me?"

"Listen!"

There was a moment's silence. Wingrave was standing upon the hearthrug, cold, passionless, Sphinx-like. Lady Ruth was seated a few feet away, but her face was hidden.

"You owe me something!" he said.

"Owe - you something?" she repeated vaguely.

"Do you deny it?" he said.

"Oh, no, no!" she declared with emotion. "Not for a moment."

"I want," he said, "to give you an opportunity of repaying some portion of that debt!"

She raised her eyes to his. Her whispered words came so softly that they were almost inaudible.

"I am waiting," she said. "Tell me what I can do!"

He commenced to speak at some length, very impassively, very deliberately.

"You will doubtless appreciate the fact," he said, "that my position, today, is a somewhat peculiar one. I have had enough of solitude. I am rich! I desire to mix once more on equal terms amongst my fellows. And against that, I have the misfortune to be a convicted felon, who has spent the last ten or a dozen years amongst the scum of the earth, engaged in degrading tasks, and with no identity save a number. The position, as you will doubtless observe, is a difficult one."

Her eyes fell from his. Once more she shivered, as

though with physical pain. Something that was like a smile, only that it was cold and lifeless, flitted across his lips.

"I have no desire," he continued, "to live in foreign countries. On the contrary, I have plans which necessitate my living in England. The difficulties by this time are, without doubt, fully apparent to you."

She said nothing. Her eyes were once more watching his face.

"My looking glass," he continued, "shows me that I am changed beyond any reasonable chance of recognition. I do not believe that the Wingrave Seton of today would readily be recognized as the Wingrave Seton of twelve years ago. But I propose to make assurance doubly sure. I am leaving this country for several years, at once. I shall go to America, and I shall return as Mr. Wingrave, millionaire - and I propose, by the way, to make money there. I desire, under that identity, to take my place once more amongst my fellows. I shall bring letters of introduction - to you."

There was a long and somewhat ominous silence! Lady Ruth's eyes were fixed upon the floor. She was thinking, and thinking rapidly, but there were no signs of it in her pale drawn face. At last she looked up.

"There is my husband," she said. "He would recognize you, if no one else did."

"You are a clever woman," he answered. "I leave it to you to deal with your husband as seems best to you."

"Other people," she faltered, "would recognize you!"

"Do me the favor," he begged her, "to look at me carefully for several moments. You doubtless have some imperfect recollection of what I was. Compare it with my present appearance! I venture to think that you will agree with me. Recognition is barely possible."

Again there was silence. Lady Ruth seemed to have no words, but there was the look of a frightened child upon her face.

"I am sorry," he continued, "that the idea does not appeal to you! I can understand that my presence may serve to recall a period which you and your husband would doubtless prefer to forget -"

"Stop!"

A little staccato cry of pain; a cry which seemed to spring into life from a tortured heart, broke from her lips. Aynesworth heard it, and, at that moment, he hated his employer. Wingrave paused for a moment politely, and then continued.

"But after all," he said, "I can assure you that you will find very little in the Mr. Wingrave of New York to remind you of the past. I shall do my utmost to win for myself a place in your esteem, which will help you to forget the other relationship, which, if my memory serves me, used once to exist between us!"

She raised her head. Either she realized that, for the present, the man was immune against all sentiment, or his calm brutality had had a correspondingly hardening effect upon her.

"If I agree," she said , "will you give me back

my letters?"

"No!" he answered.

"What are you going to do with them?"

"It depends," he said, "upon you. I enter into no engagement. I make no promises. I simply remind you that it would be equally possible for me to take my place in the world as a rehabilitated Wingrave Seton. Ten years ago I yielded to sentiment. Today I have outlived it."

"Ten years ago," she murmured, "you were a hero. God knows what you are now!"

"Exactly!" he answered smoothly. "I am free to admit that I am a puzzle to myself. I find myself, in fact, a most interesting study."

"I consent," she said, with a little shudder. "I am going now."

"You are a sensible woman," he answered. "Aynesworth, show Lady Ruth to her carriage."

She rose to her feet. Hung from her neck by a chain of fine gold, was a large Chinchilla muff. She stood before him, and her hands had sought its shelter. Timidly she withdrew one.

"Will you shake hands with me, Wingrave?" she asked timidly.

He shook his head.

E. Phillips Oppenheim

"Forgive me," he said; "I may better my manners in America, but a present I cannot."

She passed out of the room. Aynesworth followed, closing the door behind them. In the corridor she stumbled, and caught at his arm for support.

"Don't speak to me," she gasped. "Take me where I can sit down."

He found her a quiet corner in the drawing room. She sat perfectly still for nearly five minutes, with her eyes closed. Then she opened them, and looked at her companion.

"Mr. Aynesworth," she said, "are you so poor that you must serve a man like that?"

He shook his head.

"It is not poverty," he answered. "I knew his history, and I am interested in him!"

"You write novels, don't you?" she asked.

"I try," he answered. "His story fascinated me. He stands today in a unique position to life. I want to see how he will come out of it."

"You knew his story - the truth?"

"Everything," he answered. "I heard it from a journalist who was in court, his only friend, the only man who knew."

"Where is he now?"

"On his way to Japan."

She drew a little breath between her teeth.

"There were rumors," she said. "It was hard for me at first, but I lived them down. I was very young then. I ought not to have accepted his sacrifice. I wish to heaven I had not. I wish that I had faced the scandal then. It is worse to be in the power of a man like this today! Mr. Aynesworth!"

"Lady Ruth!"

"Do you think that he has the right to keep those letters?"

"I cannot answer that question."

"Will you be my friend?"

"So far as I can - in accordance with my obligations to my employer!"

She tried him no further then, but rose and walked slowly out of the room. He found her maid, and saw them to their carriage. Then he returned to the sitting room. Wingrave was smoking a cigarette.

"I am trying the humanizing influence," he remarked. "Got rid of her ladyship?"

"Lady Ruth has just gone," Aynesworth answered.

"Have you promised to steal the letters yet?" he inquired.

"Not yet!"

"Her dainty ladyship has not bid high enough, I suppose," he continued. "Don't be afraid to open your mouth. There's another woman there besides the Lady Ruth Barrington, who opens bazaars, and patronizes charity, and entertains Royalty. Ask what you want and she'll pay!"

"What a brute you are!" Aynesworth exclaimed involuntarily.

"Of course I am," he admitted. "I know that. But whose fault is it? It isn't mine. I've lived the life of a brute creature for ten years. You don't abuse a one-legged man, poor devil. I've had other things amputated. I was like you once. It seemed all right to me to go under to save a woman's honor. You never have. Therefore, I say you've no right to call me a brute. Personally, I don't object. It is simply a matter of equity."

"I admit it," Aynesworth declared. "You are acting like a brute."

"Precisely. I didn't make myself what I am. Prison did it. Go and try ten years yourself, and you'll find you will have to grope about for your fine emotions. Are you coming to America with me?"

"I suppose so," Aynesworth answered. "When do we start?"

"Saturday week."

"Sport west, or civilization east?"

"Both," Wingrave answered. "Here is a list of the kit which we shall require. Add yourself the things which I have forgotten. I pay for both!"

"Very good of you," Aynesworth answered.

"Not at all. I don't suppose you'd come without. Can you shoot?"

"A bit," he admitted.

"Be particular about the rifles. I can take you to a little corner in Canada where the bears don't stand on ceremony. Put everything in hand, and be ready to come down to Cornwall with me on Monday."

"Cornwall!" Aynesworth exclaimed. "What on earth are we going to do in Cornwall?"

"I have an estate there, the home of my ancestors, which I am going to sell. I am the last of the Setons, fortunately, and I am going to smash the family tree, sell the heirlooms, and burn the family records!"

"I shouldn't if I were you," Aynesworth said quietly. "You are a young man yet. You may come back to your own!"

"Meaning?"

"You may smoke enough cigarettes to become actually humanized! One can never tell! I have known men proclaim themselves cynics for life, who have been making idiots of themselves with their own children in five years."

E. Phillips Oppenheim

Wingrave nodded gravely.

"True enough," he answered. "But the one thing which no man can mistake is death. Listen, and I will quote some poetry to you. I think - it is something like this: -

"'The rivers of ice may melt, and the mountains crumble into dust, but the heart of a dead man is like the seed plot unsown. Green grass shall not sprout there, nor flowers blossom, nor shall all the ages of eternity show there any sign of life.'"

He spoke as though he had been reading from a child's Primer. When he had finished, he replaced his cigarette between his teeth.

"I am a dead man," he said calmly. "Dead as the wildest seed plot in God's most forgotten acre!"

LORD OF THE MANOR

She came slowly towards the two men through the overgrown rose garden, a thin, pale, wild-eyed child, dressed in most uncompromising black. It was a matter of doubt whether she was the more surprised to see them, or they to find anyone else, in this wilderness of desolation. They stood face to face with her upon the narrow path.

"Have you lost your way?" she inquired politely.

"We were told," Aynesworth answered, "that there was a gate in the wall there, through which we could get on to the cliffs."

"Who told you so?" she asked.

"The housekeeper," Aynesworth answered. "I will not attempt to pronounce her name."

"Mrs. Tresfarwin," the child said. "It is not really difficult. But she had no right to send you through here! It is all private, you know!"

"And you?" Aynesworth asked with a smile, "you have permission, I suppose?"

"Yes," she answered. "I have lived here all my life. I

E. Phillips Oppenheim

go where I please. Have you seen the pictures?"

"We have just been looking at them," Aynesworth answered.

"Aren't they beautiful?" she exclaimed. "I - oh!"

She sat suddenly down on a rough wooden seat and commenced to cry. For the first time Wingrave looked at her with some apparent interest.

"Why, what is the matter with you, child?" Aynesworth exclaimed.

"I have loved them so all my life," she sobbed; "the pictures, and the house, and the gardens, and now I have to go away! I don't know where! Nobody seems to know!"

Aynesworth looked down at her black frock.

"You have lost someone, perhaps?" he said.

"My father," she answered quietly. "He was organist here, and he died last week."

"And you have no other relatives?" he asked.

"None at all. No one - seems - quite to know - what is going to become of me!" she sobbed.

"Where are you staying now?" he inquired.

"With an old woman who used to look after our cottage," she answered. "But she is very poor, and she cannot keep me any longer. Mrs. Colson says that I must go and work, and I am afraid. I don't know anyone except at Tredowen! And I don't know how to work! And I don't want to go away from the pictures, and the garden, and the sea! It is all so beautiful, isn't it? Don't you love Tredowen?"

"Well, I haven't been here very long, you see," Aynesworth explained.

Wingrave spoke for the first time. His eyes were fixed upon the child, and Aynesworth could see that she shrank from his cold, unsympathetic scrutiny.

"What is your name?" he asked.

"Juliet Lundy," she answered.

"How long was your father organist at the church?"

"I don't know," she answered. "Ever since I was born, and before."

"And how old are you?"

"Fourteen next birthday."

"And all that time," he asked, "has there been no one living at Tredowen?"

"No one except Mrs. Tresfarwin," she answered. "It belongs to a very rich man who is in prison."

Wingrave's face was immovable. He stood on one side, however, and turned towards his companion.

"We are keeping this young lady," he remarked, "from

what seems to be her daily pilgrimage. I wonder whether it is really the pictures, or Mrs. Tresfarwin's cakes?"

She turned her shoulder upon him in silent scorn, and looked at Aynesworth a little wistfully.

"Goodbye!" she said.

He waved his hand as he strolled after Wingrave.

"There you are, Mr. Lord of the Manor," he said. "You can't refuse to do something for the child. Her father was organist at your own church, and a hard struggle he must have had of it, with an absentee landlord, and a congregation of seagulls, I should think."

"Are you joking?" Wingrave asked coldly.

"I was never more in earnest in my life," Aynesworth answered. "The girl is come from gentlefolks. Did you see what a delicate face she had, and how nicely she spoke? You wouldn't have her sent out as a servant, would you?"

Wingrave looked at his companion ominously.

"You have a strange idea of the duties of a landlord," he remarked. "Do you seriously suppose that I am responsible for the future of every brat who grows up on this estate?"

"Of course not!" Aynesworth answered. "You must own for yourself that this case is exceptional. Let us go down to the Vicarage and inquire about it."

"I shall do nothing of the sort," Wingrave answered. "Nor will you! Do you see the spray coming over the cliffs there? The sea must be worth watching."

Aynesworth walked by his side in silence. He dared not trust himself to speak. Wingrave climbed with long, rapid strides to the summit of the headland, and stood there with his face turned seawards. The long breakers were sweeping in from the Atlantic with a low, insistent roar; as far as the eye could reach the waves were crusted with white foam. Every now and then the spray fell around the two men in a little dazzling shower; the very atmosphere was salt. About their heads the seagulls whirled and shrieked. From the pebbled beach to the horizon there was nothing to break the monotony of that empty waste of waters.

Wingrave stood perfectly motionless, with his eyes fixed upon the horizon. Minute after minute passed, and he showed no signs of moving. Aynesworth found himself presently engaged in watching him. Thoughts must be passing through his brain. He wondered what they were. It was here that he had spent his boyhood; barely an hour ago the two men had stood before the picture of his father. It was here, if anywhere, that he might regain some part of his older and more natural self. Was it a struggle, he wondered, that was going on within the man? There were no signs of it in his face. Simply he stood and looked, and looked, as though, by infinite perseverance, the very horizon itself might recede, and the thing for which he sought become revealed . . . .

Aynesworth turned away at last, and there, not many yards behind, apparently watching them, stood the child. He waved his hand and advanced towards her.

E. Phillips Oppenheim

Her eyes were fixed upon Wingrave half fearfully.

"I am afraid of the other gentleman," she whispered, as he reached her side. "Will you come a little way with me? I will show you a seagull's nest."

They left Wingrave where he was, and went hand in hand, along the cliff side. She was a curious mixture or shyness and courage. She talked very little, but she gripped her companion's fingers tightly.

"I can show you," she said, "where the seagulls build, and I can tell you the very spot in the sea where the sun goes down night after night.

"There are some baby seagulls in one of the nests, but I daren't go very near for the mother bird is so strong. Father used to say that when they have their baby birds to look after, they are as fierce as eagles."

"Your father used to walk with you here, Juliet?" Aynesworth asked.

"Always till the last few months when he got weaker and weaker," she answered. "Since then I come every day alone."

"Don't you find it lonely?" he asked.

She shook her head.

"At first," she answered, "not now. It makes me unhappy. Would you like to go down on the beach and look for shells? I can find you some very pretty ones."

They clambered down and wandered hand in hand by

the seashore. She told him quaint little stories of the smugglers, of wrecks, and the legends of the fisher people. Coming back along the sands, she clung to his arm and grew more silent. Her eyes sought his every now and then, wistfully. Presently she pointed out a tiny whitewashed cottage standing by itself on a piece of waste ground.

"That is where I live now, at least for a day or two," she said. "They cannot keep me any longer. When are you going away?"

"Very soon, I am afraid, little girl," he answered. "I will come and see you, though, before I go."

"You promise," she said solemnly.

"I promise," Aynesworth repeated.

Then she held up her face, a little timidly, and he kissed her. Afterwards, he watched her turn with slow, reluctant footsteps to the unpromising abode which she had pointed out. Aynesworth made his way to the inn, cursing his impecuniosity and Wingrave's brutal indifference.

He found the latter busy writing letters.

"Doing your work, Aynesworth?" he remarked coldly. "Be so good as to write to Christie's for me, and ask them to send down a valuer to go through the pictures."

"You are really going to sell!" Aynesworth exclaimed.

"Most certainly," Wingrave answered. "Heirlooms and

family pictures are only so much rubbish to me. I am the last of my line, and I doubt whether even my lawyer could discover a next of kin for my personal property. Sell! Of course I'm going to sell! What use is all this hoarded rubbish to me? I am going to turn it into gold!"

"And what use is gold?" Aynesworth asked curiously. "You have plenty!"

"Not enough for my purpose," Wingrave declared. "We are going to America to make more."

"It's vandalism!" Aynesworth said, "rank vandalism! The place as it is is a picture! The furniture and the house have grown old together. Why, you might marry!"

Wingrave scowled at the younger man across the room.

"You are a fool, Aynesworth," he said shortly. "Take down these letters."

After dinner, Wingrave went out alone. Aynesworth followed him about an hour later, when his work was done, and made his way towards the Vicarage. It was barely nine o'clock, but the little house seemed already to be in darkness. He rang twice before anybody answered him. Then he heard slow, shuffling footsteps within, and a tall, gaunt man, in clerical attire, and carrying a small lamp, opened the door.

Aynesworth made the usual apologies and was ushered into a bare, gloomy-looking apartment which, from the fact of its containing a writing table and a few books, he imagined must be the study. His host never asked him to sit down. He was a long, unkempt-looking man with a cold, forbidding face, and his manner was the reverse of cordial.

"I have called to see you," Aynesworth explained, "with reference to one of your parishioners - the daughter of your late organist."

"Indeed!" the clergyman remarked solemnly.

"I saw her today for the first time and have only just heard her story," Aynesworth continued. "It seems to be a very sad one."

His listener inclined his head.

"I am, unfortunately, a poor man," Aynesworth continued, "but I have some friends who are well off, and I could lay my hands upon a little ready money. I should like to discuss the matter with you and see if we cannot arrange something to give her a start in life."

The clergyman cleared his throat.

"It is quite unnecessary," he answered. "A connection of her father's has come forward at the last moment, who is able to do all that is required for her. Her future is provided for."

Aynesworth was a little taken aback.

"I am very glad to hear it," he declared. "I understood that she had neither friends nor relations."

"You were misinformed , " the other answered. "She

E. Phillips Oppenheim

has both."

"May I ask who it is who has turned up so unexpectedly?" Aynesworth inquired. "I have taken a great fancy to the child."

The clergyman edged a little towards the door, and the coldness of his manner was unmistakable.

"I do not wish to seem discourteous," he said, "but I cannot recognize that you have any right to ask me these questions. You may accept my word that the child is to be fittingly provided for."

Aynesworth felt the color rising in his cheeks.

"I trust," he said, "that you do not find my interest in her unwarrantable. My visit to you is simply a matter of charity. If my aid is unneeded, so much the better. All the same, I should like to know where she is going and who her friends are."

"I do not find myself at liberty to afford you any information," was the curt reply.

Thereupon there was nothing left for Aynesworth to do but to put on his hat and walk out, which he did.

Wingrave met him in the hall on his return.

"Where have you been?" he asked a little sharply.

"On a private errand," Aynesworth answered, irritated by his words and look.

"You are my secretary," Wingrave said coldly. "I do

not pay you to go about executing private errands."

Aynesworth looked at him in surprise. Did he really wish to quarrel?

"I imagine, sir," he said, "that my time is my own when I have no work of yours on hand. If you think otherwise -"

He paused and looked at his employer significantly. Wingrave turned on his heel.

"Be so kind," he said, "as to settle the bill here tonight. We leave by the seven o'clock train in the morning."

"Tomorrow!" Aynesworth exclaimed.

"Precisely!"

"Do you mind," he asked, "if I follow by a later train?"

"I do," Wingrave answered. "I need you in London directly we arrive."

"I am afraid," Aynesworth said, after a moment's reflection, "that it is impossible for me to leave."

"Why?"

"You will think it a small thing," he said, "but I have given my promise. I must see that child again before I go!"

"You are referring," he asked, "to the black-frocked little creature we saw about the place yesterday?"

"Yes!"

Wingrave regarded his secretary as one might look at a person who has suddenly taken leave of his senses.

"I am sorry," he said, "to interfere with your engagements, but it is necessary that we should both leave by the seven o'clock train tomorrow morning."

Aynesworth reflected for a moment.

"If I can see the child first," he said, "I will come. If not, I will follow you at midday."

"In the latter case," Wingrave remarked, "pray do not trouble to follow me unless your own affairs take you to London. Our connection will have ended."

"You mean this?" Aynesworth asked.

"It is my custom," Wingrave answered, "to mean what I say."

Aynesworth set his alarm that night for half-past five. It seemed to him that his future would largely depend upon how soundly the child slept.

THE HEART OF A CHILD

The cottage, as Aynesworth neared it, showed no sign of life. The curtainless windows were blank and empty, no smoke ascended from the chimney. Its plastered front was innocent of any form of creeper, but in the few feet of garden in front a great, overgrown wild rose bush, starred with deep red blossoms, perfumed the air. As he drew near, the door suddenly opened, and with a little cry of welcome the child rushed out to him.

"How lovely of you!" she cried. "I saw you coming from my window!"

"You are up early," he said, smiling down at her.

"The sun woke me," she answered. "It always does. I was going down to the sands. Shall we go together? Or would you like to go into the gardens at Tredowen? The flowers are beautiful there while the dew is on them!"

"I am afraid," Aynesworth answered, "that I cannot do either. I have come to say goodbye."

The light died out of her face all of a sudden. The delicate beauty of her gleaming eyes and quivering mouth had vanished. She was once more the pale, wan little child he had seen coming slowly up the garden path at Tredowen.

"You are going - so soon!" she murmured.

He took her hand and led her away over the short green turf of the common.

"We only came for a few hours," he told her. "But I have good news for you, Juliet, unless you know already. Mr. Saunders has found out some of your friends. They are going to look after you properly, and you will not be alone any more."

"What time are you going?" she asked.

"Silly child," he answered, giving her hand a shake. "Listen to what I am telling you. You are going to have friends to look after you always. Aren't you glad?"

"No, I am not glad," she answered passionately. "I don't want to go away. I am - lonely."

Her arms suddenly sought his neck, and her face was buried on his shoulder. He soothed her as well as he could.

"I must go, little girl," he said, "for I am off to America almost at once. As soon as I can after I come back, I will come and see you."

"You have only been here one day," she sobbed.

"I would stay if I could, dear," Aynesworth answered. "Come, dry those eyes and be a brave girl. Think how nice it will be to go and live with people who will take care of you properly, and be fond of you. Why, you may have a pony, and all sorts of nice things."

"I don't want a pony," she answered, hanging on his arm. "I don't want to go away. I want to stay here - and wait till you come back."

He laughed.

"Why, when I come back, little woman," he answered, "you will be almost grown up. Come, dry your eyes now, and I tell you what we will do. You shall come back with me to breakfast, and then drive up to the station and see us off."

"I should like to come," she whispered, "but I am afraid of the other gentleman."

"Very likely we sha'n't see him," Aynesworth answered. "If we do, he won't hurt you."

"I don't like his face!" she persisted.

"Well, we won't look at it," Aynesworth answered. "But breakfast we must have!"

They were half way through the meal, and Juliet had quite recovered her spirits when Wingrave entered. He looked at the two with impassive face, and took his place at the table. He wished the child "Good morning" carelessly, but made no remark as to her presence there.

"I have just been telling Juliet some good news," Aynesworth remarked. "I went to see Mr. Saunders, the Vicar here, last night, and he has found out some of her father's friends. They are going to look after her."

Wingrave showed no interest in the information. But a moment later he addressed Juliet for the first time.

"Are you glad that you are going away from Tredowen?" he asked.

"I am very, very sorry," she answered, the tears gathering once more in her eyes.

"But you want to go to school, don't you, and see other girls?" he asked.

She shook her head decidedly.

"It will break my heart," she said quietly, "to leave Tredowen. I think that if I have to go away from the pictures and the garden, and the sea, I shall never be happy any more."

"You are a child," he remarked contemptuously; "you do not understand. If you go away, you can learn to paint pictures yourself like those at Tredowen. You will find that the world is full of other beautiful places!"

The sympathetic aspect of his words was altogether destroyed by the thin note of careless irony, which even the child understood. She felt that he was mocking her.

"I could never be happy," she said simply, "away from Tredowen. You understand, don't you?" she added, turning confidentially to Aynesworth.

"You think so now, dear," he said, "but remember that you are very young. There are many things for you to learn before you grow up."

"I am not a dunce," she replied. "I can talk French and German, and do arithmetic, and play the organ. Father used to teach me these things. I can learn at Tredowen very well. I hope that my friends will let me stay here."

Wingrave took no more notice of her. She and Aynesworth walked together to the station. As they passed the little whitewashed cottage, she suddenly let go his hand, and darted inside.

"Wait one moment," she cried breathlessly.

She reappeared almost at once, holding something tightly clenched in her right hand. She showed it to him shyly.

"It is for you, please," she said.

It was a silver locket, and inside was a little picture of herself. Aynesworth stooped down and kissed her. He had had as many presents in his life as most men, but never an offering which came to him quite like that! They stood still for a moment, and he held out her hands. Already the morning was astir. The seagulls were wheeling, white-winged and noiseless, above their heads; the air was fragrant with the scent of cottage flowers. Like a low, sweet undernote, the sea came rolling in upon the firm sands - out to the west it stretched like a sheet of softly swaying inland water. For those few moments there seemed no note of discord - and then the harsh whistle of an approaching train! They took hold of hands and ran.

E. Phillips Oppenheim

It was, perhaps, as well that their farewells were cut short. There was scarcely time for more than a few hurried words before the train moved out from the queer little station, and with his head out of the window, Aynesworth waved his hand to the black-frocked child with her pale, eager face already stained with tears - a lone, strange little figure, full of a sort of plaintive grace as she stood there, against a back-ground of milk cans, waving a crumpled handkerchief!

Wingrave, who had been buried in a morning paper, looked up presently.

"If our journeyings," he remarked drily, "are to contain everywhere incidents such as these, they will become a sort of sentimental pilgrimage."

Aynesworth shrugged his shoulders.

"I am sorry," he said, "that my interest in the child has annoyed you. At any rate, it is over now. The parson was mysterious, but he assured me that she was provided for."

Wingrave looked across the carriage with cold, reflective curiosity.

"Your point of view," he remarked, "is a mystery to me! I cannot see how the future of an unfledged brat like that can possibly concern you!"

"Perhaps not," Aynesworth answered, "but you must remember that you are a little out of touch with your fellows just now. I daresay when you were my age, you would have felt as I feel. I daresay that as the years go on, you will feel like it again."

Wingrave was thoughtful for a moment.

"So you think," he remarked, "that I may yet have in me the making of a sentimentalist."

Aynesworth returned his gaze as steadfastly.

"One can never tell," he answered. "You may change, of course. I hope that you will."

"You are candid, at any rate!"

"I do not think," Aynesworth answered, "that there is any happiness in life for the man who lives entirely apart from his fellow creatures. Not to feel is not to live. I think that the first real act of kindness which you feel prompted to perform will mark the opening of a different life for you."

Wingrave spread out the newspaper.

"I think," he said, with a faint sneer, "that it is quite time you took this sea voyage."

THE SWORD OF DAMOCLES

Mr. Lumley Barrington, K.C. and M.P., was in the act of stepping into his carriage to drive down to the House, when he was intercepted by a message. It was his wife's maid, who came hurrying out after him.

"I beg your pardon, sir," she said, "but her ladyship particularly wished to see you as soon as you came in."

"Is your mistress in?" Barrington asked in some surprise.

"Yes, sir!" the maid answered. "Her ladyship is resting, before she goes to the ball at Caleram House. She is in her room now."

"I will come up at once," Barrington said.

He kept the carriage waiting while he ascended to his wife's room. There was no answer to his knock. He opened the door softly. She was asleep on a couch drawn up before the fire.

He crossed the room noiselessly, and stood looking down upon her. Her lithe, soft figure had fallen into a posture of graceful, almost voluptuous ease; the ribbons and laces of her muslin dressing gown quivered gently with her deep regular breathing. She had thrown off her slippers, and one long, slender foot was exposed; the other was doubled up underneath her body. Her face was almost like the face of a child, smooth and unwrinkled, save for one line by the eyes where she laughed. He looked at her steadfastly. Could the closing of the eyes, indeed, make all the difference? Life and the knowledge of life seemed things far from her consciousness. Could one look like that - even in sleep - and underneath - ! Barrington broke away from his train of thought, and woke her quickly.

She sat up and yawned.

"Parsons managed to catch you, then," she remarked.

"Yes!" he answered. "I was just off. I got away from Wills' dinner party early, and called here for some notes. I must be at the House" - he glanced at the clock - "in three-quarters of an hour!"

She nodded. "I won't keep you as long as that."

Her eyes met his, a little furtively, full of inquiry. "I have done what you wished," he said quietly. "I called at the Clarence Hotel!"

"You saw him!"

"No! He sent back my card. He declined to see me."

She showed no sign of disappointment. She sat up and looked into the fire, smoothing her hair mechanically with her hands.

"Personally," Barrington continued, "I could see no

E. Phillips Oppenheim

object whatever in my visit. I have nothing to say to him, nor, I should think, he to me. I am sorry for him, of course, but he'd never believe me if I told him so. What happened to him was partly my fault, and unless he's changed, he's not likely to forget it."

She swayed a little towards him.

"It was partly - also - mine," she murmured.

"I don't see that at all," he objected. "You at any rate were blameless!"

She looked up at him, and he was astonished to find how pale she was.

"I was not!" she said calmly.

There was a short silence. Barrington had the air of a man who has received a shock.

"Ruth!" he exclaimed, glancing towards the door, and speaking almost in a whisper. "Do you mean - that there are things which I have never known?"

"Yes!" she answered. "I mean that he might, if he chose, do us now - both of us - an immense amount of harm."

Barrington sat down at the end of the sofa. He knew his wife well enough to understand that this was serious.

"Let us understand one another, Ruth," he said quietly. "I always thought that you were a little severe on Wingrave at the trial! He may bear you a grudge for that; it is very possible that he does. But what can he do now? He had his chance to cross examine you, and he let it go by."

"He has some letters of mine," Lady Ruth said slowly.

"Letters! Written before the trial?"

"Yes!"

"Why did he not make use of them there?"

"If he had," Lady Ruth said, with her eyes fixed upon the carpet, "the sympathy would have been the other way. He would have got off with a much lighter sentence, and you - would not have married me!"

"Good God!" Barrington muttered.

"You see," Lady Ruth continued, resting her hand upon her husband's coat sleeve, "the thing happened all in a second. I had the check in my hand when you and Sir William came crashing through that window, and Sir William's eyes were upon me. The only way to save myself was to repudiate it, and let Wingrave get out of the affair as well as he could. Of course, I never guessed what was going to happen."

"Then it was Wingrave," Barrington muttered, "who played the game?"

"Yes!" Lady Ruth answered quietly. "But I am not so sure about him now. You and I, Lumley, know one another a little better today than we did twelve years ago. We have had a few of the corners knocked off, I suppose. I can tell you things now I didn't care to then.

Wingrave had lent me money before! He has letters from me today, thanking him for it."

Barrington was a large, florid man, well built and well set up. In court he presented rather a formidable appearance with his truculent chin, his straight, firm mouth, and his commanding presence. Yet there was nothing about him now which would have inspired fear in the most nervous of witnesses. He looked like a man all broken up by some unexpected shock.

"If he had produced those letters - at the trial -"

Lady Ruth shrugged her shoulders.

"I risked it, anyhow," she said. "I had to. My story was the only one which gave me a dog's chance, and I didn't mean to go under - then. Wingrave never gave me away, but I fancy he's feeling differently about it now!"

"How do you know, Ruth?"

"I have seen him! He sent for me!" she answered. "Lumley, don't look at me like that! We're not in the nursery, you and I. I went because I had to. He's going to America for a time, and then he's coming back here. I think that when he comes back - he means mischief!"

"He is not the sort of man to forget," Barrington said, half to himself.

She shuddered ever so slightly. Then she stretched out a long white arm, and drawing his head suddenly down to her, kissed him on the lips.

"If only," she murmured, "he would give up the letters! Without them, he might say - anything. No one would believe!"

Barrington raised his eyes to hers. There was something almost pathetic in the worshiping light which shone there. He was, as he had always been, her abject slave.

"Can you think of any way?" he asked. "Shall I go to him again?"

"Useless!" she answered. "You have nothing to offer in exchange. He would not give them to me. He surely would not give them to you. Shall I tell you what is in his mind? Listen, then! He is rich now; he means to make more money there. Then he will return, calling himself Mr. Wingrave - an American - with imaginary letters of introduction to us. He has ambitions - I don't know what they are, but they seem to entail his holding some sort of a place in society. We are to be his sponsors."

"Is it practicable?" he asked.

"Quite," she answered. "He is absolutely unrecognizable now. He has changed cruelly. Can't you imagine the horror of it? He will be always in evidence; always with those letters in the background. He means to make life a sort of torture chamber for us!"

"Better defy him at once, and get over," Barrington said. "After all, don't you think that the harm he could do is a little imaginary?"

She brushed the suggestion aside with a little shiver.

"Shall I tell you what he would do, Lumley?" she said, leaning towards him. "He would have my letters, and a copy of my evidence, printed in an elegant little volume and distributed amongst my friends. It would come one day like a bomb, and nothing that you or I could do would alter it in the least. Your career and my social position would be ruined. Success brings enemies, you know, Lumley, and I have rather more than my share."

"Then we are helpless," he said.

"Unless we can get the letters - or unless he should never return from America," she answered.

Barrington moved uneasily in his seat. He knew very well that some scheme was already forming in his wife's brain.

"If there is anything that I can do," he said in a low tone, "don't be afraid to tell me."

"There is one chance," she answered, "a sort of forlorn hope, but you might try it. He has a secretary, a young man named Aynesworth. If he were on our side -"

"Don't you think," Barrington interrupted, "that you would have more chance with him than I?"

She laughed softly.

"You foolish man," she said, touching his fingers lightly. "I believe you think that I am irresistible!"

"I have seen a good many lions tamed," he reminded her.

"Nonsense! Anyhow, there is one here who seems quite insensible. I have talked already with Mr. Aynesworth. He would not listen to me!"

"Ah!"

"Nevertheless," she continued softy, "of one thing I am very sure. Every man is like every woman; he is vulnerable if you can discover the right spot and the right weapons. Mr. Aynesworth is not a woman's man, but I fancy that he is ambitious. I thought that you might go and see him. He has rooms somewhere in Dorset Street."

He rose to his feet. A glance at the clock reminded him of the hour.

"I will go," he said. "I will do what I can. I think, dear," he added, bending over her to say farewell, "that you should have been the man!"

She laughed softly.

"Am I such a failure as a woman, then?" she asked with a swift upward glance. "Don't be foolish, Lumley. My woman will be here to dress me directly. You must really go away."

He strode down the stairs with tingling pulses, and drove to the House, where his speech, a little florid in its rhetoric, and verbose as became the man, was nevertheless a great success.

"Quite a clever fellow, Barrington," one of his acquaintances remarked, "when you get him away from his wife."

A FORLORN HOPE

Aynesworth ceased tugging at the strap of his port-manteau, and rose slowly to his feet. A visitor had entered his rooms - apparently unannounced.

"I must apologize," the newcomer said, "for my intrusion. Your housekeeper, I presume it was, whom I saw below, told me to come up."

Aynesworth pushed forward a chair.

"Won't you sit down?" he said. "I believe that I am addressing Mr. Lumley Barrington."

Not altogether without embarrassment, Barrington seated himself. Something of his ordinary confidence of bearing and demeanor had certainly deserted him. His manner, too, was nervous. He had the air of being altogether ill at ease.

"I must apologize further, Mr. Aynesworth," he continued, "for an apparently ill-timed visit. You are, I see, on the eve of a journey."

"I am leaving for America tomorrow," Aynesworth answered.

"With Sir Wingrave Seton, I presume?"

E. Phillips Oppenheim

Barrington remarked.

"Precisely," Aynesworth answered.

Barrington hesitated for a moment. Aynesworth was civil, but inquiring. He felt himself very awkwardly placed.

"Mr. Aynesworth," he said, "I must throw myself upon your consideration. You can possibly surmise the reason of my visit."

Aynesworth shook his head.

"I am afraid," he said, "that I must plead guilty to denseness - in this particular instance, at any rate. I am altogether at a loss to account for it."

"You have had some conversation with my wife, I believe?"

"Yes. But -"

"Before you proceed, Mr. Aynesworth," Barrington interrupted, "one word. You are aware that Sir Wingrave Seton is in possession of certain documents in which my wife is interested, which he refuses to give up?"

"I have understood that such is the case," Aynesworth admitted. "Will you pardon me if I add that it is a matter which I can scarcely discuss?"

Barrington shrugged his shoulders.

"Let it go, for the moment , " he said. "There is

something else which I want to say to you."

Aynesworth nodded a little curtly. He was not very favorably impressed with his visitor.

"Well!"

Barrington leaned forward in his chair.

"Mr. Aynesworth," he said, "you have made for yourself some reputation as a writer. Your name has been familiar to me for some time. I was at college, I believe, with your uncle, Stanley Aynesworth."

He paused. Aynesworth said nothing.

"I want to know," Barrington continued impressively, "what has induced you to accept a position with such a man as Seton?"

"That," Aynesworth declared, "is easily answered. I was not looking for a secretaryship at all, or anything of the sort, but I chanced to hear his history one night, and I was curious to analyze, so far as possible, his attitude towards life and his fellows, on his reappearance in it. That is the whole secret."

Barrington leaned back in his chair, and glanced thoughtfully at his companion.

"You know the story of his misadventures, then?" he remarked.

"I know all about his imprisonment, and the cause of it," Aynesworth said quietly.

Barrington was silent for several moments. He felt that he was receiving but scanty encouragement.

"Is it worth while, Mr. Aynesworth?" he asked at length. "There is better work for you in the world than this."

Again Aynesworth preferred to reply by a gesture only. Barrington was watching him steadily.

"A political secretaryship, Mr. Aynesworth," he said, "might lead you anywhere. If you are ambitious, it is the surest of all stepping stones into the House. After that, your career is in your own hands. I offer you such a post."

"I am exceedingly obliged to you," Aynesworth replied, "but I scarcely understand."

"I have influence," Barrington said, "which I have never cared to use on my own account. I am willing to use it on yours. You have only to say the word, and the matter is arranged."

"I can only repeat," Aynesworth said, "that I am exceedingly obliged to you, Mr. Barrington, but I cannot understand why you should interest yourself so much on my behalf."

"If you wish me to speak in plain words," Barrington said, "I will do so. I ask you to aid me as a man of honor in the restoration of those letters to my wife."

"I cannot do it," Aynesworth said firmly. "I am sorry that you should have come to me with such an offer. It is quite out of the question!"

Barrington held out his hand.

"Do not decide too hastily," he said. "Remember this. Sir Wingrave Seton had once an opportunity of putting those letters to any use he may have thought fit. He ignored it. At that time, their tenor and contents might easily have been explained. After all these years, that task would be far more difficult. I say that no man has a right to keep a woman's letters back from her years after any friendship there may have been between them is over. It is not the action of an honorable man. Sir Wingrave Seton has placed himself outside the pale of honorable men."

"Your judgment," Aynesworth answered quietly, "seems to me severe. Sir Wingrave Seton has been the victim of peculiar circumstances."

Barrington looked at his companion thoughtfully. He was wondering exactly how much he knew.

"You defend him," he remarked. "That is because you have not yet found out what manner of man he is."

"In any case," Aynesworth answered, "I am not his judge. Mr. Barrington," he added, "You must forgive me if I remind you that this is a somewhat unprofitable discussion."

A short silence followed. With Barrington it did not appear to be a silence of irresolution. He was leaning a little forward in his chair, and his head was resting upon his hand. Of his companion he seemed for the moment to have become oblivious. Aynesworth watched him curiously. Was he looking back through the years, he wondered, to that one brief but lurid

E. Phillips Oppenheim

chapter of history; or was it his own future of which he was thinking, - a future which, to the world, must seem so full of brilliant possibilities, and yet which he himself must feel to be so fatally and miserably insecure?

"Mr. Aynesworth," he said at last, "I suppose from a crude point of view I am here to bribe you."

Aynesworth shrugged his shoulders.

"Is it worth while?" he asked a little wearily. "I have tried to be civil - but I have also tried to make you understand. Your task is absolutely hopeless!"

"It should not be," Barrington persisted. "This is one of those rare cases, in which anything is justifiable. Seton had his chance at the trial. He chose to keep silence. I do not praise him or blame him for that. It was the only course open to a man of honor. I maintain that his silence then binds him to silence for ever. He has no right to ruin my life and the happiness of my wife by subtle threats, to hold those foolish letters over our heads, like a thunderbolt held ever in suspense. You are ambitious, I believe, Mr. Aynesworth! Get me those letters, and I will make you my secretary, find you a seat in Parliament, and anything else in reason that you will!"

Aynesworth rose to his feet. He wished to intimate that, so far as he was concerned, the interview was at an end.

"Your proposition, Mr. Barrington," he said, "is absolutely impossible. In the first place, I have no idea where the letters in question are, and Sir Wingrave is never likely to suffer them to pass into my charge."

"You have opportunities of finding out," Barrington suggested.

"And secondly," Aynesworth continued, ignoring the interruption, "whatever the right or the wrong of this matter may be, I am in receipt of a salary from Sir Wingrave Seton, and I cannot betray his confidence."

Barrington also rose to his feet. He was beginning to recognize the hopelessness of his task.

"This is final, Mr. Aynesworth?" he asked.

"Absolutely!" was the firm reply.

Barrington bowed stiffly, and moved towards the door. On the threshold he paused.

"I trust, Mr. Aynesworth," he said hesitatingly, "that you will not regard this as an ordinary attempt at bribery and corruption. I have simply asked you to aid me in setting right a great injustice."

"It is a subtle distinction, Mr. Barrington," Aynesworth answered, "but I will endeavor to keep in mind your point of view."

Barrington drove straight home, and made his way directly to his study. Now that he was free from his wife's influence, and looked back upon his recent interview, he realized for the first time the folly and indignity of the whole proceedings. He was angry that, a man of common sense, keen witted and farseeing in the ordinary affairs of life, should have placed himself so completely in a false, not to say a humiliating position. And then, just as suddenly, he forgot all about himself, and remembered only her. With a breath of violets, and the delicate rustling of half-lifted skirts, she had come softly into the room, and stood looking at him inquiringly. Her manner seemed to indicate more a good-natured curiosity than real anxiety. She made a little grimace as he shook his head.

"I have failed," he said shortly. "That young man is a prig!"

"I was afraid," she said, "that he would be obstinate. Men with eyes of that color always are!"

"What are we to do, Ruth?"

"What can we?" she answered calmly. "Nothing but wait. He is going to America. It is a terrible country for accidents. Something may happen to him there! Do go and change your things, there's a dear, and look in at the Westinghams' for me for an hour. We'll just get some supper and come away."

"I will be ready in ten minutes," Barrington answered. He understood that he was to ask no questions, nor did he. But all the time his man was hurrying him into his clothes, his brain was busy weaving fancies.

PROFESSOR SINCLAIR'S DANCING ACADEMY

Mr. Sinclair, or as he preferred to be called, Professor Sinclair, waved a white kid glove in the direction of the dancing hall.

"This way, ladies and gentlemen!" he announced. "A beautiful valse just about to commence. Tickets, if you please! Ah! Glad to see you, Miss Cullingham! You'll find - a friend of yours inside!"

There was a good deal of giggling as the girls came out from the little dressing room and joined their waiting escorts, who stood in a line against the wall, mostly struggling with refractory gloves. Mr. Sinclair, proprietor of the West Islington Dancing Academy, and host of these little gatherings - for a consideration of eighteenpence - did his best, by a running fire of conversation, to set everyone at their ease. He wore a somewhat rusty frock coat, black trousers, a white dress waistcoat, and a red tie. Evening dress was not DE RIGUEUR! The money at the door, and that everyone should behave as ladies and gentlemen, were the only things insisted upon.

Mr. Sinclair's best smile and most correct bow was suddenly in evidence.

"Mademoiselle Violet ! " he exclaimed to a lady who

E. Phillips Oppenheim

came in alone, "we are enchanted. We feared that you had deserted us. There is a young gentleman inside who is going to be made very happy. One shilling change, thank you. Won't you step into the cloak room?"

The lady shook her head.

"If you don't mind, Mr. Sinclair," she said, "I would rather keep my hat and veil on. I can only stay for a few minutes. Is Mr. Richardson here, do you know? Ah! I can see him."

She stepped past the Professor into the little dancing hall. A young lady was pounding upon a piano, a boy at her side was playing the violin. A few couples were dancing, but most of the company was looking on. The evening was young, and Mr. Sinclair, who later on officiated as M.C., had not yet made his attack upon the general shyness. The lady known as Mademoiselle Violet paused and looked around her. Suddenly she caught sight of a pale, anemic-looking youth, who was standing apart from the others, lounging against the wall. She moved rapidly towards him.

"How do you do, Mr. Richardson?" she said, holding out her hand.

He started, and a sudden rush of color streamed into his cheeks. He took her hand awkwardly, and he was almost speechless with nervousness.

"I don't believe you're at all glad to see me!" she remarked.

"Oh! Miss Violet!" he exclaimed. He would have said

more, but the words stuck in his throat.

"Can we sit down somewhere?" she said. "I want to talk to you."

There were one or two chairs placed behind a red drugget curtain, where adventurous spirits led their partners later in the evening. They found a place there, and the young man recovered his power of speech.

"Not glad to see you!" he exclaimed almost vehemently. "Why, what else do you suppose I come here for every Thursday evening? I never dance; they all make game of me because they know I come here on the chance of seeing you again. I'm a fool! I know that! You just amuse yourself here with me, and then you go away, back to your friends - and forget! And I hang about round here, like the silly ass that I am!"

"My dear - George!"

The young man blushed at the sound of his Christian name. He was mollified despite himself.

"I suppose it's got to be the same thing all over again," he declared resignedly. "You'll talk to me and let me be near you - and make a fool of me all round; and then you'll go away, and heaven knows when I'll see you again. You won't let me take you home, and won't tell me where you live, or who your friends are. You do treat me precious badly, Miss Violet."

"This time," she said quietly, "it will not be the same. I have something quite serious to say to you."

"Something serious - you? Go on !" he exclaimed

in excitement.

"Have you found another place yet?"

"No. I haven't really tried. I have a little money saved, and I could get one tomorrow if -"

She stopped him with a smiling gesture.

"I don't mean that - yet," she said. "I wanted to know whether it would be possible for you to go away for a little time, if someone paid all your expenses."

"To go away!" he repeated blankly. "What for?"

Mademoiselle Violet leaned a little nearer to him.

"My mistress asked me yesterday," she said, "if I knew anyone who could be trusted who would go away, at a moment's notice, on an errand for her."

"Your mistress," he repeated. "You really are a lady's maid, then, are you?"

"Of course!" she answered impatiently. "Haven't I told you so before? Now what do you say? Will you go?"

"I dunno," he answered thoughtfully. "If it had been for you, I don't know that I'd have minded. I ain't fond of traveling."

"It is for me," she interrupted hastily. "If I can find her anyone who will do what she wants, she will make my fortune. She has promised. And then -"

"Well, and then?"

Mademoiselle Violet looked at him thoughtfully.

"I should not make any promises," she said demurely, "but things would certainly be different."

The young man's blood was stirred. Mademoiselle Violet stood to him for the whole wonderful world of romance, into which he had peered dimly from behind the counter of an Islington emporium. Her low voice - so strange to his ears after the shrill chatter of the young ladies of his acquaintance - the mystery of her coming and going, all went to give color to the single dream of his unimaginative life. Apart from her, he was a somewhat vulgar, entirely commonplace young man, of saving habits, and with some aptitude for business, in a small way. He had been well on his way to becoming a small but successful shopkeeper, thereby realizing the only ideals which had yet presented themselves to him, when Madame Violet had unconsciously intervened. Of what might become of him now he had no clear conception of himself.

"I'll go!" he declared.

Mademoiselle Violet's eyes flashed behind her veil. Her fingers touched his for a moment.

"It is a long way," she said.

"I don't care," he answered valiantly.

"To - America!"

"America!" he gasped. "But - is this a joke, Miss Violet?"

E. Phillips Oppenheim

She shook her head.

"Of course not! America is not a great journey."

"But it will cost -"

She laughed softly.

"My mistress is very rich," she said. "The cost does not matter at all. You will have all the money you can spend - and more."

He felt himself short of breath, and bereft of words.

"Gee whiz!" he murmured.

They sat there in silence for a few moments. A promenading couple put their heads behind the screen, and withdrew with the sound of feminine giggling. Outside, the piano was being thumped to the tune of a popular polka.

"But what have I go to do?" he asked.

"To watch a man who will go out by the same steamer as you," she answered. "Write to London, tell me what he does, how he spends his time, whether he is ill or well. You must stay at the same hotel in New York, and try and find out what his business is there. Remember, we want to know, my mistress and I, everything that he does."

"Who is he?" he asked. "A friend of your mistress?"

"No ! " she answered shortly , "an enemy. A cruel enemy - the cruelest enemy a woman could have!"

The subdued passion of her tone thrilled him. He felt himself bewildered - in touch with strange things. She leaned a little closer towards him, and that mysterious perfume, which was one of her many fascinations, dazed him with its sweetness.

"If you could send home word," she whispered, "that he was ill, that anything had happened to him, that he was not likely to return - our fortunes would be made - yours and mine."

"Stop!" he muttered. "You - phew! It's hot here!"

He wiped the perspiration recklessly from his forehead with a red silk handkerchief.

"What made you come to me?" he asked. "I don't even know the name of your mistress."

"And you must not ask it," she declared quietly. "It is better for you not to know. I came to you because you were a man, and I knew that I could trust you."

Her flattery sank into his soul. No one else had ever called him a man. He felt himself capable of great things. To think that, but for the coming of this wonderful Mademoiselle Violet, he might even now have been furnishing a small shop on the outskirts of Islington, with collars and ties and gloves designed to attract the youth of that populous neighborhood!

"When do I start?" he asked with a coolness which surprised himself.

She drew a heavy packet from the recesses of the muff she carried.

E. Phillips Oppenheim

"All the particulars are here," she said. "The name of the steamer, the name of the man, and money. You will be told where to get more in New York, if you need it."

He took it from her mechanically. She rose to her feet.

"You will remember," she said, looking into his eyes.

"I ain't likely to forget anything you've said tonight," he answered honestly. "But look here! Let me take you home - just this once! Give me something to think about."

She shook her head.

"I will give you something to hope for," she whispered. "You must not come a yard with me. When you come back it will, perhaps - be different."

He remained behind the partition, gripping the packet tightly. Mademoiselle Violet took a hasty adieu of Mr. Sinclair, and descended to the street. She walked for a few yards, and then turned sharply to the left. A hansom, into which she stepped at once, was waiting there. She wrapped herself hastily in a long fur coat which lay upon the seat, and thrust her hand through the trap door.

"St. Martin's Schoolroom!" she told the cabman.

Apparently Mademoiselle Violet combined a taste for philanthropy with her penchant for Islington dancing halls. She entered the little schoolroom and made her way to the platform, dispensing many smiles and nods amongst the audience of the concert, which was momentarily interrupted for her benefit. She was escorted on to the platform by a young and earnest-looking clergyman, and given a chair in the center of the little group who were gathered there. And after the conclusion of the song, the clergyman expressed his gratification to the audience that a lady with so many calls upon her time, such high social duties, should yet find time to show her deep interest in their welfare by this most kind visit. After which, he ventured to call upon Lady Barrington to say a few words.

E. Phillips Oppenheim

MEPHISTOPHELES ON A STEAMER

In some respects, the voyage across the Atlantic was a surprise to Aynesworth. His companion seemed to have abandoned, for the time at any rate, his habit of taciturnity. He conversed readily, if a little stiffly, with his fellow passengers. He divided his time between the smoke room and the deck, and very seldom sought the seclusion of his state room. Aynesworth remarked upon this change one night as the two men paced the deck after dinner.

"You are beginning to find more pleasure," he said, "in talking to people."

Wingrave shook his head.

"By no means," he answered coldly. "It is extremely distasteful to me."

"Then why do you do it?" Aynesworth asked bluntly.

Wingrave never objected to being asked questions by his secretary. He seemed to recognize the fact that Aynesworth's retention of his post was due to a desire to make a deliberate study of himself, and while his own attitude remained purely negative, he at no time exhibited any resentment or impatience.

"I do it for several reasons," he answered. "First, because misanthropy is a luxury in which I cannot afford to indulge. Secondly, because I am really curious to know whether the time will ever return when I shall feel the slightest shadow of interest in any human being. I can only discover this by affecting a toleration for these people's society, which I can assure you, if you are curious about the matter, is wholly assumed."

Aynesworth shrugged his shoulders.

"Surely," he said, "you find Mrs. Travers entertaining?"

Wingrave reflected for a moment.

"You mean the lady with a stock of epigrams, and a green veil?" he remarked. "No! I do not find her entertaining."

"Your neighbor at table then, Miss Packe?"

"If my affections have perished," Wingrave answered grimly, "my taste, I hope, is unimpaired. The young person who travels to improve her mind, and fills up the gaps by reading Baedeker on the places she hasn't been to, fails altogether to interest me!"

"Aren't you a little severe?" Aynesworth remarked.

"I suppose," Wingrave answered, "that it depends upon the point of view, to use a hackneyed phrase. You study people with a discerning eye for good qualities. Nature - and circumstances have ordered it otherwise with me. I see them through darkened glasses."

"It is not the way to happiness," Aynesworth said.

"There is no highroad to what you term happiness," Wingrave answered. "One holds the string and follows into the maze. But one does not choose one's way. You are perhaps more fortunate than I that you can appreciate Mrs. Travers' wit, and find my neighbor, who has done Europe, attractive. That is a matter of disposition."

"I should like," Aynesworth remarked, "to have known you fifteen years ago."

Wingrave shrugged his shoulders.

"I fancy," he said, "that I was a fairly average person - I mean that I was possessed of an average share of the humanities. I have only my memory to go by. I am one of those fortunate persons, you see, who have realized an actual reincarnation. I have the advantage of having looked out upon life from two different sets of windows. - By the bye, Aynesworth, have you noticed that unwholesome-looking youth in a serge suit there?"

Aynesworth nodded.

"What about him?"

"I fancy that he must know - my history. He sits all day long smoking bad cigarettes and watching me. He makes clumsy attempts to enter into conversation with me. He is interested in us for some reason or other."

Aynesworth nodded.

"Shocking young bounder," he remarked. "I've noticed

him myself."

"Talk to him some time, and find out what he means by it," Wingrave said. "I don't want to find my biography in the American newspapers. It might interfere with my operations there. Here's this woman coming to worry us! You take her off, Aynesworth! I shall go into the smoking room."

But Mrs. Travers was not so easily to be disposed of. For some reason or other, she had shown a disposition to attach herself to Wingrave.

"Please put me in my chair," she said to him, holding out her rug and cushion. "No! Not you, Mr. Aynesworth. Mr. Wingrave understands so much better how to wrap me up. Thanks! Won't you sit down yourself? It's much better for you out here than in the smoking room - and we might go on with our argument."

"I thought," Wingrave remarked, accepting her invitation after a moment's hesitation, "that we were to abandon it."

"That was before dinner," she answered, glancing sideways at him. "I feel braver now."

"You are prepared," he remarked, "for unconditional surrender?"

She looked at him again. She had rather nice eyes, quite dark and very soft, and she was a great believer in their efficacy.

"Of my argument?"

He did not answer her for a moment. He had turned his head slightly towards her, and though his face was, as usual, expressionless, and his eyes cold and hard, she found nevertheless something of meaning in his steady regard. There was a flush in her cheek when she looked away.

"I am afraid," she remarked, "that you are rather a terrible person."

"You flatter me," he murmured. "I am really quite harmless!"

"Not from conviction then, I am sure," she remarked.

"Perhaps not," he admitted. "Let us call it from lack of enterprise! The virtues are all very admirable things, but it is the men and women with vices who have ruled the world. The good die young because there is no useful work for them to do. No really satisfactory person, from a moral point of view, ever achieved greatness!"

She half closed her eyes.

"My head is going round," she murmured. "What an upheaval! Fancy Mephistopheles on a steamer!"

"He was, at any rate, the most interesting of that little trio," Wingrave remarked, "but even he was a trifle heavy."

"Do you go about the world preaching your new doctrines?" she asked.

"Not I! " he answered. "Nothing would every make a

missionary of me, for good or for evil, for the simple reason that no one else's welfare except my own has the slightest concern for me."

"What hideous selfishness!" she said softly. "But I don't think - you quite mean it?"

"I can assure you I do," he answered drily. "My world consists of myself for the central figure, and the half a dozen or so of people who are useful or amusing to me! Except that the rest are needed to keep moving the machinery of the world, they might all perish, so far as I was concerned."

"I don't think," Mrs. Travers said softly, "that I should like to be in your world."

"I can very easily believe you," he answered.

"Unless," she remarked tentatively, "I came to convert!"

He nodded.

"There is something in that," he admitted. "It would be a great work, a little difficult, you know."

"All the more interesting!"

"You see," he continued, "I am not only bad, but I admire badness. My wish is to remain bad - in fact, I should like to be worse if I knew how. You would find it hard to make a start. I couldn't even admit that a state of goodness was desirable!"

She looked at him curiously. The night air was perhaps

getting colder, for she shivered, and drew the rug a little closer around her.

"You speak like a prophet," she remarked.

"A prophet of evil then!"

She looked at him steadfastly. The lightness had gone out of her tone.

"Do you know," she said, "I am almost sorry that I ever knew you?"

He shook his head.

"You can't mean it," he declared.

"Why not?"

"I have done you the greatest service one human being can render another! I have saved you from being bored!"

She nodded.

"That may be true," she admitted. "But can you conceive no worse state in the world than being bored?"

"There is no worse state," he answered drily. "I was bored once," he added, "for ten years or so; I ought to know!"

"Were you married?" she asked.

He shook his head.

"Not quite so bad as that," he answered. "I was in prison!"

She turned a startled face towards him.

"Nonsense!"

"It is perfectly true," he said coolly. "Are you horrified?"

"What did you do?" she asked in a low tone.

"I killed a man."

"Purposely?"

He shrugged his shoulders.

"He attacked me! I had to defend myself."

She said nothing for several moments.

"Shall I go?" he asked.

"No! Sit still," she answered. "I am frightened of you, but I don't want you to go away. I want to think . . . . Yes! I can understand you better now! Your life was spoilt!"

"By no means," he answered. "I am still young! I am going to make up for those ten years."

She shook her head.

"You cannot," she answered. "The years can carry no more than their ordinary burden of sensations. If you

E. Phillips Oppenheim

try to fill them too full, you lose everything."

"I shall try what I can do!" he remarked calmly.

She rose abruptly.

"I am afraid of you tonight," she said. "I am going downstairs. Will you give my rug and cushion to the deck steward? And - good night."

She gave him her hand, but she did not look at him, and she hurried away a little abruptly.

Wingrave yawned, and lighting a cigar, strolled up and down the deck. A figure loomed out of the darkness and almost ran into him. It was the young man in the serge suit. He muttered a clumsy apology and hurried on.

A COCKNEY CONSPIRATOR

"The bar closes in ten minutes, sir!" the smoking room steward announced.

The young man who had been the subject of Wingrave's remarks hastily ordered another drink, although he had an only half-emptied tumbler in front of him. Presently he stumbled out on to the deck. It was a dark night, and a strong head wind was blowing. He groped his way to the railing and leaned over, with his head half buried in his hands. Below, the black tossing sea was churned into phosphorescent spray, as the steamer drove onwards into the night.

Was it he indeed - George Richardson? He doubted it. The world of tape measures and calico counters seemed so far away; the interior of his quondam lodgings in a by-street of Islington, so unfamiliar and impossible. He felt himself swallowed up in this new and bewildering existence, of which he was so insignificant an atom, the existence where tragedy reared her gloomy head, and the shadows of great things loomed around him. Down there in the cold restless waste of black waters - what was it that he saw? The sweat broke out upon his forehead, the blood seemed turned to ice in his veins. He knew very well that his fancy mocked him, that it was not indeed a man's white face gleaming on the crest of the waves.

E. Phillips Oppenheim

But none the less he was terrified.

Mr. Richardson was certainly nervous. Not all the brandy he had drunk - and he had never drunk half as much before in his life - afforded him the least protection from these ghastly fancies. The step of a sailor on the deck made him shiver; the thought of his empty state room was a horror. He tried to think of the woman at whose bidding he had left behind him Islington and the things that belonged to Islington! He tried to recall her soft suggestive whispers, the glances which promised more even than her spoken words, all the perfume and mystery of her wonderful presence. Her very name was an allurement. Mademoiselle Violet! How softly it fell from the lips! . . . God in heaven, what was that? He started round, trembling in every limb. It was nothing more than the closing of the smoking room door behind him. Sailors with buckets and mops were already beginning their nightly tasks. He must go to his state room! Somehow or other, he must get through the night . . .

He did it, but he was not a very prepossessing looking object when he staggered out on deck twelve hours later, into the noon sunshine. The chair towards which he looked so eagerly was occupied. He scarcely knew himself whether that little gulp of acute feeling, which shot through his veins, was of relief or disappointment. While he hesitated, Wingrave raised his head.

Wingrave did not, as a rule, speak to his fellow passengers. Of Richardson, he had not hitherto taken the slightest notice. Yet this morning, of all others, he addressed him.

"I believe," he said, holding it out towards him, "that

this envelope is yours. I found it under your chair."

Richardson muttered something inarticulate, and almost snatched it away. It was the envelope of the fatal letter which Mademoiselle Violet had written him to Queenstown.

"Sit down, Mr. Richardson, if you are not in a hurry," Wingrave continued calmly. "I was hoping that I might see you this morning. Can you spare me a few minutes?"

Richardson subsided into his chair. His heart was thumping against his ribs. Wingrave's voice sounded to him like a far-off thing.

"The handwriting upon that envelope which I have just restored to you, Mr. Richardson, is well known to me," Wingrave continued, gazing steadfastly at the young man whom he was addressing.

"The envelope! The handwriting!" Richardson faltered. "I - it was from -"

An instant's pause. Wingrave raised his eyebrows.

"Ah!" he said. "We need not mention the lady's name. That she should be a correspondent of yours, however, helps me to understand better several matters which have somewhat puzzled me lately. No! Don't go, my dear sir. We must really have this affair straightened out."

"What affair?" Richardson demanded, with a very weak attempt at bluster. "I don't understand you - don't understand you at all."

Wingrave leaned a little forward in his chair. His eyebrows were drawn close together; his gaze was entirely merciless.

"You are not well this morning," he remarked. "A little headache perhaps! Won't you try one of these phenacetine lozenges - excellent things for a headache, I believe? Warranted, in fact, to cure all bodily ailments for ever! What! You don't like the look of them?"

The young man cowered back in his chair. He was gripping the sides tightly with both hands, and the pallor of a ghastly fear had spread over his face.

"I - don't know what you mean," he faltered. "I haven't a headache!"

Wingrave looked thoughtfully at the box between his fingers.

"If you took one of these, Mr. Richardson," he said, "you would never have another, at any rate. Now, tell me, sir, how you came by them!"

"I know nothing about -" the young man began.

"Don't lie to me, sir," Wingrave said sharply. "I have been wondering what the - you meant by hanging around after me, giving the deck steward five shillings to put your chair next mine, and pretending to read, while all the time you were trying to overhear any scraps of conversation between my secretary and myself. I thought you were simply guilty of impertinent curiosity. This, however, rather alters the look of affairs."

"What does?" Richardson asked faintly. "That box ain't mine."

"Perhaps not," Wingrave answered, "but you found it in my state room and filled it up with its present contents. My servant saw you coming out, and immediately went in to see what you had stolen, and report you. He found nothing missing, but he found this box full of lozenges, which he knows quite well was half full before you went in. Now, what was your object, Mr. Richardson, in tampering with that box upon my shelf?"

"I have - I have never seen it before," Richardson declared. "I have never been in your state room!"

The deck steward was passing. Wingrave summoned him.

"I wish you would ask my servant to step this way," he said. "You will find him in my state room."

The man disappeared through the companion way. Richardson rose to his feet.

"I'm not going to stay here to be bullied and cross examined," he declared. "I'm off!"

"One moment," Wingrave said. "If you leave me now, I shall ask the captain to place you under arrest."

Richardson looked half fearfully around.

"What for?"

"Attempted murder ! Very clumsily attempted, but

E. Phillips Oppenheim

attempted murder none the less."

The young man collapsed. Wingrave's servant came down the deck.

"You sent for me, sir?" he inquired respectfully.

Wingrave pointed towards his companion.

"Was that the person whom you saw coming out of my state room?" he asked.

"Yes sir," the man replied at once.

"You could swear to him, if necessary?"

"Certainly, sir."

"That will do, Morrison."

The man withdrew. Wingrave turned to his victim. "A few weeks ago," he remarked, "I had a visit from the lady whose handwriting is upon that envelope. I had on the table before me a box of phenacetine lozenges. She naturally concluded that I was in the habit of using them. That lady has unfortunately cause to consider me, if not an enemy, something very much like it. You are in correspondence with her. Only last night you placed in my box of these lozenges some others, closely resembling them, but fortunately a little different in shape. Mine were harmless - as a matter of fact, a single one of yours would kill a man in ten minutes. Now, Mr. Richardson, what have you to say about all this? Why should I not send for the captain, and have you locked up till we arrive at New York?"

Richardson drew his handkerchief across his damp forehead.

"You can't prove nothing," he muttered.

"I am afraid that I must differ from you," Wingrave answered. "We will see what the captain has to say."

He leaned forward in his chair, to attract the attention of a seaman.

Richardson interposed.

"All right," he said thickly. "Suppose I own up! What then?"

"A few questions - nothing terrifying. I am not very frightened of you."

"Go on!"

"How did you become acquainted with the writer of that letter?"

Richardson hesitated.

"She came to a dancing class at Islington," he said.

Wingrave's face was expressionless, but his tone betrayed his incredulity.

"A dancing class at Islington! Nonsense!"

"Mind," the young man asserted, "it was her mistress who put her up to this! It was nothing to do with her. It was for her mistress's sake."

"Do you know the mistress?" Wingrave asked.

"No; I don't know her name even. Never heard it."

"Your letter, then, was from the maid?"

"Of course, it was," Richardson answered. "If you recognize the writing, you must know that yourself."

Wingrave looked reflectively seaward. The matter was not entirely clear to him. Yet he was sure that this young man was telling the truth, so far as he could divine it.

"Well," he said, "you have made your attempt and failed. If fortune had favored you, you might at this moment have been a murderer. I might have warned you, by the bye, that I am an exceedingly hard man to kill."

Richardson looked uneasily around.

"I ain't admitting anything, you know," he said.

"Precisely! Well, what are you going to do now? Are you satisfied with your first reverse, or are you going to renew the experiment?"

"I've had enough," was the dogged answer. "I've been made a fool of. I can see that. I shall return home by the next steamer. I never ought to have got mixed up in this."

"I am inclined to agree with you," Wingrave remarked calmly. "Do I understand that if I choose to forget this little episode, you will return to England by the next steamer?"

"I swear it," Richardson declared.

"And in the meantime, that you make no further attempt of a similar nature?"

"Not I!" he answered with emphasis. "I've had enough."

"Then," Wingrave said, "we need not prolong this conversation. Forgive my suggesting, Mr. Richardson, that whilst I am on deck, the other side of the ship should prove more convenient for you!"

The young man rose, and without a word staggered off. Wingrave watched him through half-closed eyes, until he disappeared.

"It was worth trying," he said softly to himself. "A very clever woman that! She looks forward through the years, and she sees the clouds gathering. It was a little risky, and the means were very crude. But it was worth trying!"

E. Phillips Oppenheim

THE MOTH AND THE CANDLE

"Tomorrow morning," Aynesworth remarked, "we shall land."

Wingrave nodded.

"I shall not be sorry," he said shortly.

Aynesworth fidgeted about. He had something to say, and he found it difficult. Wingrave gave him no encouragement. He was leaning back in his steamer chair, with his eyes fixed upon the sky line. Notwithstanding the incessant companionship of the last six days, Aynesworth felt that he had not progressed a single step towards establishing any more intimate relations between his employer and himself.

"Mrs. Travers is not on deck this afternoon," he remarked a trifle awkwardly.

"Indeed!" Wingrave answered. "I hadn't noticed."

Aynesworth sat down. There was nothing to be gained by fencing.

"I wanted to talk about her, sir, if I might," he said.

Wingrave withdrew his eyes from the sea, and looked

at his companion in cold surprise.

"To me?" he asked.

"Yes! I thought, the first few days, that Mrs. Travers was simply a vain little woman of the world, perfectly capable of taking care of herself, and heartless enough to flirt all day long, if she chose, without any risk, so far as she was concerned. I believe I made a mistake!"

"This is most interesting," Wingrave said calmly, "but why talk to me about the lady? I fancy that I know as much about her as you do."

"Very likely; but you may not have realized the same things. Mrs. Travers is a married woman, with a husband in Boston, and two little children, of whom, I believe, she is really very fond. She is a foolish, good-natured little woman, who thinks herself clever because her husband has permitted her to travel a good deal, and has evidently been rather fascinated by the latitudinarianism of continental society. She is a little afraid of being terribly bored when she gets back to Boston, and she is very sentimental."

"I had no idea," Wingrave remarked, "that you had been submitting the lady and her affairs to the ordeal of your marvelous gift of analysis. I rather fancied that you took no interest in her at all."

"I did not," Aynesworth answered, "until last night."

"And last night?" he repeated questioningly.

"I found her on deck - crying. She had been tearing up some photographs, and she talked a little wildly. I

E. Phillips Oppenheim

talked to her then for a little time."

"Can't you be more explicit?" Wingrave asked.

Aynesworth looked him in the face.

"She gave me the impression," he said, "that she did not intend to return to her husband."

Wingrave nodded.

"And what have you to say to me about this?" he asked.

"I have no right to say anything, of course," Aynesworth answered. "You might very properly tell me that it is no concern of mine. Mrs. Travers has already compromised herself, to some extent, with the people on board who know her and her family. She never leaves your side for a moment if she can help it, and for the last two or three days she has almost followed you about. You may possibly derive some amusement from her society for a short time, but - afterwards!"

"Explain yourself exactly," Wingrave said.

"Is it necessary?" Aynesworth declared brusquely. "Talk sensibly to her! Don't encourage her if she should really be contemplating anything foolish!"

"Why not?"

"Oh, hang it all!" Aynesworth declared. "I'm not a moralist, but she's a decent little woman. Don't ruin her life for the sake of a little diversion!"

Wingrave, who had been holding a cigar case in his hand for the last few minutes, opened it, and calmly selected a cigar.

"Aren't you a little melodramatic, Aynesworth?" he said.

"Sounds like it, no doubt," his companion answered, "but after all, hang it, she's not a bad little sort, and you wouldn't care to meet her in Piccadilly in a couple of years' time."

Wingrave turned a little in his chair. There was a slight hardening of the mouth, a cold gleam in his eyes.

"That," he remarked, "is precisely where you are wrong. I am afraid you have forgotten our previous conversations on this or a similar subject. Disconnect me in your mind at once from all philanthropic notions! I desire to make no one happy, to assist at no one's happiness. My own life has been ruined by a woman. Her sex shall pay me where it can. If I can obtain from the lady in question a single second's amusement, her future is a matter of entire indifference to me. She can play the repentant wife, or resort to the primeval profession of her sex. I should not even have the curiosity to inquire which."

"In that case," Aynesworth said slowly, "I presume that I need say no more."

"Unless it amuses you," Wingrave answered, "it really is not worth while."

"Perhaps," Aynesworth remarked, "it is as well that I should tell you this. I shall put the situation before

Mrs. Travers exactly as I see it. I shall do my best to dissuade her from any further or more intimate intercourse with you."

"At the risk, of course," Wingrave said, "of my offering you - this?"

He drew a paper from his pocket book, and held it out. It was the return half of a steamer ticket.

"Even at that risk," Aynesworth answered without hesitation.

Wingrave carefully folded the document, and returned it to his pocket.

"I am glad," he said, "to find that you are so consistent. There is Mrs. Travers scolding the deck steward. Go and talk to her! You will scarcely find a better opportunity."

Aynesworth rose at once. Wingrave in a few moments also left his seat, but proceeded in the opposite direction. He made his way into the purser's room, and carefully closed the door behind him.

Mrs. Travers greeted Aynesworth without enthusiasm. Her eyes were resting upon the empty place which Wingrave had just vacated.

"Can I get your chair for you, Mrs. Travers," Aynesworth asked, "or shall we walk for a few minutes?"

Mrs. Travers hesitated. She looked around, but there was obviously no escape for her.

"I should like to sit down," she said. "I am very tired this morning. My chair is next Mr. Wingrave's there."

Aynesworth found her rug and wrapped it around her. She leaned back and closed her eyes.

"I shall try to sleep," she said. "I had such a shocking night."

He understood at once that she was on her guard, and he changed his tactics.

"First," he said, "may I ask you a question?"

She opened her eyes wide, and looked at him. She was afraid.

"Not now," she said hurriedly. "This afternoon."

"This afternoon I may not have the opportunity," he answered. "Is your husband going to meet you at New York, Mrs. Travers?"

"No!"

"Are you going direct to Boston?"

She looked at him steadily. There was a slight flush of color in her cheeks.

"I find your questions impertinent, Mr. Aynesworth," she answered.

There was a short silence. Aynesworth hated his task and hated himself. But most of all, he pitied the woman who sat by his side.

"No!" he said, "they are not impertinent. I am the looker-on, you know, and I have seen - a good deal. If Wingrave were an ordinary sort of man, I should never have dared to interfere. If you had been an ordinary sort of woman, I might not have cared to."

She half rose in her chair.

"I shall not stay here," she began, struggling with her rug.

"Do!" he begged. "I am - I want to be your friend, really!"

"You are supposed to be his," she reminded him.

He shook his head.

"I am his secretary. There is no question of friendship between us. For the rest, I told him that I should speak to you."

"You have no right to discuss me at all," she declared vehemently.

"None whatever," he admitted. "I have to rely entirely upon your mercy. This is the truth. People are thrown together a good deal on a voyage like this. You and Mr. Wingrave have seen a good deal of one another. You are a very impressionable woman; he is a singularly cold, unimpressionable man. You have found his personality attractive. You fancy - other things. Wingrave is not the man you think he is. He is selfish and entirely without affectionate impulses. The world has treated him badly, and he has no hesitation in saying that he means to get some part of his own back again. He does not care for you, he does not care for anyone. If you should be contemplating anything ridiculous from a mistaken judgment of his character, it is better that you should know the truth."

The anger had gone. She was pale again, and her lips were trembling.

"Men seldom know one another," she said softly. "You judge from the surface only."

"Mine is the critical judgment of one who has studied him intimately," Aynesworth said. "Yours is the sentimental hope of one fascinated by what she does not understand. Wingrave is utterly heartless!"

"That," she answered steadfastly, "I do not believe."

"You do not because you will not," he declared. "I have spoken because I wish to save you from doing what you would repent of for the rest of your days. You have the one vanity which is common to all women. You believe that you can change what, believe me, is unchangeable. To Wingrave, women are less than playthings. He owes the unhappiness of his life to one, and he would see the whole of her sex suffer without emotion. He is impregnable to sentiment. Ask him and I believe that he would admit it!"

She smiled and regarded him with the mild pity of superior knowledge.

"You do not understand Mr. Wingrave," she remarked.

Aynesworth sighed. He realized that every word he had spoken had been wasted upon this pale, pretty woman, who sat with her eyes now turned seawards, and the smile still lingering upon her lips. Studying her for a moment, he realized the danger more acutely than ever before. The fretfulness seemed to have gone from her face, the weary lines from her mouth. She had the look of a woman who has come into the knowledge of better things. And it was Wingrave who had done this! Aynesworth for the first time frankly hated the man. Once, as a boy, he had seen a keeper take a rabbit from a trap and dash its brains out against a tree. The incident flashed then into his mind, only the face of the keeper was the face of Wingrave!

"DEVIL TAKE THE HINDMOST"

Wingrave and Aynesworth were alone in a private room of the Waldorf Astoria Hotel. The table at which the former was seated was covered with letters and papers. A New York directory and an atlas were at his elbow.

"I propose," Wingrave said, leaning back in his chair, "to give you some idea of the nature of my business in this country. You will be able then, I trust, to carry out my instructions more intelligibly."

Aynesworth nodded.

"I thought," he said, "that you came here simply to remain in seclusion for a time."

"That is one of my reasons," Wingrave admitted, "but I had a special purpose in coming to America. During my - enforced seclusion - I made the acquaintance of a man called Hardwell. He was an Englishman, but he had lived in America for some years, and had got into trouble over some company business. We had some conversation, and it is upon his information that I am now going to act."

"He is trustworthy?" Aynesworth asked.

E. Phillips Oppenheim

"I take the risk," Wingrave answered coolly. "There is a small copper mine in Utah called the Royal Hardwell Copper Mine. The shares are hundred dollar ones, and there are ten thousand of them. They are scarcely quoted now, as the mine has become utterly discredited. Hardwell managed this himself with a false report. He meant to have the company go into liquidation, and then buy it for a very small amount. As a matter of fact, the mine is good, and could be worked at a large profit."

"You have Hardwell's word for that," Aynesworth remarked.

"Exactly!" Wingrave remarked. "I am proceeding on the assumption that he told me the truth. I wish to buy, if possible, the whole of the shares, and as many more as I can get brokers to sell. The price of the shares today is two dollars!"

"I presume you will send out an expert to the mine first?" Aynesworth said.

"I shall do nothing of the sort," Wingrave answered. "The fact that I was buying upon information would send the shares up at once. I mean to buy first, and then go out to the mine. If I have made a mistake, I shall not be ruined. If Hardwell's story is true, there will be millions in it."

Aynesworth said nothing, but his face expressed a good deal.

"Here are the names of seven respectable brokers," Wingrave continued, passing a sheet of paper towards him. "I want you to buy five hundred shares from each of them. The price may vary a few points. Whatever it is, pay it. Here are seven signed checks. I shall buy myself as many as I can without spoiling the market. You had better start out in about a quarter of an hour and see to this. You have my private ledger?"

"Yes."

"Open an account to Hardwell in it; a quarter of all the shares I buy are to be in his name, and a quarter of all the profits I make in dealing in the shares is to be credited to him."

"A fairly generous arrangement for Mr. Hardwell," Aynesworth remarked.

"There is nothing generous about it," Wingrave answered coldly. "It is the arrangement I made with him, and to which I propose to adhere. You understand what I want you to do?"

"Perfectly," Aynesworth answered; "I still think, however, that much the wiser course would be to send an expert to the mine first."

"Indeed!" Wingrave remarked politely. "That is all, I think. I shall expect to see you at luncheon time. If you are asked questions as to why you are dealing in these shares to such an extent, you can say that the friend for whom you are acting desires to boom copper, and is going on the low price of the metal at the moment. They will think you a fool, and perhaps may not trouble to conceal their opinion after they have finished the business. You must endeavor to support the character. I have no doubt but that you will be successful."

Aynesworth moved towards the door.

Once more Wingrave called him back. He was leaning a little forward across the table. His face was very set and cold.

"There is a question which I wish to ask you, Aynesworth," he said. "It concerns another matter altogether. Do you know who sent the Marconigram to Dr. Travers, which brought him to New York to meet his wife?"

"I do not," Aynesworth answered.

"It was sent by someone on board the ship," Wingrave continued. "You have no suspicion as to whom it could have been?"

"None!" Aynesworth answered firmly. "At the same time, I do not mind telling you this. If I had thought of it, I would have sent it myself."

Wingrave shrugged his shoulders.

"It is perhaps fortunate for the continuation of our mutual relations that you did not think of it," he remarked quietly. "I accept your denial. I shall expect you back at one o'clock."

At a few minutes after that hour the two men sat down to luncheon. Wingrave at that time was the possessor of six thousand shares in the Royal Hardwell Copper Mine, which had cost him, on an average, two dollars twenty-five. The news of the dealing, however, had got about, and although derision was the chief sentiment amongst the brokers, the price steadily mounted. A dozen telegrams were sent out to the mine, and on receipt of the replies, the dealing became the joke of the day. The mine was still deserted, and no fresh inspection had been made. The price dropped a little. Then Wingrave bought a thousand more by telephone, and it rose again to four. A few minutes before closing time, he threw every share of which he was possessed upon the market, and the next morning Royal Hardwells stood at one dollar seventy-five.

For a week Wingrave pursued the same tactics, and at the end of that time he had made twenty thousand dollars. The brokers, however, now understood, or thought they understood, the situation. No one bought for the rise; they were all sellers. Wingrave at once changed his tactics. He bought five thousand shares in one block, and sold none. Even then, the market was only mildly amused. In a fortnight he was the nominal owner of sixteen thousand shares in a company of which only ten thousand actually existed. Then he sat still, and the panic began. The shares in a company which everyone believed to be worthless stood at thirty dollars, and not a share was offered.

A small pandemonium reigned in Wingrave's sitting room. The telephone rang all the time; the place was besieged with brokers. Then Wingrave showed his hand. He had bought these shares to hold; he did not intend to sell one. As to the six thousand owed to him beyond the number issued, he was prepared to consider offers. One broker left him a check for twenty thousand dollars, another for nearly forty thousand. Wingrave had no pity. He had gambled and won. He would accept nothing less than par price. The air in his sitting room grew thick with curses and tobacco smoke.

Aynesworth began by hating the whole business, but insensibly the fascination of it crept over him. He grew used to hearing the various forms of protest, of argument and abuse, which one and all left Wingrave so unmoved. Sphinx-like he lounged in his chair, and listened to all. He never condescended to justify his position, he never met argument by argument. He had the air of being thoroughly bored by the whole proceedings. But he exacted always his pound of flesh.

On the third afternoon, Aynesworth met on the stairs a young broker, whom he had come across once or twice during his earlier dealings in the shares. They had had lunch together, and Aynesworth had taken a fancy to the boy - he was little more - fresh from Harvard and full of enthusiasm. He scarcely recognized him for a moment. The fresh color had gone from his cheeks, his eyes were set in a fixed, wild stare; he seemed suddenly aged. Aynesworth stopped him.

"Hullo, Nesbitt!" he exclaimed. "What's wrong?"

The young man would have passed on with a muttered greeting, but Aynesworth turned round with him, and led the way into one of the smaller smoking rooms. He called for drinks and repeated his question.

"Your governor has me six hundred Hardwells short," Nesbitt answered curtly.

"Six hundred! What does it mean?" Aynesworth asked.

"Sixty thousand dollars, or thereabouts," the young man answered despairingly. "His brokers won't listen to me, and your governor - well, I've just been to see him. I won't call him names! And we thought that some fool of an Englishman was burning his fingers with those shares. I'm not the only one caught, but the others can stand it. I can't, worse luck!"

"I'm beastly sorry," Aynesworth said truthfully. "I wish I could help you."

Nesbitt raised his head. A sudden light flashed in his eyes; he spoke quickly, almost feverishly.

"Say, Aynesworth," he exclaimed, "do you think you could do anything with your governor for me? You see - it's ruin if I have to pay up. I wouldn't mind - for myself, but I was married four months ago, and I can't bear the thought of going home - and telling her. All the money we have between us is in my business, and we've got no rich friends or anything of that sort. I don't know what I'll do if I have to be hammered. I've been so careful, too! I didn't want to take this on, but it seemed such a soft thing! If I could get off with twenty thousand, I'd keep my head up. I hate to talk like this. I'd go down like a man if I were alone, but - but - oh! Confound it all - !" he exclaimed with an ominous break in his tone.

Aynesworth laid his hand upon the boy's arm.

"Look here," he said, "I'll try what I can do with Mr. Wingrave. Wait here!"

Aynesworth found his employer alone with his broker, who was just hastening off to keep an appointment. He plunged at once into his appeal.

"Mr. Wingrave," he said, "you have just had a young broker named Nesbitt on."

Wingrave glanced at a paper by his side.

"Yes," he said. "Six hundred short! I wish they wouldn't come to me."

"I've been talking to him downstairs," Aynesworth said. "This will break him."

"Then I ought not to have done business with him at all," Wingrave said coolly. "If he cannot find sixty thousand dollars, he has no right to be in Wall street. I daresay he'll pay, though! They all plead poverty - curs!"

"I think Nesbitt's case is a little different from the others," Aynesworth continued. "He is quite young, little more than a boy, and he has only just started in business. To be hammered would be absolute ruin for him. He seems such a decent young fellow, and he's only just married. He's in an awful state downstairs. I wish you'd have another talk with him. I think you'd feel inclined to let him down easy."

Wingrave smiled coldly.

"My dear Aynesworth," he said, "you astonish me. I am not interested in this young man's future or in his matrimonial arrangements. He has gambled with me and lost. I presume that he would have taken my money if I had been the fool they all thought me. As it is, I mean to have his - down to the last cent!"

"He isn't like the others," Aynesworth protested doggedly. "He's only a boy - and it seems such jolly hard luck, doesn't it, only four months married! New York hasn't much pity for paupers. He looks mad enough to blow his brains out. Have him up, sir, and see if you can't compromise!"

"Fetch him," Wingrave said curtly.

Aynesworth hurried downstairs. The boy was walking restlessly up and down the room. The look he turned upon Aynesworth was almost pitiful.

"He'll see you again," Aynesworth said hurriedly. "Come along."

The boy wrung his hand.

"You're a brick!" he declared.

THE HIDDEN HAND

Wingrave glanced up as they entered. He motioned Nesbitt to a chair by his side, but the young man remained standing.

"My secretary tells me," Wingrave said curtly, "that you cannot pay me what you owe."

"It's more than I possess in the world, sir," Nesbitt answered.

"It is not a large amount," Wingrave said. "I do not see how you can carry on business unless you can command such a sum as this."

Nesbitt moistened his dry lips with his tongue.

"I have only been doing a very small business, sir," he answered, "but quite enough to make a living. I don't speculate as a rule. Hardwells seemed perfectly safe, or I wouldn't have touched them. I sold at four. They are not worth one. I could have bought thousands last week for two dollars."

"That is beside the question," Wingrave answered. "If you do not pay this, you have cheated me out of my profits for I should have placed the commission with brokers who could. Why did you wish to see me again?"

"I thought that you might give me time," Nesbitt answered, raising his head and looking Wingrave straight in the face. "It seems rather a low down thing to come begging. I'd rather cut my right hand off than do it for myself, but I've - someone else to think about, and if I'm hammered, I'm done for. Give me a chance, Mr. Wingrave! I'll pay you in time."

"What do you ask for?" Wingrave said.

"I thought that you might give me time," Nesbitt said, "and I'll pay you the rest off with the whole of my profits every year."

"A most absurd proposal," Wingrave said coolly. "I will instruct my brokers to take twenty thousand dollars down, and wait one week for the balance. That is the best offer I can make you. Good day!"

The young man stood as though he were stunned.

"I - I can't find it," he faltered. "I can't indeed."

"Your resources are not my affair," Wingrave said. "I shall instruct my broker to do as I have said. If the money is not forthcoming, you know the alternative."

"You mean to ruin me, then?" Nesbitt said slowly.

"I mean to exact the payment of what is due to me," Wingrave said curtly. "If you cannot pay, it seems to me that I am the person to be pitied - not you. Show Mr. Nesbitt out, Aynesworth."

Nesbitt turned towards the door. He was very pale, but he walked steadily. He did not speak another word to Wingrave.

"I'm beastly sorry," Aynesworth said to him on the stairs. "I wish I could help you!"

"Thank you," Nesbitt answered. "No one can help me. I'm through."

Aynesworth returned to the sitting room. Wingrave had lit a cigarette and watched him as he arranged some papers.

"Quite a comedy, isn't it?" he remarked grimly.

"It doesn't present itself in that light to me," Aynesworth answered.

Wingrave blew the smoke away from in front of his face. "Ah!" he said, "I forgot that you were a sentimentalist. I look upon these things from my own point of view. From yours, I suppose I must seem a very disagreeable person. I admit frankly that the sufferings of other people do not affect me in the slightest."

"I am sorry for you," Aynesworth said shortly. "If there is going to be much of this sort of thing, though, I must ask you to relieve me of my post. I can't stand it."

"Whenever you like, my dear fellow," Wingrave answered. " I think that you would be very foolish to leave me, though. I must be a most interesting study."

"You are - what the devil made you!" Aynesworth muttered.

Wingrave laid down his cigarette.

"I am what my fellows have made me," he said slowly. "I tasted hell for a good many years. It has left me, I suppose, with a depraved taste. Ring up my brokers, Aynesworth! I want to speak to Malcolmson. He had better come round here."

The day dragged on. Aynesworth hated it all, and was weary long before it was half over. Everyone who came was angry, and a good many came whom Wingrave refused to see. Just before five o'clock, young Nesbitt entered the room unannounced. Aynesworth started towards him with a little exclamation. The young man's evident excitement terrified him, and he feared a tragedy. Malcolmson, too, half rose to his feet. Wingrave alone remained unmoved.

Nesbitt walked straight up to the table at which Malcolmson and Wingrave were sitting. He halted in front of the latter.

"Mr. Wingrave," he said, "you will give me my receipt for those shares for fifty-seven thousand six hundred dollars."

Wingrave turned to a paper by his side, and ran his forefinger down the list of names.

"Mr. Nesbitt," he said. "Yes! sixty thousand dollars."

The young man laid a slip of paper upon the table.

"That is a certified check for the amount," he said. "Mr. Malcolmson, please give me my receipt."

"Ah!" Mr. Wingrave remarked. "I thought that you would find the money."

Nesbitt bit his lip, but he said nothing till he had the receipt and had fastened it up in his pocket. Then he turned suddenly round upon Wingrave.

"Look here!" he said. "You've got your money. I don't owe you a cent. Now I'm going to tell you what I think of you."

Wingrave rose slowly to his feet. He was as tall as the boy, long, lean, and hard. His face expressed neither anger nor excitement, but there was a slight, dangerous glitter in his deep-set eyes.

"If you mean," he said, "that you are going to be impertinent, I would recommend you to change your mind."

Nesbitt for a moment hesitated. There was something ominous in the cool courage of the older man. And before he could collect himself, Wingrave continued: -

"I presume," he said, "that you chose your own profession. You knew quite well there was no place in it for men with a sense of the higher morality. It is a profession of gamblers and thieves. If you'd won, you'd have thought yourself a smart fellow and pocketed your winnings fast enough. Now that you've lost - don't whine. You sat down willingly enough to play the game with me. Don't call me names because you lost. This is no place for children. Pocket your defeat, and be more careful next time."

Nesbitt was silent for a moment. Wingrave, cool and immovable, dominated him. He gave a little laugh, and turned towards the door.

"Guess you're right," he declared; "we'll let it go at that."

Aynesworth followed him from the room.

"I'm awfully glad you're out of the scrape," he said.

Nesbitt caught him by the arm.

"Come right along," he said. "I haven't had a drink in the daytime for a year, but we're going to have a big one now. I say, do you know how I got that money?"

Aynesworth shook his head.

"On easy terms, I hope."

They sat down in the American Bar, and a colored waiter in a white linen suit brought them whisky and Apollinaris in tall tumblers.

"Listen," Nesbitt said. "My brain is on the reel still. I went back to my office, and if it hadn't been for the little girl, I should have brought a revolver by the way. Old Johnny there waiting to see me, no end of a swell, Phillson, the uptown lawyer. He went straight for me.

"'Been dealing in Hardwells?' he asked.

"I nodded.

"'Short, eh?'

"'Six hundred shares,' I answered. There was no harm in telling him for the Street knew well enough.

"'Bad job,' he said. 'How much does Wingrave want?'

"'Shares at par,' I answered. 'It comes to close on fifty-seven thousand six hundred dollars.'

"'I'm going to find you the money,' he said.

"Then I can tell you the things in my office began to swim. I'd an idea somehow that he was there as a friend, but nothing like this. I couldn't answer him.

"'It's a delicate piece of business,' he went on. 'In fact, the fewer questions you ask the better. All I can say is there's a chap in Wall Street got his eye on you. Your old dad once helped him over a much worse place than this. Anyhow, I've a check here for sixty thousand dollars, and no conditions, only that you don't talk.'

"'But when am I to pay it back?' I gasped.

"'If my client ever needs it, and you can afford it, he will ask for it.' Phillson answered. 'That's all.'

"And before I could say another darned word, he was gone, and the check was there on my desk."

Aynesworth sipped his whisky and Apollinaris, and lit a cigarette.

"And they say," he murmured, "that romance does not exist in Wall Street. You're a lucky chap, Nesbitt."

"Lucky! Do you think I don't realize it? Of course, I know the old governor had lots of friends on the Street, but he was never in a big way, and he got hit awfully hard himself before he died. I can't understand it anyway."

"I wouldn't try," Aynesworth remarked, laughing. "By the bye, your friend, whoever he was, must have got to know pretty quickly."

Nesbitt nodded.

"I thought of that," he said. "Of course, Phillsons are lawyers for Malcolmson, Wingrave's broker, so I daresay it came from him. Say, Aynesworth, you don't mind if I ask you something?"

"Not at all," Aynesworth answered. "What is it?"

"Why the devil do you stop with a man like Wingrave? He doesn't seem your sort at all."

Aynesworth hesitated.

"Wingrave interests me," he answered. "He has had a curious life, and he is a man with very strange ideas."

Nesbitt finished his drink, and rose up.

"Well," he said, "he's not a man I should care to be associated with. Not but what I daresay he was right upstairs. He's strong, too, and he must have a nerve. But he's a brute for all that!"

Nesbitt went his way, and Aynesworth returned upstairs. Wingrave was alone.

"Have we finished this miserable business?" Aynesworth asked.

"For the present," Wingrave answered. "Mr. Malcolmson will supply you with a copy of the accounts. See that Hardwell is credited with a quarter share of the profits. Our dealings are over for the present. Be prepared to start on Saturday for the West. We are going to look for those bears."

"But the mine?" Aynesworth exclaimed. "It belongs to you now. Aren't you going out to examine it?"

Wingrave shook his head.

"No," he said, "I know nothing about mines. My visit could not teach me anything one way or the other. I have sent a commission of experts. I am tired of cities and money-making. I want a change."

Aynesworth looked at him suddenly. The weariness was there indeed - was it his fancy, or was it something more than weariness which shone out of the dark, tired eyes?

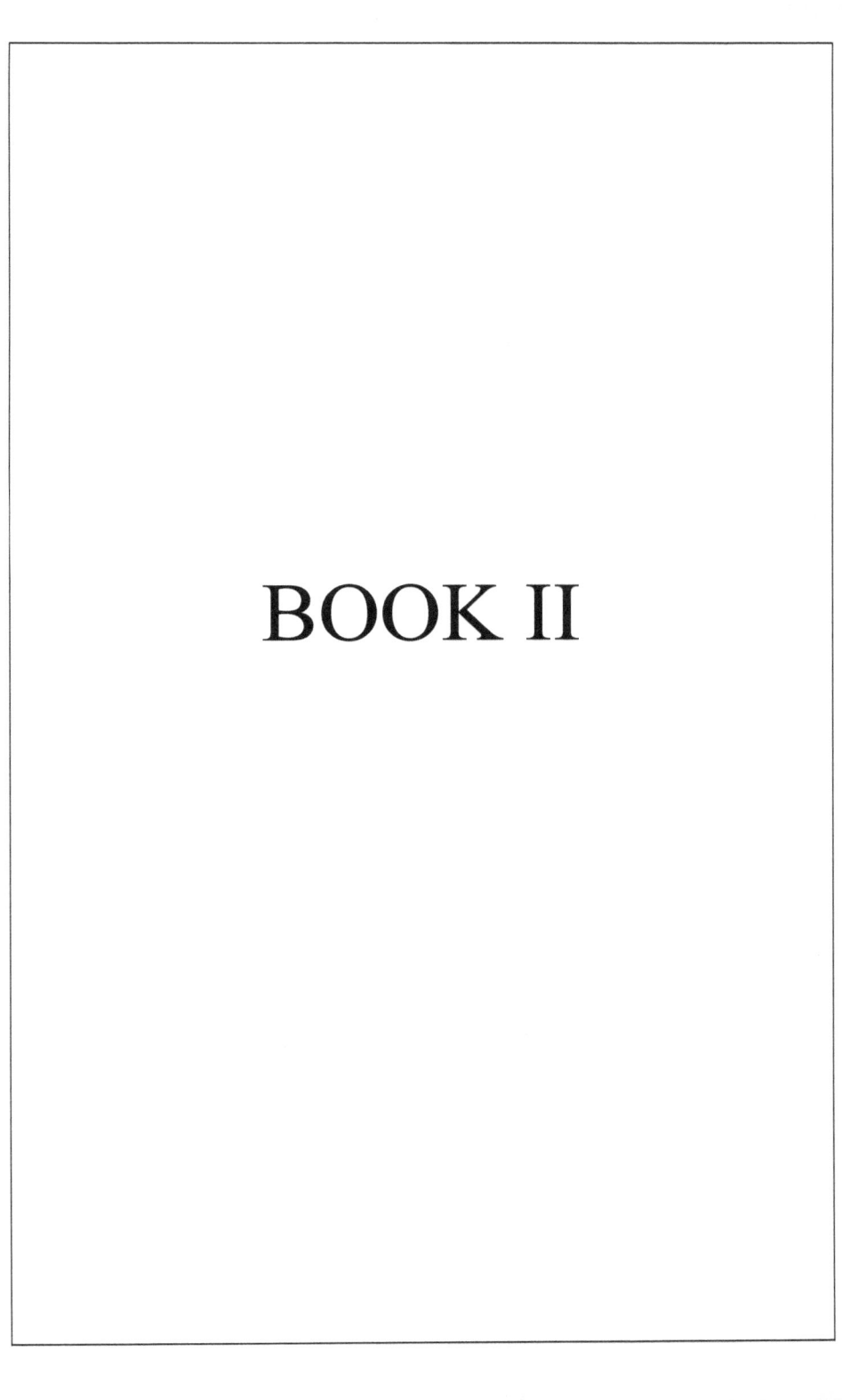

BOOK II

"MR. WINGRAVE FROM AMERICA"

"Four years ago tonight," Aynesworth said, looking round the club smoking room thoughtfully, "we bade you farewell in this same room!"

Lovell, wan and hollow-eyed, his arm in a sling, his once burly frame gaunt and attenuated with disease, nodded.

"And I told you the story," he remarked, "of - the man who had been my friend."

"Don't let us talk of Wingrave tonight!" Aynesworth exclaimed with sudden emphasis.

"Why not?" Lovell knocked the ashes from his pipe, and commenced leisurely to refill it. "Why not, indeed? I mean to go and see him as soon as I can get about a little better."

"If your description of him," Aynesworth said, "was a faithful one, you will find him changed."

Lovell laughed a little bitterly.

"The years leave their mark," he said, "upon us all - upon all of us, that is, who step out into the open where the winds of life are blowing. Look at me! I weighed eighteen stone when I left England. I had the muscles of a prize fighter and nerves of steel. Today I turn the scale at ten stone and am afraid to be alone in the dark."

"You will be yourself again in no time," Aynesworth declared cheerfully.

"I shall be better than I am now, I hope," Lovell answered, "but I shall never be the man I was. I have seen - God grant that I may some day forget what I have seen! No wonder that my nerves have gone! I saw a Russian correspondent, a strong brutal-looking man, go off into hysterics; I saw another run amuck through the camp, shooting right and left, and, finally, blow his own brains out. Many a night I sobbed myself to sleep. The men who live through tragedies, Aynesworth, age fast. I expect that I shall find Wingrave changed."

"I would give a good deal," Aynesworth declared, "to have known him when you did."

Lovell nodded.

"You should be able to judge of the past," he said, "by the present. Four years of - intimate companionship with any man should be enough!"

"Perhaps!" Aynesworth declared. "And yet I can assure you that I know no more of Wingrave today than when I was first attracted to him by your story and became his secretary. It is a humiliating confession, but it is the truth."

"That is why you remain with him," Lovell remarked.

"I suppose so! I have often meant to leave, but somehow, when the time comes, I stay on. His life seems to be made up of brutalities, small and large. He ruins a man with as little compunction as one could fancy him, in his younger days, pulling the legs from a fly. I have never seen him do a kindly action. And yet, all the time I find myself watching for it. A situation arises, and I say to myself: 'Now I am going to see something different.' I never do, and yet I always expect it. Am I boring you, Lovell?"

"Not in the least! Go on! Anything concerning Wingrave interests me."

"It is four years ago, you know, since I went to him. My first glimpse of his character was the cold brutality with which he treated Lady Ruth when she went to see him. Then we went down to his country place in Cornwall. There was a small child there, whose father had been the organist of the village, and who had died penniless. There was no one to look after her, no one to save her from the charity schools and domestic service afterwards. The church was on Wingrave's estate, it should have been his duty to augment the ridiculous salary the dead man had received. Would you believe it, Wingrave refused to do a single thing for that child! He went down there like a vandal to sell the heirlooms and pictures which had belonged to his family for generations. He had no time, he told me coldly, for sentiment."

"It sounds brutal enough," Lovell admitted. "What became of the child?"

"One of her father's relations turned up after all and took care of her," Aynesworth said. "Wingrave knew nothing about that, though. Then on the voyage across the Atlantic, there was a silly, pretty little woman on board who was piqued by Wingrave's indifference and tried to flirt with him. In a few days she was his slave. She was going home to her husband, and you would have thought that any decent fellow would have told her that she was a little fool, and let her go. But not Wingrave! She was landing with him at New York, but someone amongst the passengers, who guessed what was up, sent a Marconigram to her husband, and he met us at the landing stage."

"Nothing came of that, then?"

"No, but it wasn't Wingrave's fault. Then he began dealing with some shares in a mine - THE mine, you know. They were supposed to be worthless, and one boy, who was a little young to the game, sold him too many. Wingrave was bleeding these brokers for hundreds of thousands of dollars, and the boy came and asked to be let off by paying his whole fortune to escape being hammered. Wingrave refused. I believe if the boy hadn't just been married, he'd have blown his brains out!"

Lovell laughed.

"I don't envy you your job," he remarked. "Is there nothing to set down on the credit side of the ledger?"

"Not much," Aynesworth answered. "He is a fine sportsman, and he saved my life in the Rockies, which makes me feel a bit uncomfortable sometimes. He has a sense of justice, for he heard of this mine from a man in prison, and he has kept accounts showing the fellow's share down to the last halfpenny. But I have

E. Phillips Oppenheim

never yet known him to speak a kindly word or do a kindly deed. He seems intent upon carrying out to the letter his own principles - to make as many people as possible suffer for his own broken life. Now he is back here, a millionaire, with immense power for good or for evil, I am almost afraid of him. I wouldn't be Lady Ruth or her husband for something."

Lovell smoked thoughtfully for a time.

"Wingrave was always a little odd," he remarked, "but I never thought that he was a bad chap."

"Go and see him now!" Aynesworth said. "Tell me if you think he wears a mask or whether he is indeed what he seems."

The hall porter entered the room and addressed Aynesworth.

"Gentleman called for you, sir," he announced.

"It is Wingrave," Aynesworth declared. "Come and speak to him!"

They descended the stairs together. Outside, Wingrave was leaning back in the corner of an electric brougham, reading the paper. Aynesworth put his head in at the window.

"You remember Lovell, Mr. Wingrave?" he said. "We were just talking when your message came up. I've brought him down to shake hands with you."

Wingrave folded his paper down at the precise place where he had been reading and extended a very limp hand. His manner betrayed not the slightest interest or pleasure.

"How are you, Lovell?" he asked. "Some time since we met!"

"A good many years," Lovell answered.

"Finished your campaigning?" Wingrave inquired. "Knocked you about a bit, haven't they?"

"They very nearly finished me," Lovell admitted. "I shall pick up all right over here, though."

There was a moment's silence. Lovell's thoughts had flashed backwards through the years, back to the time when he had sat within a few feet of this man in the crowded court of justice and listened through the painful stillness of that heavy atmosphere, charged with tragedy, to the slow unfolding of the drama of his life. There had been passion enough then in his voice and blazing in his eyes, emotion enough in his twitching features and restless gestures to speak of the fire below. And now, pale and cold, the man who had gripped his fingers then and held on to them like a vise, seemed to find nothing except a slight boredom in this unexpected meeting.

"I shall see you again, I hope," Wingrave remarked at last. "By the bye, if we do meet, I should be glad if you would forget our past acquaintance. Sir Wingrave Seton does not exist any longer. I prefer to be known only as Mr. Wingrave from America."

Lovell nodded.

E. Phillips Oppenheim

"As you wish, of course," he answered. "I do not think," he added, "that you need fear recognition. I myself should have passed you in the street."

Wingrave leaned back in the carriage.

"Aynesworth," he said, "if you are ready, will you get in and tell the man to drive to Cadogan Square? Good night, Mr. Lovell!"

Lovell re-entered the club with a queer little smile at his lips. The brougham glided up into the Strand, and turned westwards.

"We are going straight to the Barringtons'?" Aynesworth asked.

"Yes," Wingrave answered. "While I think of it, Aynesworth, I wish you to remember this. Both Lady Ruth and her husband seem to think it part of the game to try and make a cat's paw of you. I am not suggesting that they are likely to succeed, but I do think it possible that one of them may ask you questions concerning certain investments in which I am interested. I rely upon you to give them no information."

"I know very little about your investments - outside the mine," Aynesworth answered. "They couldn't very well approach a more ignorant person. Are you going to help Barrington to make a fortune?"

Wingrave turned his head. There was a slight contraction of the forehead, an ominous glitter in his steel grey eyes.

"I think , " he said, "you know that I am not likely to

do that."

The two men did not meet again till late in the evening. Lady Ruth's rooms were crowded for it was the beginning of the political season, and her parties were always popular. Nevertheless, she found time to beckon Wingrave to her before they had been in the room many minutes.

"I want to talk to you," she said a little abruptly. "You might have come this afternoon as you promised."

Lady Ruth was a wonderful woman. A well-known statesman had just asked a friend her age.

"I don't know," was the answer, "but whatever it is, she doesn't look it."

Tonight she was almost girlish. Her complexion was delicate and perfectly natural, the graceful lines of her figure suggested more the immaturity of youth than any undue slimness. She wore a wonderful collar of pearls around her long, shapely neck, but very little other jewelry. The touch of her fingers upon Wingrave's coat sleeve was a carefully calculated thing. If he had thought of it, he could have felt the slight appealing pressure with which she led him towards one of the smaller rooms.

"There are two chairs there," she said. "Come and sit down. I have something to say to you."

THE SHADOW OF A FEAR

For several minutes Lady Ruth said nothing. She was leaning back in the farthest corner of her chair, her head resting slightly upon her fingers, her eyes studying with a curious intentness the outline of Wingrave's pale, hard face. He himself, either unconscious of, or indifferent to her close scrutiny, had simply the air of a man possessed of an inexhaustible fund of patience.

"Wingrave," she said quietly, "I think that the time has gone by when I was afraid of you."

He turned slightly towards her, but he did not speak.

"I am possessed," she continued, "at present, of a more womanly sentiment. I am curious."

"Ah!" he murmured, "you were always a little inclined that way."

"I am curious about you," she continued. "You are, comparatively speaking, young, well-looking enough, and strong. Your hand is firmly planted upon the lever which moves the world. What are you going to do?"

"That," he said, "depends upon many things."

"You may be ambitious," she remarked. "If so, you conceal it admirably. You may be devoting your powers to the consummation of vengeance against those who have treated you ill. There are no signs of that, either, at present."

"We have excellent authority," he remarked, "for the statement that a considerable amount of satisfaction is derivable from the exercise of that sentiment."

"Perhaps," she answered, "but the pursuit of vengeance for wrongs of the past is the task of a fool. Now, you are not a fool. You carry your life locked up within you as a strong man should. But there are always some who may look in through the windows. I should like to be one."

"An empty cupboard," he declared. "A cupboard swept bare by time and necessity."

She shook her head.

"Your life," she said, "is molded towards a purpose. What is it?"

"I must ask myself the question," he declared, "before I can tell you the answer!"

"No," she said, "the necessity does not exist. Your reckless pursuit of wealth, your return here, the use you are making of my husband and me, are all means towards some end. Why not tell me?"

"Your imagination," he declared, "is running away with you."

E. Phillips Oppenheim

"Are you our enemy?" she asked. "Is this seeming friendship of yours a cloak to hide some scheme of yours to make us suffer? Or -" She drew a little closer to him, and her eyes drooped.

"Or what?" he repeated.

"Is there a little left," she whispered, "of the old folly?"

"Why not?" he answered quietly. "I was very much in love with you."

"It is dead," she murmured. "I believe that you hate me now!"

Her voice was almost a caress. She was leaning a little towards him; her eyes were seeking to draw his.

"Hate you! How impossible!" he said calmly. "You are still a beautiful woman, you know, Ruth."

He turned and studied her critically. Lady Ruth raised her eyes once, but dropped them at once. She felt herself growing paler. A spasm of the old fear was upon her.

"Yes," he continued, "age has not touched you. You can still pour, if you will, the magic drug into the wine of fools. By the bye, I must not be selfish. Aren't you rather neglecting your guests?"

"Never mind my guests," she answered. "I have been wanting to talk to you alone for days. Why have you done this? Why are you here? What is it that you are seeking for in life?"

"A little amusement only," he declared. "I cannot find it except amongst my own kind."

"You have not the appearance of a pleasure seeker," she answered.

"Mine is a passive search," he said. "I have some years to live - and of solitude, well, I have tasted at once the joys and the depths."

"You are not in love with me any longer, are you?" she asked.

"I am not bold enough to deny it," he answered, "but do not be afraid that I shall embarrass you with a declaration. To tell you the truth, I have not much feeling left of any sort."

"You mean to keep your own counsel, then?" she asked.

"It is so little to keep," he murmured, "and I have parted with so much!"

She measured the emotion of his tone, the curious yet perfectly natural indifference of his manner, and she shivered a little. Always she feared what she could not understand.

"I had hoped," she said sadly, "that we might at least have been friends."

He shook his head.

"I have no fancy," he declared, "for the cemeteries of affection. You must remember that I am beginning life anew. I do not know myself yet, or you! Let us drift into the knowledge of one another, and perhaps -"

"Well! Perhaps?"

"There may be no question of friendship!"

Lady Ruth went back to her guests, and with the effortless ease of long training, she became once more the gracious and tactful hostess. But in her heart, the fear had grown a little stronger, and a specter walked by her side. Once during the evening, her husband looked at her questioningly, and she breathed a few words to him. He laughed reassuringly.

"Oh! Wingrave's all right, I believe," he said, "it's only his manner that puts you off a bit. He's just the same with everyone! I don't think he means anything by it!"

Lady Ruth shivered, but she said nothing. Just then Aynesworth came up, and with a motion of her fan she called him to her.

"Please take me into the other room," she said "I want a glass of champagne, and on the way you can tell me all about America."

"One is always making epigrams about America," he protested, smiling. "Won't you spare me?"

"Tell me, then, how you progress with your great character study!"

"Ah!" he remarked quietly, "you come now to a more interesting subject."

"Yes?"

"Frankly, I do not progress at all."

"So far as you have gone?"

"If," he said, "I were to take pen and paper and write down, at this moment, my conclusions so far as I have been able to form any, I fancy that they would make evil reading. Permit me!"

They stood for a few minutes before the long sideboard. A footman had poured champagne into their glasses, and Lady Ruth talked easily enough the jargon of the moment. But when they turned away, she moved slowly, and her voice was almost a whisper.

"Tell me this," she said, "is he really as hard and cold as he seems? You have lived with him now for four years. You should know that, at least."

"I believe that he is," Aynesworth answered. "I can tell you that much, at least, without breach of faith. So far as one who watches him can tell, he lives for his own gratification - and his indulgence in it does not, as a rule, make for the happiness of other people."

"Then what does he want with us?" she asked almost sharply. "I ask myself that question until - I am terrified."

Aynesworth hesitated.

"It is very possible," he said, "that he is simply making use of you to re-enter the world. Curiously enough, he has never seemed to care for solitude. He makes numberless acquaintances. What pleasure he finds in it I do not know, but he seldom avoids people. He may be simply making use of you."

"What do you think yourself?"

"I cannot tell," Aynesworth answered. "Indeed I cannot tell."

She left him a little impatiently, and Aynesworth joined the outside of the circle of men who had gathered round Wingrave. He was answering their questions readily enough, if a little laconically. He was quite aware that he occupied in society the one unique place to which princes might not even aspire - there was something of divinity about his millions, something of awe in the tone of the men with whom he talked. Women pretended to be interested in him because of the romance of his suddenly acquired wealth - the men did not trouble to deceive themselves or anyone else. A break up of the group came when a certain great and much-talked-about lady sent across an imperative message by her cavalier for the moment. She desired that Mr. Wingrave should be presented to her.

They passed down the room together a few moments later, the Marchioness wonderfully dressed in a gown of strange turquoise blue, looking up at her companion, and talking with somewhat unusual animation. Everyone made remarks, of course - exchanged significant glances and unlovely smiles. It was so like the Marchioness to claim, as a matter of course, the best of everything that was going. Lady Ruth watched them with a curious sense of irritation for which she could not altogether account. It was impossible that she should be jealous, and yet it was equally certain that she was annoyed. If Wingrave resisted his present fair captor, he would enjoy a notability equal to that which his wealth already conferred upon him. No man as yet had done it. Was it likely that Wingrave would wear two crowns? Lady Ruth beckoned Aynesworth to her.

"Tell me," she said, "what is Mr. Wingrave's general attitude towards my sex?"

" Absolute indifference , " he declared promptly, "unless -"

He stopped short.

"You must go on," she told him.

"Unless he is possessed of the ability to make them suffer," he answered after a moment's hesitation.

"Then Emily will never attract him," she declared almost triumphantly, "for she has no more heart that he has."

"He has yet to discover it," Aynesworth remarked. "When he does, I think you will find that he will shrug his shoulders - and say farewell."

"All the same," Lady Ruth murmured to herself, "Emily is a cat."

Lady Ruth spoke to one more man that night of Wingrave - and that man was her husband. Their guests had departed, and Lady Ruth, in a marvelous white dressing gown, was lying upon the sofa in her room.

"How do you get on with Wingrave?" she asked. "What do you think of him?"

Barrington shrugged his shoulders.

"What can one think of a man," he answered, "who goes about like an animated mummy? I have done my best; I talked to him for nearly half an hour at a stretch today when I took him to the club for lunch. He is the incarnation of indifference. He won't listen to politics; women, or tales about them, at any rate, seem to bore him to extinction; he drinks only as a matter of form, and he won't talk finance. By the bye, Ruth, I wish you could get him to give you a tip. I scarcely see how we are going to get through the season unless something turns up."

"Is it as bad as that?" she asked.

"Worse!" her husband answered gloomily. "We've been living on our capital for years. Every acre of Queen's Norton is mortgaged, and I'm shot if I can see how we're going to pay the interest."

She sighed a little wearily.

"Do you think that it would be wise?" she asked. "Let me tell you something, Lumley. I have only known what fear was once in my life. I am afraid now. I am afraid of Wingrave. I have a fancy that he does not mean any good to us."

Barrington frowned and threw his cigarette into the fire with a little jerk.

"Nonsense ! " he exclaimed. "The man's not quite so

bad as that. We've been useful to him. We've done exactly what he asked. The other matter's dead and buried. We don't want his money, but it is perfectly easy for him to help us make a little."

She looked up at him quietly.

"I think, Lumley, that it is dangerous!" she said.

"Then you're not the clever woman I take you for," he answered, turning to leave the room. "Just as you please. Only it will be that or the bankruptcy court before long!"

Lady Ruth lay quite still, looking into the fire. When her maid came, she moved on tiptoe for it seemed to her that her mistress slept. But Lady Ruth was wide awake though the thoughts which were flitting through her brain had, perhaps, some kinship to the land of dreams.

JULIET ASKS QUESTIONS

"Any place," the girl exclaimed as she entered, "more unlike a solicitor's office, I never saw! Flowers outside and flowers on your desk, Mr. Pengarth! Don't you have to apologize to your clients for your surroundings? There's absolutely nothing, except the brass plate outside, to show that this isn't an old-fashioned farmhouse, stuck down in the middle of a village. Fuchsias in the window sill, too!"

He placed a chair for her, and laid down the deed which he had been examining, with a little sigh of relief. It really was very hard work pretending to be busy.

"You see, Miss Juliet," he explained with twinkling eyes, "my clients are all country folk, and it makes them feel more at home to find a lawyer's office not very different from their own parlor."

She nodded.

"What would the great man say?" she inquired, pointing to the rows of black tin boxes which lined the walls.

"Sir Wingrave Seton is never likely to come here again, I am afraid," he answered. "If he did, I don't think he'd mind. To tell you the truth, I'm rather proud of my office, young lady!"

She looked around.

"They are nice," she said decidedly, "but unbusinesslike."

"You're going to put up the pony and stay to lunch, of course?" he said. "I'll ring for the boy."

She stopped him.

" Please don't!" she exclaimed. "I have come to see you - on business!"

Mr. Pengarth, after his first gasp of astonishment, was a different man. He fumbled about on the desk, and produced a pair of gold spectacles, which he adjusted with great nicety on the edge of his very short nose.

"On business, my dear!" he repeated. "Well, well! To be sure! Is it Miss Harrison who has sent you?"

Mr. Pengarth's visitor looked positively annoyed. She leaned across the table towards him so that the roses in her large hat almost brushed his forehead. Her wonderful brown eyes were filled with reproach.

"Mr. Pengarth," she said, "do you know how old I am?"

"How old, my dear? Why, let me see!" he exclaimed. "Fourteen and - why, God bless my soul, you must be eighteen!"

"I am nineteen years old, Mr. Pengarth," the young lady announced with dignity. "Perhaps you will be kind enough to treat me now - er - with a little more respect."

"Nineteen!" he repeated vaguely. "God bless my - nineteen years old?"

"I consider myself," she repeated, "of age. I have come to see you about my affairs!"

"Yes, yes!" he said. "Quite natural."

"For four years," she continued, "I seem to have been supported by some relative of my father, who has never vouchsafed to send me a single line or message except through you. I have written letters which I have given to you to forward. There has been no reply. Have you sent on those letters, Mr. Pengarth?"

"Why certainly, my dear, certainly!"

"Can you tell me how it is that I have had no answer?"

Mr. Pengarth coughed. He was not at all comfortable.

"Your guardian, Miss Juliet, is somewhat eccentric," he answered, "and he is a very busy man."

"Can you tell me, Mr. Pengarth, exactly what relation he is to me?"

There was a dead silence. Mr. Pengarth found the room suddenly warm, and mopped his forehead with a large silk handkerchief.

"I have no authority," he declared, "to answer any questions."

"Then can you tell me of your own accord," she said, "why there is all this mystery? Why may I not know who he is, why may I not write to him? Am I anything to be ashamed of, that he will not trust me even with his name? I am tired of accepting so much and not being able to offer even my thanks in return. It is too much like charity! I have made up my mind that if this is to go on, I will go away and earn my own living! There, Mr. Pengarth!"

"Rubbish!" he exclaimed briskly. "What at?"

"Painting!" she declared triumphantly. "I have had this in my mind for some time, and I have been trying to see what I can do best. I have quite decided, now, to be an artist."

"Pictures," he declared sententiously, "don't sell!"

"Mine do," she answered, smiling. "I have had a check for three guineas from a shop in London for a little sea piece I did in two afternoons!"

He regarded her admiringly.

"You are a wonderful child!" he exclaimed.

"I am not a child at all," she interrupted warmly, "and you can just sit down and write to your silly client and tell him so."

"I will certainly write to him," he affirmed. "I will do so today. You will not do anything rash until I have had time to get a reply?"

"No!" she answered graciously. "I will wait for a week. After that - well, I might do anything!"

"You wouldn't leave Tredowen, Miss Juliet!" he protested.

"It would break my heart, of course," she declared, "but I would do it and trust to time to heal it up again. Tredowen seems like home to me, but it isn't really, you know. Some day, Sir Wingrave Seton may want to come back and live there himself. Are you quite certain, Mr. Pengarth, that he won't be angry to hear that we have been living at the house all this time?"

"Certain," Mr. Pengarth declared firmly. "He left everything entirely in my hands. He did not wish me to let it, but he did not care about its being altogether uninhabited. The arrangement I was able to make with your guardian was a most satisfactory one."

"But surely he will come back himself some time?" she asked,

The lawyer shook his head sorrowfully.

"I am afraid," he said, "that Sir Wingrave has no affection for the place whatever."

"No affection for Tredowen," she repeated wonderingly. "Do you know what I think, Mr. Pengarth? I think that it is the most beautiful house in the world!"

"And yet you talk of leaving it."

"I don't want to go," she answered, "but I don't want to be accepting things all my life from someone whose name even I do not know."

"Well, well," he said, "you must wait until I have written my letter. Time enough to talk about that later on. Now, if you won't stay to lunch, you must come and see Rachael and have some cake and a glass of wine."

"How sweet of you," she exclaimed. "I'm frightfully hungry. Can I do anything to stop growing, Mr. Pengarth? I'm getting taller and taller!"

She stood up. She was head and shoulders taller than the little lawyer, slim as a lath, and yet wonderfully graceful. She laughed down at him and made a little grimace.

"I'm a giraffe, am I not?" she declared; "and I'm still growing. Do show me your garden, Mr. Pengarth. I want to see your hollyhocks. Everyone is talking about them."

They were joined in a few minutes by a prim, dignified little lady, ridiculously like Mr. Pengarth, whom he called sister, and she Miss Rachael. Juliet walked down the garden between them.

"Sister," Mr. Pengarth said, "Juliet has come today to see me on business. In effect, she has come to remind me that she is grown up."

"Grown up," Miss Rachael protested vigorously, "rubbish!"

"I am nineteen years old," Juliet declared.

"And what if you are," Miss Rachael replied briskly. "In my young days we were in the nursery at nineteen."

"Quite so," Mr. Pengarth assented with relief. "You took me by storm just now, Miss Juliet. After all, you are only a child."

"I am old enough to feel and to mean all that I said to you, Mr. Pengarth," she answered gravely. "And that reminds me, too - there was something else I meant to ask you."

"Sister," Mr. Pengarth said, "have you ordered the wine and the cake?"

"Bless me, no!" Miss Rachael declared. "It shall be ready in five minutes."

She entered the house. Mr. Pengarth stooped to pick some lavender.

"The only time I ever saw Sir Wingrave Seton," she said, "was on the day before I was told that a relation of my father had been found, who was willing to take charge of me. There was a younger man with him, someone very, very different from Sir Wingrave. Do you know who he was?"

"A sort of secretary of Sir Wingrave, I believe, dear. I never met him. I was, unfortunately, away at the time they came."

"He was very nice and kind to me," the girl continued,

"just as nice as Sir Wingrave was horrid. I suppose it was because they came on that day, but I have always connected him somehow with this mysterious relation of mine. Mr. Aynesworth didn't help to find him, did he?"

"Certainly not!" the lawyer answered. "The instructions I had came first from Mr. Saunders, the vicar of the parish. It was he who appeared to have made the necessary inquiries."

"Horrid old man!" she declared. "He used to make me feel that I wanted to cry every time that I saw him."

"Miss Rachael is calling us," the lawyer declared with obvious relief.

"New cake!" Juliet declared, "I can smell it! Delicious!"

LADY RUTH'S LAST CARD

"There are two letters," Aynesworth announced, "which I have not opened. One, I think, is from the Marchioness of Westhampton, the other from some solicitors at Truro. They were both marked private."

Wingrave was at breakfast in his flat; Aynesworth had been in an adjoining room sorting his correspondence. He accepted the two letters, and glanced them through without remark. But whereas he bestowed scarcely a second's consideration upon the broad sheet of white paper with the small coronet and the faint perfume of violets, the second letter apparently caused him some annoyance. He read it through for a second time with a slight frown upon his forehead.

"You must cancel my engagements for two days, Aynesworth," he said. "I have to go out of town."

Aynesworth nodded.

"There's nothing very special on," he remarked. "Do you want me to go with you?"

"It is not necessary," Wingrave answered. "I am going," he added, after a moment's pause, "to Cornwall."

Aynesworth was immediately silent. The one time when Wingrave had spoken to him as an employer, was in answer to some question of his as to what had eventually become of the treasures of Tredowen. He had always since scrupulously avoided the subject.

"Be so good as to look out the trains for me," Wingrave continued. "I cannot go until the afternoon," he added after a momentary pause. "I have an engagement for luncheon. Perhaps, if you are not too busy, you will see that Morrison packs some things for me."

He moved to the writing table, and wrote a few lines to the Marchioness, regretting that his absence from town would prevent his dining with her on the following day. Then he studied the money column in several newspapers for half an hour, and telephoned to his broker. At eleven o'clock, he rode for an hour in the quietest part of the park, avoiding, so far as possible, anyone he knew, and galloping whenever he could. It was the only form of exercise in which he was known to indulge although the knowledge of English games, which he sometimes displayed, was a little puzzling to some of his acquaintances. On his return, he made a simple but correct toilet, and at half-past one he met Lady Ruth at Prince's Restaurant.

Lady Ruth's gown of dove color, with faint touches of blue, was effective, and she knew it. Nevertheless, she was a little pale, and her manner lacked that note of quiet languor which generally characterized it. She talked rather more than usual, chattering idly about the acquaintances to whom she was continually nodding and bowing. Her face hardened a little as the Marchioness, on her way through the room with a party of friends, stopped at their table.

E. Phillips Oppenheim

The two women exchanged the necessary number of inanities, then the Marchioness turned to Wingrave.

"You won't forget that you are dining with me tomorrow?"

Wingrave shook his head regretfully.

"I am sorry," he said, "but I have to go out of town. I have just written you."

"What a bore," she remarked. "Business, of course!"

She nodded and passed on. Her farewell to Lady Ruth was distinctly curt. Wingrave resumed his seat and his luncheon without remark.

"Hateful woman," Lady Ruth murmured.

"I thought you were friends," Wingrave remarked.

"Yes, we are," Lady Ruth assented, "the sort of friendship you men don't know much about. You see a good deal of her, don't you?"

Wingrave raised his head and looked at Lady Ruth contemplatively.

"Why do you ask me that?" he asked.

"Curiosity!"

"I do," he remarked; "you should be grateful to her."

"Why?"

"It may save you a similar infliction."

Lady Ruth was silent for several moments.

"Perhaps," she said at last, "I do not choose to be relieved."

Wingrave bowed, his glass in his hand. His lips were curled into the semblance of a smile, but he did not say a word. Lady Ruth leaned a little across the table so that the feathers of her hat nearly brushed his forehead.

"Wingrave," she asked, "do you know what fear is? Perhaps not! You are a man, you see. No one has ever called me a coward. You wouldn't, would you?"

"No!" he said deliberately, "you are not a coward."

"There is only one sort of fear which I know," she continued, "and that is the fear of what I do not understand. And that is why, Wingrave, I am afraid of you."

He set down his glass, and his fingers trifled for a moment with its stem. His expression was inscrutable.

"Surely," he said, "you are not serious!"

"I am serious," she declared, "and you know that I am."

"You are afraid of me," he repeated softly. "I wonder why."

She looked him straight in the eyes.

"Because," she said, "I did you once a very grievous wrong. Because I know that you have not forgiven me. Because I am very sure that all the good that was in you lies slain."

"By whose hand?" he asked quietly. "No! You need not answer. You know. So do I. Yes, I can understand your fear. But I do not understand why you confess it to me."

"Nor I," she answered. "Nor do I understand why I am here - at your bidding, nor why I keep you always by my side whenever you choose to take your place there. Are you a vain man, Wingrave? Do you wish to pose as the friend of a woman whom the world has thought too ambitious to waste time upon such follies? There is the Marchioness! She would do you more credit still."

"Thank you," he answered. "I like to choose the path myself when I pass into the maze of follies!"

"You have not yet explained yourself," she reminded him. "Of all people in world, you have chosen us for your presumptive friends. Why? You hate us both. You know that you do. Is it part of a scheme? Lumley is investing money on your advice, I am allowing myself to be seen about with you more than is prudent - considering all things. Do you want to rake out the ashes of our domestic hearth - to play the part of - melodramatic villain? You are ingenious enough, and powerful enough."

"You put strange ideas into my head," he told her lightly. "Why should I not play the part that you suggest? It might be amusing, and you certainly deserve all the evil which I could bring upon you."

She leaned a little across the table towards him. Her eyes were soft and bright, and they looked full into his. The color in her cheeks was natural. The air around him was faintly fragrant with the perfume of her clothes and hair.

"We couldn't leave off playing at the game - and act it, could we?" she murmured. "We couldn't really - be friends?"

Lady Ruth had played her trump card. She had touched his fingers with hers, her eyes shone with the promise of unutterable things. But if Wingrave was moved, he did not show it.

"I wish," he said, "that I could accept your offer in the spirit with which you tender it. Unfortunately, I am a maimed person. My sensibilities have gone. Friendship, in the more intimate sense of the word, I may never hope to feel again. Enmity - well, that is more comprehensible; even enmity," he continued slowly, "which might prompt a woman to disguise herself as her own lady's maid, to seek out a tool to get rid of the man she feared. Pardon me, Lady Ruth, you are eating nothing."

She pulled down her veil.

"Thank you, I have finished," she said in a low tone.

He called for the bill.

"Pray, don't let my little remark distress you," he said. "I had almost forgotten the circumstance until something you said brought it into my mind. It is you yourself, you must remember, who set the example

E. Phillips Oppenheim

of candor."

"I deserve everything you can say," she murmured, "everything you can do. There is nothing left, I suppose, but suffering. Will you take me out to my carriage? You can come back and have your coffee with the Marchioness! She keeps looking across at you, and it will please her to think that you got rid of me."

He glanced at his watch.

"I am afraid," he said, rising, "that I must deny myself the pleasure of seeking the Marchioness again today. I have a train to catch in half an hour. You are ready?"

"Quite!"

They made their way through the maze of tables towards the door, Lady Ruth exchanging greetings right and left with her friends, although the tall, grave-looking man who followed her was by far the greater object of interest.

"Just like Ruth to keep him in her pocket," remarked her dearest friend, looking after them; "they say that he has millions."

She sighed a little enviously.

"The Barrington menage needs a little backing up," her companion remarked. "I should say that he had come just in time. The Marchioness has her eye upon him too. There may be some fun presently."

Lady Ruth's dearest friend smiled.

"I will back Ruth," she said drily. "Emily is beautiful, but she is too obvious, and too eager! Ruth's little ways are more subtle. Besides, look at the start she has. She isn't the sort of woman men tire of."

Lady Ruth held out her hand through the window of her electric coupe.

"Thank you for my luncheon," she said. "When shall we see you again?"

"In a few days," he answered, standing bareheaded upon the pavement. "I shall call directly I return."

Lady Ruth nodded and leaned back. Wingrave smiled faintly as he turned away. He had seen the little shudder which she had done her best to hide!

Lady Ruth found her husband at home, writing letters in his study. She sank wearily into a chair by his side.

"Been lunching out?" he inquired.

She nodded.

"At Prince's, with Wingrave."

He made no remark, but he seemed far from displeased.

"If I'd only had the pluck," he remarked a little disconsolately, "I might have made thousands by following his advice this week. It was you who put me off, too!"

"It turned out all right?" she asked.

"Exactly as he said. I made five hundred! I might just as well have made five thousand."

"Can you let me have a couple of hundred?" she asked. "The people are all bothering so."

"You know that I can't," he answered irritably. "I had to send the lot to Lewis, and then it wasn't a quarter of what he is pressing for. We shall never get through the season, Ruth, unless -"

She raised her eyes.

"Unless what?"

"Unless something turns up!"

There was a short, uncomfortable silence. Lady Ruth rose to her feet and stood facing the fireplace with her back to him.

"Lumley," she said, "let's face it!"

He gave a little start.

"Face what?" he inquired.

"Ruin, the Bankruptcy Court, and all the rest of it!" she declared, a note of defiance creeping into her tone.

Her husband's face was white with astonishment. He stared across at her blankly.

"Are you mad, Ruth?" he exclaimed. "Do you know what you are saying?"

"Quite well," she answered. "I'm a little sick of the whole show. The tradespeople are getting impertinent. I don't even know where to get flowers for dinner tonight or where to go for my Ascot gowns. It must come sooner or later."

"You're talking like a fool," he declared harshly. "Do you know that I should have to give up my seat and my clubs?"

"We could live quietly in the country."

"Country be - hanged!" he exclaimed savagely. "What use is the country to you and me? I'd sooner put a bullet through my brain. Ruth, old lady," he added more gently, "what's gone wrong? You're generally such a well plucked'un! Have you - had a row with Wingrave?" he asked, looking at her anxiously.

"No!"

"Then what is it?"

"Nothing! I've lost my nerve, I suppose!"

"You want a change! It isn't so very long to Cowes now and, thank heavens, that'll cost us nothing. We're going on Wingrave's yacht, aren't we?"

"Yes! We did accept."

Barrington fidgeted for a moment with a paper knife.

"Ruth," he asked, "what's wrong between you and Wingrave?"

"Nothing," she answered; "I'm afraid of him, that's all!"

"Afraid of him! Afraid of Wingrave!" he repeated.

"Yes! I do not think that he has forgotten. I think that he means to make us suffer."

Barrington was almost dignified.

"I never heard such nonsense in my life, Ruth!" he exclaimed. "I have watched Wingrave closely, and I have seen no trace of anything of the sort. Nonsense! It is worse than nonsense! You must be getting hysterical. You must get all this rubbish out of your head. To tell you the truth -"

"Well?"

"I was thinking that you might ask Wingrave to help us a bit. I don't believe he'd hesitate for a moment."

Ruth looked her husband in the face. There was a curious expression in her eyes.

"Do you think that it would be wise of me to ask him?" she demanded.

"Why not?" he answered. "You can take care of yourself. I can trust you."

"I told you that I was afraid of Wingrave," she reminded him. "I can take care of myself as a rule - and I do - as you know. I have elected to be one of the unfashionables in that respect. But to ask Wingrave for money is more than I dare do."

"Then I shall ask him myself," Barrington declared.

She picked up her gloves and turned to leave the room.

"I should prefer even that," she said.

E. Phillips Oppenheim

GUARDIAN AND WARD

"Up to the present, then," Wingrave remarked, "the child has no idea as to who has been responsible for the charge of her?"

"No idea at all, Sir Wingrave," the lawyer declared. "Your wishes have been strictly carried out, most strictly. She imagines that it is some unknown connection of her father. But, as I explained to you in my letter, she has recently exhibited a good deal of curiosity in the matter. She is - er - a young lady of considerable force of character for her years, and her present attitude - as I explained in my letter - is a trifle difficult."

Wingrave was sitting in the lawyer's own chair. Mr. Pengarth, who was a trifle nervous, preferred to stand.

"She shows, I think, a certain amount of ingratitude in forcing this journey and explanation upon me," Wingrave declared coldly. "It should have been sufficient for her that her benefactor preferred to remain anonymous."

"I regret, Sir Wingrave, that I must disagree with you," Mr. Pengarth answered boldly. "Miss Juliet, Miss Lundy I should say, is a young lady of character - and - er - some originality of disposition. She is a great favorite with everyone around here."

Wingrave remained silent. He had the air of one not troubling to reply to what he considered folly. Through the wide open window floated in the various sounds of the little country town, the rumbling of heavy carts passing along the cobbled streets, the shrill greetings of neighbors and acquaintances meeting upon the sidewalk. And then the tinkling bell of a rubber-tired cart pulling up outside, and a clear girlish voice speaking to some one of the passers-by.

Wingrave betrayed as much surprise as it was possible for him to show when at last she stood with outstretched hand before him. He had only an imperfect recollection of an ill-clad, untidy-looking child, with pale tear-stained cheeks, and dark unhappy eyes. The march of the years had been a thing whose effects he had altogether underestimated. The girl who stood now facing him was slight, and there was something of the child left in her bright eager face, but she carried herself with all the graceful assurance of an older woman. Her soft, dark eyes were lit with pleasure and excitement, her delicately traced eyebrows and delightful smile were somehow suggestive of her foreign descent. Her clothes were country-made, but perfect as regarded fit and trimness, her beflowered hat was worn with a touch of coquettish grace, a trifle un-English, but very delightful. She had not an atom of shyness or embarrassment. Only there was a great surprise in her face as she held out her hands to Wingrave.

"I know who you are," she exclaimed. "You are Sir Wingrave Seton. To think that I never guessed."

E. Phillips Oppenheim

"You remember seeing me, then?" he remarked, and his tone sounded all the colder after the full richness of her young voice.

"I just remember it - only just," she answered. "You see you did not take much notice of me that time, did you? But I have lived amongst your ancestors too long to make any mistake. Why have you stayed away from Tredowen so long?"

"I have been abroad," Wingrave answered. "I am not fond of England."

"You had trouble here, I know," she said frankly. "But that is all past and over. I think that you must forget how beautiful your home is or you would never bear to live away from it. Now, please, may I ask you a question?"

"Any that you think necessary," Wingrave answered. "Spare me as much as possible; I am not fond of them."

"Shall I leave you two together for a little time?" Mr. Pengarth suggested, gathering up some papers.

"Certainly not," Wingrave said shortly. "There is not the slightest necessity for it."

Mr. Pengarth resumed his seat.

"Just as you please," he answered. "But you must sit down, Juliet. There, you shall have my clients' chair."

The girl accepted it with a little laugh. There was no shadow of embarrassment about her manner, notwithstanding the cold stiffness of Wingrave's deportment. He sat where the sunlight fell across his chair, and the lines in his pale face seemed deeper than usual, the grey hairs more plentiful, the weariness in his eyes more apparent. Yet she was not in the least afraid of him.

"First of all, then, Sir Wingrave, may I ask you why you have been so extraordinarily kind to me?"

"There is nothing extraordinary about it at all," he answered. "Your father died and left you friendless in a parish of which I am Lord of the Manor. He received a starvation pittance for his labors, which it was my duty to augment, a duty which, with many others, I neglected. I simply gave orders that you should be looked after."

She laughed softly.

"Looked after! Why, I have lived at Tredowen. I have had a governess, a pony to drive. Heaven knows how many luxuries!"

"That," he interrupted hastily, "is nothing. The house is better occupied. What I have done for you is less in proportion than the sixpence you may sometimes have given to a beggar for I am a rich, a ridiculously rich man, with no possible chance of spending one-quarter of my income. You had a distinct and obvious claim upon me, and, at no cost or inconvenience to myself, I have endeavored, through others, to recognize it."

"I will accept your view of the situation," the girl said, still smiling, but with a faint note of disappointment in her tone. "I do not wish to force upon you expressions of gratitude which you would only find wearisome. But I must thank you! It is in my heart, and I must speak of it. There, it is over, you see! I shall say no more."

"You are a sensible young lady," Wingrave said, making a motion as though to rise. "I have only one request to make to you, and that is that you keep to yourself the knowledge which Mr. Pengarth informs me that you insisted upon acquiring. You are nearly enough of age now, and I will make you your own mistress. That is all, I think."

The smile died away from her lips. Her tone became very earnest.

"Sir Wingrave," she said, "for all that you have done for me, I am, as you know grateful. I would try to tell you how grateful, only I know that it would weary you. So we will speak only of the future. I cannot continue to accept - even such magnificent alms as yours."

"What do you mean, child?" he asked, frowning across at her.

"I mean," she said, "that now I am old enough to work, I cannot accept everything from one upon whom I have no claim. If you will help me a little still, I shall be more than grateful. But it must be in my own way."

"You talk about work," he said. "What can you do?"

"I can paint," she answered, "fairly well. I should like to go to London and have a few lessons. If I cannot make a living at that, I shall try something else."

"You disappoint me," Wingrave said. "There is no place for you in London. There are thousands starving there already because they can paint a little, or sing a little, or fancy they can. Do you find it dull down here?"

"Dull!" she exclaimed wonderingly. "I think that there can be no place on earth so beautiful as Tredowen."

"You are happy here?"

"Perfectly!"

"Then, for heaven's sake, forget all this folly," Wingrave said hardly. "London is no place for children. Miss Harrison can take you up for a month when you choose. You can go abroad if you want to. But for the rest -"

She rose suddenly, and sweeping across the office with one graceful movement, she leaned over Wingrave's chair. Her hands rested upon his shoulders, her eyes, soft with gathering tears, pleaded with his. Wingrave sat with all the outward immobility of a Sphinx.

"Dear Sir Wingrave," she said, "you have been so generous, so kind, and I may not even speak of my gratitude. Don't please think me unreasonable or ungracious. I can't tell you how I feel, but I must, I must, I must go away. I could not live here any longer now that I know. Fancy for a moment that I am your sister, or your daughter! Don't you believe, really, that she would feel the same? And I think you would wish her to. Don't be angry with me, please."

Wingrave's face never changed; but his fingers gripped

the arms of his chair so that a signet ring he wore cut deep into his flesh. When he spoke, his tone sounded almost harsh. The girl turned away to dash the tears from her eyes.

"What do you think of this - folly, Pengarth?"

The lawyer looked his best client squarely in the face. "I do not call it folly, Sir Wingrave. I think that Miss Lundy is right."

There was a pause. Her eyes were still pleading with him.

"Against the two of you," Wingrave remarked, "I am, of course, powerless. After all, it is no concern of mine. I shall leave you, Pengarth, to make such arrangements as Miss Lundy desires!"

He rose to his feet. Juliet now was pale. She dashed the tears from her eyes and looked at him in amazement mingled with something which was almost like despair.

"You don't mean," she exclaimed, "you are going away without coming to Tredowen?"

"Why not?" he asked. "I never had any intention of going there!"

"You are very angry with me," she cried in despair. "I - I -"

Her lip quivered. Wingrave interposed.

"I shall be happy to go and have a look at the place,"

he said carelessly, "if you will drive me back. I fancy I have almost forgotten what it is like."

She looked at him as at one who had spoken irreverently. Her eyes were full of wonder.

"I think that you must have indeed forgotten," she said, "how very beautiful it is. It is your home too! There is no one else," she added softly, "who can live there, amongst all those wonderful things, and call it really - home!"

"I am afraid," he said, "you will find that I have outlived all sentiment; but I will certainly come to Tredowen with you!"

E. Phillips Oppenheim

GHOSTS OF DEAD THINGS

"It was here," she said, as they passed through the walled garden seawards, "that I saw you first - you and the other gentleman who was so kind to me."

Wingrave nodded.

"I believe that I remember it," he said; "you were a mournful-looking object in a very soiled pinafore and most untidy hair."

"I had been out on the cliffs," she reminded him, "where I am taking you now. If you are going to make unkind remarks about my hair, I think that I had better fetch a hat."

"Pray don't leave me," he answered. "I should certainly lose my way. Your hair in those days was, I fancy, a little more - unkempt!"

She laughed.

"It used to be cut short," she said. "Hideous! There! Isn't that glorious?"

She had opened the postern gate in the wall, and through the narrow opening was framed a wonderful picture of the Cornish sea, rolling into the rock-studded bay. Its soft thunder was in their ears; salt and fragrant, the west wind swept into their faces. She closed the gate behind her, and stepped blithely forward.

"Come!" she cried. "We will climb the cliffs where we left you alone once before."

Side by side they stood looking over the ocean. Her head was thrown back, her lips a little parted. He watched her curiously.

"You must have sea blood in your veins," he remarked. "You listen as though you heard music all the time."

"And what about you?" she asked him, smiling. "You are the grandson of Admiral Sir Wingrave Seton who commanded a frigate at Trafalgar, and an ancestor of yours fought in the Armada."

"I am afraid," he said quietly, "that there is a hiatus in my life somewhere. There are no voices which call to me any more, and my family records are so much dead parchment."

Trouble passed into her glowing face and clouded her eyes.

"Ah!" she said, "I do not like to hear you talk so. Do you know that when you do, you make me afraid that something I have always hoped for will never come to pass?"

"What is it?" he asked.

"I have always hoped," she said, "that some day you would come once more to Tredowen. I suppose I am

rather a fanciful person. This is a country of super-
stitions and fancies, you know; but sometimes when I
have been alone in the picture gallery with all that long
line of dark faces looking down upon me from the
walls, I have felt like an interloper. Always they seem
to be waiting! Tonight, after dinner, I will take you
there. I will try and show you what I mean."

He shook his head.

"I shall never come back," he said, "and there are no
more of my name."

She hesitated. When at last she spoke, the color was
coming and going in her cheeks.

"Sir Wingrave," she said, "I am only an ignorant girl,
and I have no right to talk to you like this. Please be
angry with me if you want to. I deserve it. I know all
about - that ten years! Couldn't you forget it, and come
back? None of the country people round here, your
own people, believe anything evil about you. You were
struck, and you struck back again. A man would do
that. You could be as lonely as you liked here, or you
could have friends if you wished for them. But this is
the place where you ought to live. You would be
happier here, I believe, than in exile. The love of it all
would come back, you would never be lonely. It is the
same sea which sang to you when you were a child,
and to your fathers before you. It would bring you
forgetfulness when you wanted it, or -"

Wingrave interrupted her. His tone was cold, but not
unkind.

"My dear young lady," he said, "it is very good of you

to be so sympathetic, but I am afraid I am not at all the sort of person you imagine me to be. What I was before those ten years - well, I have forgotten. What I am now, I unfortunately know. I am a soured, malevolent being whose only pleasure lies in the dealing out to others some portion of the unhappiness which was dealt out to me."

"I do not believe it," she declared briskly.

He shrugged his shoulders.

"Nevertheless, it is true," he declared coolly. "Listen! More or less you interest me. I will tell you something which I have never yet told to a single human being. I need not go into particulars. You will probably believe a broad statement. My ten years' imprisonment was more or less an injustice!"

"Sir Wingrave!"

He checked her. There was not a tremor in his tone. The gesture with which he had repelled her was stiff and emotionless.

"I went into prison one man, I came out another. While I live, I shall never be able to think kindly again of a single one of my fellow creatures. It was not my fault. So far as our affections are concerned, we are machines, all of us. Well, my mainspring has broken."

"I don't believe it," she declared.

"It is, nevertheless, true," he affirmed calmly. "I am living in exile because I have no friends, because friends have become an impossibility to me. I shall not tell you any more of my life because you are young and you would not believe me if I did. Some day," he added grimly, "you will probably hear for yourself."

"I shall never believe anything," she declared, "which I do not choose to believe. I shall never believe, for instance, that you are quite what you think yourself."

"We will talk of other things," he said. "Five years ago, you showed Aynesworth where the seagulls built."

"And now I will show you," she exclaimed, "if you are sure that your head is steady enough. Come along!" . . .

It was after dinner that she took him into the picture gallery. Miss Harrison, very much disturbed by the presence of the master of Tredowen, and still more so by the hint which she had already received as to coming changes, followed them at a little distance.

"I am so sorry," Juliet said, "that we have no cigars or cigarettes."

"I seldom smoke," Wingrave answered.

"If only we had had the slightest idea of your coming," Miss Harrison said for the tenth time, "we would have made more adequate preparations. The wine cellar, at least, could have been opened. I allowed Mr. and Mrs. Tresfarwin to go for their holiday only yesterday, and the cellars, of course, are never touched."

"Your claret was excellent," Wingrave assured her.

"I am quite sure," Miss Harrison said, "that claret from the local grocer is not what you are accustomed to -"

"My dear madam," Wingrave protested, "I seldom touch wine. Show me which picture it is, Juliet, that you - ah!"

She had led him to the end of the gallery and stopped before what seemed to be a plain oak cupboard surrounded by a massive frame. She looked at him half fearfully.

"You want to see that picture?" he asked.

"If I might."

He drew a bunch of keys from his pocket and calmly selected one. It was a little rusty, but the cupboard turned at once on its hinges. A woman's face smiled down upon them, dark and splendid, from the glowing touch of a great painter. Juliet studied it eagerly, and then stole a sidelong glance at the man by her side. He was surveying it critically and without any apparent emotion.

"Herkomer's, I think," he remarked. "Quite one of his best."

"It is your mother?" she whispered.

He nodded.

"I'm not great at genealogy," he said, "but I can go as far back as that. She was by way of being a great lady, the daughter of the Duke of Warminster."

"You were an only son," she said softly. "She must have been very fond of you."

"Customary thing, I suppose," he remarked. "Lucky for her, under the circumstances, that she died young."

He closed the oaken door in front of the picture, and locked it.

"I should like to see the armory," he said; "but I really forget - let me see, it is at the end of the long gallery, isn't it?"

She led him there without a word. She was getting a little afraid of him. They inspected the library and wandered back into the picture gallery. It was she, now, who was silent. She had shown him all her favorite treasures without being able to evoke a single spark of enthusiasm.

"Once," she remarked, "we all had a terrible fright. We were told that everything was going to be sold."

He nodded.

"I did think of it," he admitted; "but there seemed to be no hurry. All these things are growing into money year by year. Some day I shall send everything to Christie's."

She looked at him in horror.

"You cannot - oh, you cannot mean it?" she cried.

"Why not? They are no use to me."

"No use?" she faltered.

"Not a bit. I don't suppose I shall see them again for

many years. And the money - well, one can use that."

"But I thought - that you were rich?" she faltered.

"So I am," he answered, "and yet I go on making more and more, and I shall go on. Money is the whip with which its possessor can scourge humanity. It is with money that I deal out my - forgive me, I forgot that I was talking aloud, and to a child," he wound up suddenly.

She looked at him, dry-eyed, but with a strained look of sorrow strangely altering her girlish face.

"You must be very unhappy," she said.

"Not at all," he assured her. "I am one of those fortunate persons who have outlived happiness and unhappiness. I have nothing to do but live - and pay off a few little debts."

He rose directly afterwards, and she walked with him out to the gardens whence a short cut led to the village.

"I have not tried again to make you change your mind," he said as they stood for a moment on the terrace. "If my wishes have any weight with you, I trust that you will do nothing without consulting Mr. Pengarth."

"And you -" she faltered, "are you - never in London? Sha'n't I see you again any time?"

"If you care to, by all means," he answered. "Tell Mr. Pengarth to let me have your address. Goodbye! Thank you for taking care of my treasures so well."

E. Phillips Oppenheim

She held his cold hand in hers and suddenly raised it to her lips. Then she turned away and hurried indoors.

Wingrave stood still for a moment and gazed at his hand through the darkness as though the ghosts of dead things had flitted out from the dark laurel shrubs. Then he laughed quietly to himself.

SPREADING THE NETS

"By the bye," the Marchioness asked him, "have you a Christian name?"

"Sorry," Wingrave answered, "if I ever had, I've forgotten it."

"Then I must call you Wingrave," she remarked. "I hate calling anyone I know decently well Mr. anything."

"Charmed," Wingrave answered; "it isn't a bad name."

"It isn't," she admitted. "By the bye," she continued, looking at him critically, "you are rather a surprising person, aren't you?"

"Glad you've found it out," Wingrave answered. "I always thought so."

"One associates all sorts of terrible things with millionaires - especially African and American ones," she remarked. "Now you could pass anywhere for the ordinary sort of decent person."

Wingrave nodded.

"I was told the other day," he remarked reflectively,

E. Phillips Oppenheim

"that if I would only cultivate two things, I might almost pass as a member of the English aristocracy."

"What were they?" she asked rashly.

"Ignorance and impertinence," he answered.

The Marchioness was silent for a moment. There was a little more color than usual in her beautiful cheeks and a dangerous glitter in her eyes.

"You can go home, Mr. Wingrave," she said.

He rose to his feet imperturbably. The Marchioness stretched out a long white hand and gently forced him back again.

"You mustn't talk like that to me," she said quietly. "I am sensitive."

He bowed.

"A privilege, I believe, of your order," he remarked.

"Of course, if you want to quarrel -" she began.

"I don't," he assured her.

"Then be sensible! I want to talk to you."

"Sensible, alone with you!" he murmured. "I should establish a new record."

"You certainly aren't in the least like a millionaire," she declared, smiling at him, "you are more like a -"

"Please go on," he begged.

"I daren't," she answered, shaking her head.

"Then you aren't in the least like a marchioness," he declared. "At least, not like our American ideas of one."

She laughed outright.

"Bring your chair quite close to mine," she ordered, "I really want to talk to you."

He obeyed, and affected to be absorbed in the contemplation of the rings on the hand which a great artist had called the most beautiful in England. She withdrew it a little peevishly, after a moment's pause.

"I want to talk about the Barringtons," she said. "Do you know that they are practically ruined?"

"I heard that Barrington had been gambling on the Stock Exchange the last few days," he answered.

"He has lost a great deal of money," she answered, "and they were almost on their last legs before. Are you going to set them straight again?"

"No idea," he answered. "I haven't been asked, for one thing."

"Ruth will ask you, of course," the Marchioness said impatiently. "I expect that she is waiting at your flat by now. I want to know whether you are going to do it."

The hand was again very close to his. Again Wingrave

E. Phillips Oppenheim

contemplated the rings.

"I forgot that you were her friend, and are naturally anxious," he remarked.

" I am not her friend , " the Marchioness answered, "and - I do not wish you to help them."

Wingrave was silent. The hand was insistent, and he held it for a moment lightly, and then let it go.

"Well, I don't know," he said doubtfully. "The Barringtons have been very hospitable to me."

"Rubbish!" the Marchioness answered. "You have done quite enough for them already. Of course, you are a man - and you must choose. I am sure that you understand me."

He rose to his feet.

"I must think this out," he said. "The Barringtons have a sort of claim on me. I will let you know which way I decide."

She stood close to him, and her hand fell upon his shoulder.

"You are not going!" she exclaimed. "I have told them that I am at home to no one, and I thought that you would stay and entertain me. Sit down again, Wingrave!"

"Sorry," he answered, "I have a lot to do this afternoon. I came directly I had your note; but I have had to keep some other people waiting."

"You are going to see Lady Ruth!"

"Not that I know of," he declared. "I have heard nothing from her. By the bye, I lost some money to you at bridge the other evening. How much was it? Do you remember?"

She looked at him for a second, and turned away.

"Do you really want to know?" she asked.

"If you please. Put the amount down on a piece of paper, and then I sha'n't forget it."

She crossed the room to her desk, and returned with a folded envelope. He stuffed it into his waistcoat pocket.

"I shall be at the opera tonight," she said. "Will you come there and tell me what - which you decide?"

"With pleasure," he answered, "if I can get away from a stupid dinner in time."

She let him go reluctantly. Afterwards she passed into her own room, and stood looking at herself in the pier glass. Artists and the society papers called her the most beautiful woman in England; fashion had placed her upon such a pinnacle that men counted it a distinction to be seen speaking to her. She dealt out her smiles and favors like Royalty itself; she had never once known a rebuff. This afternoon she felt that she had received one. Had she been too cold or too forward? Perhaps she had underestimated the man himself. She rang for her maid.

E. Phillips Oppenheim

"Celeste," she said, "I shall wear my new Paquin gown tonight at the opera, and my pearls."

"Very good, your ladyship."

"And I am going to lie down for an hour or two now. Don't let me be disturbed. I want to look my best tonight. You understand?"

"Perfectly, your ladyship."

The Marchioness rested, but she did not sleep. She was thinking of Wingrave!

It was not Lady Ruth, but her husband, who was waiting to see Wingrave on his return. Aynesworth was talking to him, but at once withdrew. Wingrave nodded with slightly upraised eyebrows. He never shook hands with Barrington.

"You wanted to see me?" he inquired, carelessly turning over a little pile of letters.

Barrington was ill at ease. He hated himself and he hated his errand.

"Yes, for a moment or two - if you're not busy," he said. "May I smoke? I'm nervous this morning."

"Help yourself," Wingrave said shortly. "Cigarettes and cigars on the sideboard. Touch the bell if you'll take anything to drink."

"Thanks - Aynesworth gave me a brandy and soda. Capital fellow, Aynesworth!"

"Have another," Wingrave said shortly.

He crossed the room to the sideboard. Wingrave glanced up from his letters, and smiled coldly as he saw the shaking fingers.

"I don't often indulge like this," Barrington said, turning away from the sideboard with a tumbler already empty in his hands. "The fact is, I've had rather a rude knock, and Ruth thought I'd better come and see you."

Wingrave remained a study of impassivity. His guest's whole demeanor, his uneasy words and nervous glances were an unspoken appeal to be helped out in what he had come to say. And Wingrave knew very well what it was. Nevertheless, he remained silent - politely questioning. Barrington sat down a little heavily. He was not so carefully dressed as usual; he looked older, his appearance lacked altogether that air of buoyant prosperity which was wont to inspire his friends and creditors with confidence.

"I've been a fool, Wingrave," he said. "You showed me how to make a little money a few weeks ago, and it seemed so easy that I couldn't resist having a try by myself, only on rather a larger scale. I lost! Then I went in again to pull myself round, and I lost again. I lost - more than I can easily raise before settlement."

"I am sorry," Wingrave said politely. "It is very unwise to meddle in things you know so little about."

For a moment the worm turned. Barrington rose to his feet, and with a deep flush upon his cheeks moved towards the door. But his spark of genuine feeling died out almost as soon as it had been kindled. Outside that door was ruin; within, as he very well knew, lay his only chance of salvation. He set down his hat, and turned round.

"Wingrave," he said, "will you lend me some money?"

Wingrave looked at him with upraised eyebrows.

"I," he remarked, "lend you money? Why should I?"

"Heaven knows," Barrington answered. "It is you who have chosen to seek us out. You have forced upon us something which has at least the semblance of friendship. There is no one else whom I could ask. It isn't only this damned Stock Exchange transaction. Everything has gone wrong with me for years. If I could have kept going till next July, I should have been all right. I have made a little success in the House, and I am promised a place in the next government. I know it seems queer that I should be asking you, but it is that - or ruin. Now you know how things are with me."

"You are making," Wingrave said quietly, "a mistake. I have not pretended or given the slightest evidence of any friendship for yourself."

Barrington looked at him with slowly mounting color.

"You mean -"

"Precisely," Wingrave interrupted. "I do not know what I might or might not do for Lady Ruth. I have not considered the subject. It has not, in fact, been presented to me."

"It is the same thing," Barrington declared hoarsely.

"Pardon me - it is not," Wingrave answered.

"What I ask you to do," Barrington said, "I ask on behalf of my wife."

"As an ambassador," Wingrave said coldly, "you are not acceptable to me. It is a matter which I could only discuss with Lady Ruth herself. If Lady Ruth has anything to say to me, I will hear it."

Barrington stood quite still for several moments. The veins on his forehead stood out like tightly drawn cords, his breath came with difficulty. The light in his eyes, as he looked at Wingrave, was almost murderous.

"If Lady Ruth desires to see me," Wingrave remarked slowly, "I shall be here at nine o'clock this evening. Tomorrow my movements are uncertain. You will excuse me if I hurry you away now. I have an engagement which is already overdue."

Barrington took up his hat and left the room without a word. Wingrave remained in his chair. His eyes followed the departing figure of his visitor. When he was absolutely sure that he was alone, he covered his face with one hand. His engagement seemed to have been with his thoughts for he did not stir for nearly an hour later. Then he rang the bell for Aynesworth.

E. Phillips Oppenheim

IN THE TOILS

Wingrave did not speak for several moments after Aynesworth had entered the room. He had an engagement book before him and seemed to be deep in its contents. When at last he looked up, his forehead was furrowed with thought, and he had the weary air of a man who has been indulging in unprofitable memories.

"Aynesworth," he said, "be so good as to ring up Walters and excuse me from dining with him tonight."

Aynesworth nodded.

"Any particular form of excuse?" he asked.

"No! Say that I have an unavoidable engagement. I will see him tomorrow morning."

"Anything else?" Aynesworth asked, preparing to leave the room.

"No! You might see that I have no visitors this evening. Lady Ruth is coming here at nine o'clock."

"Lady Ruth is coming here," Aynesworth repeated in a colorless tone. "Alone?"

"Yes."

Aynesworth shrugged his shoulders, but made no remark. He turned towards the door, but Wingrave called him back.

"Your expression, Aynesworth," he said, "interests me. Am I or the lady in question responsible for it?"

"I am sorry for Lady Ruth," Aynesworth said. "I think that I am sorry, too, for her husband."

"Why? She is coming of her own free will."

"There are different methods of compulsion," Aynesworth answered.

Wingrave regarded him thoughtfully.

"That," he said, "is true. But I still do not understand why you are sorry for her."

"Because," Aynesworth said, "I know the history of a certain event, and I know you. It is, I suppose, for this end that you made use of them."

Wingrave nodded.

"Quite right," he declared. "I think that the time is not far off when that dear lady and I can cry quits. This time, too, I see nothing to impair my satisfaction at the probable finale. In various other cases, as you might remember, I have not been entirely successful."

"It depends," Aynesworth remarked drily, "upon what you term success."

Wingrave shrugged his shoulders.

"I think," he said coldly, "that you are aware of what my feelings and desired course of action have been with regard to those of my fellow creatures with whom I have happened to come into contact. It seems to me that I have been a trifle unfortunate in several instances."

"As for instance?" Aynesworth asked.

"Well, to take a few cases only," Wingrave continued, "there was the child down at Tredowen whom you were so anxious for me to befriend. Of course, I declined to do anything of the sort, and she ought, by rights, to have gone to some charitable institution, founded and supported by fools, and eventually become, perhaps, a domestic servant. Instead of which, some relation of her father turns up and provides for her lavishly. You must admit that that was unfortunate."

"It depends upon the point of view," Aynesworth remarked drily. "Personally, I considered it a most fortunate occurrence."

"Naturally," Wingrave agreed. "But then you are a sentimentalist. You like to see people happy, and you would even help to make them so if you could without any personal inconvenience. I am at the other pole. If I could collect humanity into one sentient force, I would set my heel upon it without hesitation. I try to do what I can with the atoms, but I have not the best of fortune. There was Mrs. Travers, now! There I should have been successful beyond a doubt if some busybody hadn't sent that cable to her husband. I wonder if you were idiot enough to do that, Aynesworth?"

"If I had thought of the Marconigram," Aynesworth said, "I am sure I should have done it. But as a matter of fact, I did not."

"Just as well, so far as our relations are concerned," Wingrave said coldly. "I did manage to make poor men of a few brokers in New York, but my best coup went wrong. That boy would have blown his brains out, I believe, if some meddling idiot hadn't found him all that money at the last moment. I have had a few smaller successes, of course, and there is this affair of Lady Ruth and her estimable husband. You know that he came to borrow money of me, I suppose?"

"I guessed it," Aynesworth answered. "You should be modern in your revenge and lend it to him."

Wingrave smiled coldly.

"I fancy," he said, "that Lumley Barrington will find my revenge modern enough. I may lend the money they need - but it will be to Lady Ruth! I told her husband so a few minutes ago. I told him to send his wife to me. He has gone to tell her now!"

"I wonder," Aynesworth remarked, "that he did not thrash you - or try to."

Again Wingrave's lips parted.

"Moral deterioration has set in already," he remarked. "When he pays his bills with my money, he will lose the little he has left of his self-respect."

Aynesworth turned abruptly away. He was strongly tempted to say things which would have ended his connection with Wingrave, and as yet he was not ready to leave. For the sake of a digression, he took up a check book from the table.

"There are three checks," he remarked, "which I cannot trace. One for ten thousand pounds, another for five, and a third for a thousand pounds. What account shall I put them to?"

"Private drawing account," Wingrave answered. "They represent a small speculation. By the bye, you'd better go and ring up Walters."

"Do you wish the particulars entered in your sundry investment book?" Aynesworth asked.

Wingrave smiled grimly.

"I think not," he answered. "You can put them to drawing account. If you want me again this evening, I shall dine at the Cafe Royal at eight o'clock, and shall return here at five minutes to nine."

. . . .

Lady Ruth was punctual. At a few minutes past nine, Morrison announced that a lady had called to see Mr. Wingrave by appointment.

"You can show her in," Wingrave said. "See that we are not disturbed."

Lady Ruth was scarcely herself. She was dressed in a high-necked muslin gown, and she wore a hat and veil, which somewhat obscured her features. The latter she raised, however, as she accepted the chair which

Wingrave had placed for her. He saw then that she was pale, and her manner betrayed an altogether unfamiliar nervousness. She avoided his eyes.

"Did you expect me?" she asked.

"Yes!" he answered, "I thought that you would come."

Her foot, long and slender, beat impatiently upon the ground. She looked up at him once, but immediately withdrew her eyes.

"Why did you bring me here?" she asked in a low tone.

"My dear Lady Ruth!" he protested.

"If you want to play at being friends," she said, "for heaven's sake call me Ruth. You found it easy enough once."

"You are very kind," he answered. "Ruth, by all means."

"Now will you answer my question?" she said. "Do you mean - to help us?"

"Us - no!" he answered; "you - perhaps yes!" he added.

Then she looked at him, and found herself puzzled by the perfect impassivity of his features. Surely he would drop the mask now. He had insisted upon her coming!

"Perhaps?" she repeated. "What then - are the conditions?"

He bent over towards her. Curiously enough , there

was, mingled with many other sensations, a certain sense of triumph in the thought, it was almost a hope, that at last he was going to betray himself, that he was going to admit tacitly, or by imputation, that her power over him was not wholly dead. It was a terrible situation - in her heart she felt so, but it had its compensations. Wingrave had been her constant attendant for months. He had seen her surrounded by men, all anxious to secure a smile from her; he had seen her play the great lady in her own house, and she played it very well. She knew that she was a past mistress in the arts which fascinate his sex, she understood the quiet speeches, the moods, every trick of the gamester in emotions, from the fluttering of eyelids to the unchaining of the passions. And he had loved her. Underneath it all, he must love her now. She was determined that he should tell her so. It was genuine excitement which throbbed in her pulses, a genuine color which burned in her cheeks.

"The conditions?" he repeated. "You believe, then, that I mean to make conditions?"

She raised her eyes to his, eloquent eyes she knew, and looked at him. The mask was still there - but he had moved a little nearer to her.

"I do not know," she said softly. "You must tell me."

There was a moment's silence. She had scarcely given herself credit for such capacity for emotion. He was on his feet. Surely the mask must go now! And then - she felt that it must be a nightmare. It was incredible! He had struck a match and was calmly lighting a cigarette.

"One ," he said coolly, "is that Mademoiselle Violet

employs no more amateur assassins to make clumsy attempts upon my life."

She sat in her place rigid - half frozen with a cold, numbing fear. He had sent for her, then, only to mock her. She had failed! They were not even to have the money! Speech was quite impossible. Then he continued.

"I will take your assent for granted," he said. "Do you know how much you require to free yourself?"

"About eight thousand pounds!" she answered mechanically.

He sat down and wrote a check, which he laid before her.

"You will have to endorse that," he remarked in a matter-of-fact tone. "Your name at the back will do instead of a receipt."

She sprang to her feet.

"Keep your money," she cried. "I will not touch it. Please open the door for me! I am going."

"By all means - if you wish it," he answered undisturbed. "At the same time, I am curious to know why you came here at all if you did not intend to accept it."

She faced him, hot and angry.

"I did intend to accept it," she declared. "It is that or ruin. But you are too cruel! You make it - impossible."

"You surprise me," he answered. "I suppose you know best."

"For heaven's sake tell me," she cried passionately, "what has come to you, what manner of a man are you? You loved me once! Now, even, after all these years, you cannot deny it. You have gone out of your way to be with me, to be my companion wherever we are. People are beginning to smile when they see us together. I don't mind. I - for God's sake tell me, Wingrave! Why do you do it? Why do you lend me this money? What can I do for you? What do you want me to be? Are you as cold as a stone? Have you no heart - no heart even for friendship!"

"I would not seek," he answered, "to buy - your friendship with a check!"

"But it is yours already," she cried, holding out her hands. "Give me a little kindness, Wingrave! You make me feel and seem a perfect idiot. Why, I'd rather you asked me anything that treated me like this."

"I was under the impression," Wingrave remarked, "that I was behaving rather well. I wonder what would really satisfy you!"

"To have you behave as you are doing, and want to behave differently," she cried. "You are magnificent - but it is because you are indifferent. Will you kiss me, Wingrave?"

"With pleasure!" he answered.

She drew away from him quickly.

"Is it - another woman?" she asked. "The Marchioness?"

Her eagerness was almost painful. He did not answer her at once. She caught hold of his wrist and drew him towards her. Her eyes searched his face.

"The Marchioness," he said, "is a very beautiful woman. She does not, however, affect the situation as between you and me."

"If she dared!" Lady Ruth murmured. "Wingrave, won't you try and be friends with me?"

"I will try - certainly," he answered. "You would be surprised, however, if you could realize the effect of a long period of enforced seclusion upon a man of my -"

"Don't!" she shrieked; "stop!"

"My temperament, I was about to say," he concluded. "There was a time when I am afraid I might have been tempted, under such circumstances as these, to forget that you were no longer free, to forget everything that except we were alone, and that you - are as beautiful as ever you were!"

"Yes!" she murmured, moving imperceptibly a little nearer towards him.

He picked up the check and gave it to her.

"I am no actor," he said, looking at her steadily. "At present, I make no conditions. But -"

She leaned towards him. He took her face between his

hands and kissed her on the lips.

"I may make them later," he said. "I reserve my right."

She looked at him for a moment, and dropped her veil.

"Please take me down to my carriage," she asked.

THE INDISCRETION OF THE MARCHIONESS

"I am perfectly certain," Juliet declared, "that we ought not to be here."

"That," Aynesworth remarked, fanning himself lightly with his pocket handkerchief, "may account for the extraordinary sense of pleasure which I am now experiencing. At the same time, I can't see why not."

"I only met you this afternoon - a few hours ago. And here we are, absolutely wedged together on these seats - and my chaperon is dozing half the time."

"Pardon me," Aynesworth objected. "I knew you when you were a child."

"For one day!"

"Nevertheless," Aynesworth persisted, "the fact remains. If you date our acquaintance from this afternoon, I do not. I have never forgotten the little girl in short frocks and long black hair, who showed me where the seagulls built, and told me Cornish fairy stories."

"It was a very long time ago," she remarked.

"Four years," he answered; "for you, perhaps, a long

time, because you have changed from a child - into a woman. But for a man approaching middle age - as I am - nothing!"

"That is all very well," she answered, "but I am not sure that we ought to be in the gallery at Covent Garden together, with a chaperon who will sleep!"

"She will wake up," he declared, "with the music."

"And I," she murmured, "will dream. Isn't it lovely?"

He smiled.

"I wonder how it really seems to you," he remarked. "We are breathing an atmosphere hot with gas, and fragrant with orange peel. We are squashed in amongst a crowd of people of a class whom I fancy that neither you nor I know much about. And I saw you last in a wilderness! We saw only the yellow sands, and the rocks, and the Atlantic. We heard only the thunder of the sea and the screaming of seagulls. This is very different."

"Wonderfully, wonderfully different," she answered. "I miss it all! Of course I do, and yet one is so much nearer to life here, the real life of men and women. Oh, one cannot compare it. Why should one try? Ah, listen!"

The curtain went up. The music of the orchestra subsided, and the music of the human voice floated through the Opera House - the human voice, vibrant with joy and passion and the knowledge which lies behind the veil. Juliet found no time to talk then, no time to think even of her companion. Her young cheeks were flushed, her eyes were bright with excitement. She leaned a little forward in her place, she passed with all the effortless facility of her ingenuous youth, into the dim world of golden fancies which the story of the opera was slowly unfolding. Beside her, Mrs. Tresfarwin dozed and blinked and dozed again - and on her left Aynesworth himself, a little affected by the music, still found time to glance continually at his companion, so radiant with life and so fervently intent upon realizing to the full this, the first of its unknown joys. So with crashing of chords and thunder of melody the act went on. And when it was over, Juliet thought no more of the Cornish sea and the lullaby of the waves. A new music was stirring in her young blood.

They were in the front row of the gallery, and presently she leaned over to gaze down at the panorama below, the women in the boxes and stalls, whose bare shoulders and skillfully coiffured hair flashed with jewels. Suddenly her hand fell upon Aynesworth's arm.

"Look!" she cried in some excitement, "do you see who that is in the box there - the one almost next to the stage?"

Aynesworth, too, uttered a little exclamation. The lights from beneath were falling full upon the still, cold face of the man who had just taken a vacant chair in one of the boxes.

"Wingrave!" he exclaimed, and glanced at once at his watch.

"Sir Wingrave Seton," she murmured. "Isn't it strange that I should see him here tonight?"

E. Phillips Oppenheim

"He comes often," Aynesworth answered. "Music is one of his few weaknesses."

There was a movement in the box, and a woman's head and shoulders appeared from behind the curtain. Juliet gave a little gasp.

"Mr. Aynesworth," she exclaimed, "did you ever see such a beautiful woman? Do tell me who she is!"

"A very great lady in London society," Aynesworth answered. "That is Emily, Marchioness of Westchester."

Juliet's eyes never moved from her until the beautiful neck and shoulders were turned away. She leaned over towards her companion, and she did not again, for some few minutes, face the house.

"She is the loveliest woman I ever saw in my life," Juliet said with a little sigh. "Is she a great friend of Sir Wingrave Seton, Mr. Aynesworth?"

"He has no friends," Aynesworth answered. "I believe that they are very well acquainted."

"Poor Sir Wingrave!" Juliet murmured softly.

Aynesworth looked at her in some surprise.

"It is odd that you should have recognized him from up here," he remarked thoughtfully. "He has changed so much during the last few years."

Juliet smiled, but she did not explain. She felt that she was obeying Wingrave's wishes.

"I should have recognized him anywhere," she answered simply. "I wonder what they are talking about. She seems so interested, and he looks so bored."

Aynesworth looked at his watch. It was barely ten o'clock.

"I am very glad to see him here this evening," he remarked.

"I should like so much," she said, still gazing at them earnestly, "to know that they are talking about."

. . . .

"So you will not tell me," the Marchioness murmured, ceasing for a moment the graceful movements of her fan, and looking at him steadily. "You refuse me this - almost the first thing I have ever asked you?"

"It is scarcely," Wingrave objected, "a reasonable question."

"Between you and me," she murmured, "such punctiliousness is scarcely necessary - is it?"

He withstood the attack of those wonderful eyes lifted swiftly to his, and answered her gravely.

"You are Lady Ruth's friend," he remarked. "Probably, therefore, she will tell you all about it."

The Marchioness laughed softly, yet with something less than mirth.

"Friends , " she exclaimed, "Lady Ruth and I? There

E. Phillips Oppenheim

was never a woman in this world who was less my friend - especially now!"

He asked for no explanation of her last words, but in a moment or two she vouchsafed it. She leaned a little forward, her eyes flashed softly through the semi-darkness.

"Lady Ruth is afraid," she said quietly, "that I might take you away from her."

"My dear lady," he protested, "the slight friendship between Lady Ruth and myself is not of the nature to engender such a fear."

She shrugged her beautiful shoulders. Her hands were toying with the rope of pearls which hung from her neck. She bent over them, as though examining the color of the stones.

"How long have you known Ruth?" she asked quietly.

He looked at her steadfastly. He could not be sure whether it was his fancy, or whether indeed there was some hidden meaning in her question.

"Since I came to live in England," he answered.

"Ah!"

There was a moment's silence. Then with a little wave of her hands and a brilliant smile, she figuratively dismissed the subject.

"We waste time," she remarked lightly, "and we may have callers at any moment. I will ask you no more questions save those which the conventions may permit you to answer truthfully. We can't depart from our code, can we, even for the sake of an inquisitive woman?"

"I can assure you -" he began.

"But I will have no assurances," she interrupted smilingly. "I am going to talk of other things. I am going to ask you a ridiculous question. Are you fond of music? - seriously!"

"I believe so," he answered. "Why?"

"Because," she answered, "I sometimes wonder what there is in the world that interests you! Certainly, none of the ordinary things seem to. Tonight, almost for the first time, I saw you look a little drawn out of yourself. I was wondering whether it was the music or the people. I suppose, until one gets used to it," she added, looking a little wearily around the house, "an audience like this is worth looking at."

"It certainly is not the people," he said. "Do you make as close a study of all your acquaintances?"

"Naturally not," she answered, "and I do not class you amongst my acquaintances at all. You interest me, my friend - very much indeed!"

"I am flattered," he murmured.

"You are not - I wish that you were," she answered simply. "I can understand why you have succeeded where so many others have failed. You are strong. You have nerves of steel - and very little heart. But

now - what are you going to do with your life, now that
wealth must even have lost its meaning to you? I
should like to know that. Will you tell me?"

"What is there to do?" he asked. "Eat and drink, and
juggle a little with the ball of fate."

"You are not ambitious?"

"Not in the least."

"Pleasure, for itself, does not attract you. No! I know
that it does not. What are you going to do, then?"

"I have no idea," he answered. "Won't you direct me?"

"Yes, I will," she answered, "if you will pay my price."

He looked at her more intently. He himself had been
attaching no particular importance to this conversation,
but he was suddenly conscious that it was not so with
the woman at his side. Her eyes were shining at him,
soft and full and sweet; her beautiful bosom was rising
and falling quickly; there had come to her something
which even he was forced to recognize, that curious
and voluptuous abandonment which a woman rarely
permits herself, and can never assume. He was a little
bewildered. His speech lost for a moment its cold
precision.

"Your price?" he repeated. "I - I am stupid. I'm afraid I
don't understand."

"Marry me," she whispered in his ear, "and I will take
you a little further into life than you could ever go
alone You don't care for me, of course - but you shall.

You don't understand this world, Wingrave, or how to make the best of it. I do! Let me be your guide!"

Wingrave looked at her in grave astonishment.

"You are not by any chance - in earnest?" he asked.

"You know very well that I am," she answered swiftly. "And yet you hesitate! What is it that you are afraid of? Don't you like to give up your liberty? We need not marry unless you choose. That is only a matter of form nowadays at any rate. I have a hundred chaperons to choose from. Society expects strange things from me. It is your companionship I want. Your money is fascinating, of course. I should like to see you spend it, to spend it with both hands. Don't be afraid that we should be talked about. I am not Lady Ruth! I am Emily, Marchioness of Westchester, and I live and choose my friends as I please; will you be chief amongst them? Hush!"

For Wingrave it was providential. The loud chorus which had heralded the upraising of the curtain died away. Melba's first few notes were floating through the house. Silence was a necessity. The low passion of the music rippled from the stage, through the senses and into the hearts of many of the listeners. But Wingrave listened silent and unmoved. He was even unconscious that the woman by his side was watching him half anxiously every now and then.

The curtain descended amidst a thunder of applause. Wingrave turned slowly towards his companion. And then there came a respite - a knock at the door.

The Marchioness frowned, but Wingrave was already

holding it open. Lady Ruth, followed by an immaculate young guardsman, a relative of her husband, was standing there.

"Mr. Wingrave!" she exclaimed softly, with upraised eyebrows, "why have you contrived to render yourself invisible? We thought you were alone, Emily," she continued, "and took pity on you. And all the time you had a prize."

The Marchioness looked at Lady Ruth, and Lady Ruth looked at the Marchioness. The young guardsman was a little sorry that he had come, but Lady Ruth never turned a hair.

"You must really have your eyes seen to, dear," the Marchioness remarked in a tone of tender concern. "When you can't see such an old friend as Mr. Wingrave from a few yards away, they must be very bad indeed. How are you, Captain Kendrick? Come and tell me about the polo this afternoon. Sorry I can't offer you all chairs. This is an absurd box - it was only meant for two!"

"Come into ours," Lady Ruth said; "we have chairs for six, I think."

The Marchioness shook her head.

"I wish I had a millionaire in the family," she murmured. "All the same, I hate large parties. I am old-fashioned enough to think that two is a delightful number."

Lady Ruth laid her hand upon Wingrave's arm.

"A decided hint, Mr. Wingrave," she declared. "Come and let me introduce you to my sister. Our box is only a few yards off."

E. Phillips Oppenheim

"I AM MISANTHROPOS, AND HATE MANKIND"

Wingrave had just come in from an early gallop. His pale cheeks were slightly flushed, and his eyes were bright. He had been riding hard to escape from disconcerting thoughts. He looked in at the study, and found Aynesworth with a mass of correspondence before him.

"Anything important?" he asked.

"Not yet," Aynesworth answered. "The letters marked private I have sent up to your room. By the bye, there was something I wanted to tell you."

Wingrave closed the door.

"Well?" he said.

"I was up in the gallery of the Opera House last night," Aynesworth said, "with a - person who saw you only once, soon after I first came to you - before America. You were some distance away, and yet - my friend recognized you."

Wingrave shrugged his shoulders.

"That, of course, is possible," he answered. "It really does not matter so very much unless they knew me - as

Wingrave Seton!"

"My friend," Aynesworth said, "recognized you as Sir Wingrave Seton."

Wingrave frowned thoughtfully for a moment.

"Who was it?" he asked.

"A most unlikely person," Aynesworth remarked smiling. "Do you remember, when we went down to Tredowen just before we left for America, a little, long-legged, black-frocked child, whom we met in the gardens - the organist's daughter, you know?"

"What of her?" Wingrave asked.

"It was she who was with me," Aynesworth remarked. "It was she who saw you in the box with the Marchioness of Westchester."

Aynesworth was puzzled by the intentness with which Wingrave was regarding him. Impenetrable though the man was, Aynesworth, who had not yet lost his early trick of studying him closely, knew that, for some reason or other, his intelligence had proved disturbing.

"Have you then - kept up your acquaintance with this child?" he demanded.

Aynesworth shook his head.

"She is not a child any longer, but a very beautiful young woman," he said. "I met her again quite by accident. She is up in London, studying art at the studio of an old friend of mine who has a class of girls.

E. Phillips Oppenheim

I called to see him the other afternoon, and recognized her."

"Your acquaintance," Wingrave remarked, "has progressed rapidly if she accepts your escort - to the gallery of the Opera!"

"It was scarcely like that," Aynesworth explained. "I met her and Mrs. Tresfarwin on the way there, and asked to be allowed to accompany them. Mrs. Tresfarwin was once your housekeeper, I think, at Tredowen."

"And did you solve the mystery of this relation of her father who turned up so opportunely?" Wingrave asked.

Aynesworth shook his head.

"She told me nothing about him," he answered.

Wingrave passed on to his own room. His breakfast was on the table awaiting him, and a little pile of letters and newspapers stood by his plate. His servant, his head groom, and his chauffeur were there to receive their orders for the morning. About him were all the evidences of his well-ordered life. He sent both the men away and locked the door. It was half an hour before he touched either his breakfast or his letters . . .

He lunched at Westchester House in obedience to a somewhat imperative summons. There were other guests there, whom, however, he outstayed. As soon as they were alone, his hostess touched him on the arm and led him to her own room.

"At last!" she exclaimed, with an air of real relief. "There, sit down opposite to me, please - I want to watch your face."

She was a little paler than usual, and he noticed that she had avoided talking much to him at luncheon time. And yet he thought that he had never seen her more beautiful. Something in her face had altered. He could not tell what it was for he was not a man of much experience as regarded her sex. Yet, in a vague sort of way, he understood the change. A certain part of the almost insolent quietness, the complete self-assurance of her manner, had gone. She was a little more like an ordinary woman!

"Lady Ruth proved herself an excellent tactician last night," she remarked. "She has given me an exceedingly uncomfortable few hours. For you, well for you it was a respite, wasn't it?"

"I don't know that I should call it exactly that," he answered thoughtfully.

She looked at him steadfastly, almost wistfully.

"Well," she said, "I am not going to make excuses for myself. But the things which one says naturally enough when the emotions provoke them sound crude enough in cold blood and colder daylight. We women are creatures of mood, you know. I was feeling a little lonely and a little tired last night, and the music stole away my common sense."

"I understand," he murmured. "All that you said shall be forgotten."

"Then you do not understand," she answered, smiling at him. "What I said I do not wish to be forgotten. Only - just at that moment, it sounded natural enough - and today - I think that I am a little ashamed."

He rose from his seat. Her eyes leaped up to his expectantly, and the color streamed into her cheeks. But he only stood by her side. He did nothing to meet the half-proffered embrace.

"Dear Lady Emily," he said, "all the kind things that you said were spoken to a stranger. You did not know me. I did not mean anyone to know me. It is you who have commanded the truth. You must have it. I am not the person I seem to be. I am not the person to whom words such as yours should have been spoken. Even my name is an assumed one. I should prefer to leave it at that - if you are content."

"I am not content," she answered quietly; "I must hear more."

He bowed.

"I am a man," he said, "who spent ten years in prison, the ten best years of my life. A woman sent me there - a woman swore my liberty away to save her reputation. I was never of a forgiving disposition, I was never an amiably disposed person. I want you to understand this. Any of the ordinary good qualities with which the average man may be endowed, and which I may have possessed, are as dead in me as hell fire could burn them. You have spoken of me as of a man who failed to find a sufficient object in life. You were wrong. I have an object, and I do my best to live up to it. I hate the whole world of men and women who laughed their way through life whilst I suffered - tortures. I hate the woman who sent me there. I have no heart, nor any sense of pity. Now perhaps you can understand my life and the manner of it."

Her hands were clasped to the side of her head. Something of horror had stolen into the steadfast gaze with which she was still regarding him. Yet there were other things there which puzzled him.

"This - is terrible!" she murmured. "Then you are not - Mr. Wingrave at all?"

He hesitated. After all, it was scarcely worth while concealing anything now.

"I am Sir Wingrave Seton," he said. "You may remember my little affair!"

She caught hold of his hands.

"You poor, poor dear!" she cried. "How you must have suffered!"

Wingrave had a terrible moment. What he felt he would never have admitted, even to himself. Her eyes were shining with sympathy, and it was so unexpected. He had expected something in the nature of a cold withdrawal; her silence was the only thing he had counted upon. It was a fierce, but short battle. His sudden grasp of her hands was relaxed. He stood away from her.

"You are very kind," he said. "As you can doubtless imagine, it is a little too late for sympathy. The years have gone, and the better part of me, if ever there was a better part, with them."

"I am not so sure of that!" she whispered.

He looked at her coldly.

"Why not?"

"If you were absolutely heartless," she said, "if you were perfectly consistent, why did you not make me suffer? You had a great chance! A little feigned affection, and then a few truths. You could have dragged me down a little way into the pit of broken hearts! Why didn't you?"

He frowned.

"One is forced to neglect a few opportunities!"

She smiled at him - delightfully.

"You foolish man!" she murmured. "Some day or other, you will turn out to be a terrible impostor. Do you know, I think I am going to ask you again - what I asked you last night?"

"I scarcely think that you will be so ill-advised," he declared coldly. "Whether you believe it or not, I can assure you that I am incapable of affection."

She sighed.

"I am not so sure about that," she said with protesting eyebrows, "but you are terribly hard-hearted?"

He was entirely dissatisfied with the impression he had

produced. He considered the attitude of the Marchioness unjustifiably frivolous. He had an uneasy conviction that she was not in the least inclined to take him seriously.

"I don't think," he said, glancing at the clock, "that I need detain you any longer."

"You are really going away, then?" she asked him softly.

"Yes."

"To call on Lady Ruth, perhaps?"

"As it happens, no," he answered.

Suddenly her face changed - she had remembered something.

"It was Lady Ruth!" she exclaimed.

"Exactly!" he interrupted.

"What a triumph of inconsistency!" she declared scornfully. "You are lending them money!"

"I am lending money to Lady Ruth," he answered slowly.

Their eyes met. She understood, at any rate, what he intended to convey. Certainly his expression was hard and merciless enough now!

"Poor Ruth," she murmured.

"Some day," he answered, "you will probably say that in earnest."

JULIET GAINS EXPERIENCE

"Of course," Juliet said, "after Tredowen it seems very small, almost poky, but it isn't, really, and Tredowen was not for me all my days. It was quite time I got used to something else."

Wingrave looked around him with expressionless face. It was a tiny room, high up on the fifth floor of a block of flats, prettily but inexpensively furnished. Juliet herself, tall and slim, with all the fire of youth and perfect health on her young face, was obviously contented.

"And your work?" he asked.

She made a little grimace.

"I have a good deal to unlearn," she said, "but Mr. Pleydell is very kind and encouraging."

"You will go down to Cornwall for the hot weather, I hope?" he said. "London is unbearable in August."

"The class are going for a sketching tour to Normandy," she said, "and Mr. Pleydell thought that I might like to join them. It is very inexpensive, and I should be able to go on with my work all the time."

E. Phillips Oppenheim

He nodded thoughtfully.

"I hear," he said, "that you have met Mr. Aynesworth again."

"Wasn't it delightful?" she exclaimed. "He is quite an old friend of Mr. Pleydell. I was so glad to see him."

"I suppose," he remarked, "you are a little lonely sometimes?"

"Sometimes," she admitted. "But I sha'n't be when I get to know the girls in the class a little better."

"I have some friends," he said thoughtfully, "women, of course, who would come and see you with pleasure. And yet," he added, "I am not sure that you would not be better off without knowing them."

"They are fashionable ladies, perhaps?" she said simply.

He nodded.

"They belong to the Juggernaut here which is called society. They would probably try to draw you a little way into its meshes. I think, yes, I am sure," he added, looking at her, "that you are better off outside."

"And I am quite sure of it," she answered laughing. "I haven't the clothes or the time or the inclination for that sort of thing. Besides, I am going to be much too happy ever to be lonely."

"I myself," he said, "am not an impressionable person. But they tell me that most people, especially of your age, find London a terribly lonely place."

"I can understand that," she answered, "unless they really had something definite to do. I have felt a little of that myself. I think London frightens me a little. It is so different from the country, and there is a great deal that is difficult to understand."

"For instance?"

"The great number of poor people who find it so hard to live," she answered. "Some of the small houses round here are awful, and Mr. Malcolm - he is the vicar of the church here, and he called yesterday - tells me that they are nothing like so bad as in some other parts of London. And then you take a bus, it is such a short distance - and the shops are full of wonderful things at such fabulous prices, and the carriages and houses are so lovely, and people seem to be showering money right and left everywhere."

"It is the same in all large cities," he answered, "more or less. There must always be rich and poor, when a great community are herded together. As a rule, the extreme poor are a worthless lot."

"There must be some of them, though," she answered, "who deserve to have a better time. Of course, I have never been outside Tredowen, where everyone was contented and happy in their way, and it seems terrible to me just at first. I can't bear to think that everyone hasn't at least a chance of happiness."

"You are too young," he said, "to bother your head about these things yet. Wait until you have gathered in a little philosophy with the years. Then you will

E. Phillips Oppenheim

understand how helpless you are to alter by ever so little the existing state of things, and it will trouble you less."

"I," she answered, "may, of course, be helpless, but what about those people who have huge fortunes, and still do nothing?"

"Why should they?" he answered coldly. "This is a world for individual effort. No man is strong enough to carry even a single one of his fellows upon his shoulders. Charity is the most illogical and pernicious of all weaknesses."

"Now you are laughing at me," she declared. "I mean men like that Mr. Wingrave, the American who has come to England to spend all his millions. I have just been reading about him," she added, pointing to an illustrated paper on the table. "They say that his income is too vast to be put into figures which would sound reasonable; that he has estates and shooting properties, and a yacht which he has never yet even seen. And yet he will not give one penny away. He gives nothing to the hospitals, nothing to the poor. He spends his money on himself, and himself alone!"

Wingrave smiled grimly.

"I am not prepared to defend my namesake," he said; "but every man has a right to do what he likes with his own, hasn't he? And as for hospitals, Mr. Wingrave probably thinks, like a good many more, that they should be state endowed. People could make use of them, then, without loss of self respect."

She shook her head a little doubtfully.

"I can't argue about it yet," she said, "because I haven't thought about it long enough. But I know if I had all the money this man has, I couldn't be happy to spend thousands and thousands upon myself while there were people almost starving in the same city."

"You are a sentimentalist, you see," he remarked, "and you have not studied the laws on which society is based. Tell me, how does Mrs. Tresfarwin like London?"

Juliet laughed merrily.

"Isn't it amusing?" she declared. "She loves it! She grumbles at the milk, and we have the butter from Tredowen. Everything else she finds perfection. She doesn't even mind the five flights of stone steps."

"Social problems," Wingrave remarked, "do not trouble her."

"Not in the least," Juliet declared. "She spends all her pennies on beggars and omnibus rides, and she is perfectly happy."

Wingrave rose to go in a few minutes. Juliet walked with him to the door.

"I am going to be really hospitable," she declared. "I am going to walk with you to the street."

"All down those five flights?" he exclaimed.

"Every one of them!"

They commenced the descent.

"There is something about a flat," she declared, "which makes one horribly curious about one's neighbors - especially if one has never had any. All these closed doors may hide no end of interesting people, and I have never seen a soul go in or out. How did you like all this climbing?"

"I'm afraid I didn't appreciate it," he admitted.

"Perhaps you won't come to see me again, then?" she asked. "I hope you will."

"I will come," he said a little stiffly, "with pleasure!"

They were on the ground floor, and Juliet opened the door. Wingrave's motor was outside, and the man touched his hat. She gave a little breathless cry.

"It isn't yours?" she exclaimed.

"Certainly," he answered. "Do you want to come and look at it?"

"Rather!" she exclaimed. "I have never seen one close to in my life."

He hesitated.

"I'll take you a little way, if you like," he said.

Her cheeks were pink with excitement.

"If I like! And I've never been in one before! I'll fly up for my hat. I sha'n't be a moment."

She was already halfway up the first flight of stairs,

with a whirl of skirts and flying feet. Wingrave lit a cigarette and stood for a moment thoughtfully upon the pavement. Then he shrugged his shoulders. His face had grown a little harder.

"She must take her chances," he muttered. "No one knows her. Nobody is likely to find out who she is."

She was down again in less time than seemed possible. Her cheeks were flushed and her eyes bright with excitement. Wingrave took the wheel himself, and she sat up by his side. They glided off almost noiselessly.

"We will go up to the Park," he said. "It is just the time to see the people."

"Anywhere!" she exclaimed. "This is too lovely!"

They passed from Battersea northwards into Piccadilly, and down into the Park. Juliet was too excited to talk; Wingrave had enough to do to drive the car. They passed plenty of people who bowed, and many who glanced with wondering admiration at the beautiful girl who sat by Wingrave's side. Lady Ruth, who drive by quickly in a barouche, almost rose from her seat; the Marchioness, whose victoria they passed, had time to wave her hand and flash a quick, searching glance at Juliet, who returned it with her dark eyes filled with admiration. The Marchioness smiled to herself a little sadly as the car shot away ahead.

"If one asked," she murmured to herself, "he would try to persuade one that it was another victim."

NEMESIS AT WORK

Wingrave was present that evening at a reception given by the Prime Minister to some distinguished foreign guests. He had scarcely exchanged the usual courtesies with his host and hostess before Lady Ruth, leaning over from a little group, whispered in his ear.

"Please take me away. I am bored. I want to talk to you."

He paused at once. Lady Ruth nodded to her friends.

"Mr. Wingrave is going to take me to hear Melba sing," she said. "See you all again, I suppose, at Hereford House!"

They made slow progress through the crowded rooms. Once or twice Wingrave fancied that his companion hung a little heavily upon his arm. She showed no desire to talk. She even answered a remark of his in a monosyllable. Only when they passed the Marchioness, on the arm of one of the foreign guests in whose honor the reception was given, she seemed to shiver a little, and her grasp upon his arm was tightened. Once, in a block, she was forced to speak to some acquaintances, and during those few seconds, Wingrave studied her curiously. She was absolutely colorless, and her strange brilliant eyes seemed to have lost all their fire. Her gown was black, and the decorations of her hair were black except for a single diamond. There was something almost spectral about her appearance. She walked stiffly - for the moment she had lost the sinuous grace of movement which had been one of her many fascinations. Her neck and shoulders alone remained, as ever, dazzlingly beautiful.

They reached a quiet corner at last. Lady Ruth sank with a little gesture of relief into an easy chair. Wingrave stood before her.

"You are tired tonight," he remarked.

"I am always tired," she answered wearily. "I begin to think that I always shall be."

He said nothing. Lady Ruth closed her eyes for a moment as though from sheer fatigue. Suddenly she opened them again and looked him full in the face.

"Who was she?" she asked.

"I do not understand," he replied.

"The child you were with - the ingenue, you know - with the pink cheeks and the wonderful eyes! Is she from one of the theaters, or a genuine article?"

"The young lady to whom you refer," he answered, "is the daughter of an old friend of mine. I am practically her guardian. She is in London studying painting."

"You are her guardian?" Lady Ruth repeated. "I am sorry for her."

"You need not be," he answered. "I trust that I shall be able to fulfill my duties in a perfectly satisfactory manner."

"Oh! I have no doubt of it," she answered. "Yet I am sorry for her."

"You are certainly," he remarked, "not in an amiable mood."

"I am in rather a desperate one if that is anything," she said, looking at him with something of the old light in her tired eyes.

"You made a little error, perhaps, in those calculations?" he suggested. "It can be amended."

"Don't be a brute," she answered fiercely.

He shrugged his shoulders.

"That sounds a little severe," he remarked.

"Don't take any notice of anything I say tonight," she murmured softly. "I am a little mad. I think that everything is going against me! I know that you haven't a grain of sympathy for me - that you would rather see me suffer than not, and yet you see I give myself away entirely. Why shouldn't I? Part of it is through you in a way."

"I rather fancied," he remarked, "that up to now -"

"Yes! Of course!" she interrupted, "you saved me from ruin, staved it off at any rate. And you held over the reckoning! I - I almost wish -"

She paused. Again her eyes were searching his.

"I am a little tired of it all, you see," she continued. "I don't suppose Lumley and I can ever be the same again since I brought him - that check. He avoids being alone with me - I do the same with him. One would think - to watch the people, that the whole transaction was in the Morning Post. They smile when they see us together, they grin when they see you with anybody else. It's getting hateful, Wingrave!"

"I am afraid," he said quietly, "that you are in a nervous, hypersensitive state. No one else can possibly know of the little transaction between us, and, so far as I am concerned, there has been nothing to interfere with your relations with your husband."

"You are right," she answered, "I am losing my nerve. I am only afraid that I am losing something else. I haven't an ounce of battle left in me. I feel that I should like to close my eyes and wake up in a new world, and start all over again."

"It is nothing but a mood," he assured her. "Those new worlds don't exist any longer. They generally consist of foreign watering places where the sheep and the goats house together now and then. I think I should play the game out, Lady Ruth, until -"

"Until what?"

"Perhaps to the end," he answered. "Who can tell? Not I! By this time tomorrow, it might be I who would be reminding you -"

"Yes?"

"That there are other worlds, and other lives to live!"

"I should like," she whispered very softly, "to hear of them. But I fancy somehow that you will never be my instructor. What of your ward?"

"Well! What of her?" he answered calmly.

She shivered a little.

"You were very frank with me once, Wingrave," she said. "You are a man whose life fate has wrecked, fate and I! You have no heart left, no feeling. You can create suffering and find it amusing. I am beginning to realize that."

He nodded.

"There is some truth," he declared, "In what you say."

"What of that child? Is she, too, to be a victim?"

"I trust," he answered, "that you are not going to be melodramatic."

"I don't call it that. I really want to know. I should like to warn her."

"I am not at war with children," he answered. "Her life and mine are as far apart as the poles."

"I had an odd fancy when I saw you with her," Lady Ruth said slowly. "She is very good-looking - and not so absurdly young."

"The fancy was one , " he remarked coldly, "which I

think you had better get rid of."

"In a way," she continued thoughtfully, "I should like to get rid of it, and yet - how old are you, Wingrave? Well, I know. You are very little over forty. You are barely in the prime of life, you are strong, you have the one thing which society today counts almost divine - great, immeasurable wealth! Can't you find someone to thaw the snows?"

"I loved a woman once," he answered. "It was a long time ago, and it seems strange to me now."

Lady Ruth lifted her eyes to his, and their lambent fires were suddenly rekindled.

"Love her again," she murmured. "What is past is past, but there are the days to come! Perhaps the woman, too, is a little lonely."

"I think not," he answered calmly. "The woman is married, she has lived with her husband more or less happily for a dozen years or so! She is a little ambitious, a little fond of pleasure, but a leader of society, and, I am sure, a very reputable member of it. To love her again would be as embarrassing to her - as it would be difficult for me. You, my dear Lady Ruth, I am convinced, would be the last to approve of it."

"You mock me," she murmured, bending her head. "Is forgiveness also an impossibility?"

"I think," he said, "that any sentiment whatever between those two would be singularly misplaced. You spoke of Melba, I think! She is singing in the further room."

Lady Ruth rose up, still and pale. There was fear in her eyes when she looked at him.

"Is it to be always like this, then?" she said.

"Ah!" he answered, "I am no prophet. Who can tell what the days may bring? In the meantime..."

The Marchioness was very much in request that evening, and she found time for only a few words with Wingrave.

"What have you been doing to poor Ruth?" she asked. "I never saw her look so ill!"

"Indeed!" he answered, "I had not noticed it."

"If I didn't know her better," she remarked, "I might begin to suspect her of a conscience. Whose baby were you driving about this afternoon? I didn't know that your taste ran to ingenues to such an extent. She's sweetly pretty, but I don't think it's nice of you to flaunt her before us middle-aged people. It's enough to drive us to the rouge box. Come to lunch tomorrow!"

"I shall be delighted," he answered, and passed on.

An hour or so later, on his way out, he came upon Lady Ruth sitting a little forlornly in the hall.

"I wonder whether I dare ask you to drop me in Cadogan Square?" she asked. "Is it much out of your way? I am leaving a little earlier than I expected."

"I shall be delighted," he answered, offering his arm.

They passed out of the door and down the covered way into the street. A few stragglers were loitering on the pavement, and one, a tall, thin young man in a long ulster, bent forwards as they came down the steps. Wingrave felt his companion's grasp tighten upon his arm; a flash of light upon the pale features and staring eyes of the young man a few feet off, showed him to be in the act of intercepting them. Then, at a sharp word from Wingrave, a policeman stretched out his arm. The young man was pushed unceremoniously away. Wingrave's tall footman and the policeman formed an impassable barrier - in a moment the electric brougham was gliding down the street. Lady Ruth was leaning back amongst the cushions, and the hand which fell suddenly upon Wingrave's was cold as ice!

E. Phillips Oppenheim

RICHARDSON TRIES AGAIN

"You saw - who that was?"

Lady Ruth's voice seemed to come from a greater distance. Wingrave turned and looked at her with calm curiosity. She was leaning back in the corner of the carriage, and she seemed somehow to have shrunk into an unusual insignificance. Her eyes alone were clearly visible through the semi-darkness - and the light which shone from their depths was the light of fear.

"Yes," he answered slowly, "I believe that I recognized him. It was the young man who persists in some strange hallucination as to a certain Mademoiselle Violet."

"It was no hallucination," she answered. "You know that! I was Mademoiselle Violet!"

He nodded.

"It amazes me," he said thoughtfully, "that you should have stooped to such folly. That my demise would have been a relief to you I can, of course, easily believe, but the means - they surely were not worthy of your ingenuity."

"Don't!" she cried sharply. "I must have been utterly,

miserably mad!"

"Even the greatest of schemers have their wild moments," he remarked consolingly. "This was one of yours. You paid me a very poor compliment, by the bye, to imagine that an insignificant creature like that -"

"Will you - leave off?" she moaned.

"I daresay," he continued after a moment's pause, "that you find him now quite an inconvenient person to deal with."

She shuddered.

"Oh, I am paying for my folly, if that is what you mean," she declared. "He knows - who I am - that he was deceived. He follows me about - everywhere."

Wingrave glanced out of the carriage window.

"Unless I am very much surprised," he answered, "he is following us now!"

She came a little closer to him.

"You won't leave me? Promise!"

"I will see you home," he answered.

"You are coming on to Hereford House."

"I think not," he answered; "I have had enough of society for one evening."

"Emily will be there later," she said quietly.

"Even Lady Emily," he answered, "will not tempt me. I will see you safely inside. Afterwards, if your persistent follower is hanging about, I will endeavor to talk him into a more reasonable frame of mind."

She was silent for a moment. Then she turned to him abruptly.

"You are more kind to me sometimes than I deserve, Wingrave," she remarked.

"It is not kindness," he answered. "I dislike absurd situations. Here we are! Permit me!"

Wingrave kept his word. He saw Lady Ruth to her front door, and then turned back towards his carriage. Standing by the side of the footman, a little breathless, haggard and disheveled-looking, was the young man who had attempted to check their progress a few minutes ago.

Wingrave took hold of his arm firmly.

"Get in there," he ordered, pointing to the carriage.

The young man tried to escape, but he was held as though in a vise. Before he well knew where he was, he was in the carriage, and Wingrave was seated by his side.

"What do you want with me?" he asked hoarsely.

"I want to know what you mean by following that lady about?" Wingrave asked.

The young man leaned forward. His hand was upon the door.

"Let me get out," he said sullenly.

"With pleasure - presently," Wingrave answered. "I can assure you that I am not anxious to detain you longer than necessary. Only you must first answer my question."

"I want to speak to her! I shall follow her about until I can!" the young man declared.

Wingrave glanced at him with a faint derisive smile. His clothes were worn and shabby, he was badly in need of a shave and a wash. He sat hunched up in a corner of the carriage, the picture of mute discomfort and misery.

"Do you know who she is?" Wingrave asked.

"Mademoiselle Violet!" the young man answered.

"You are mistaken," Wingrave answered. "She is Lady Ruth Barrington, wife of Lumley Barrington and daughter of the Earl of Haselton."

The young man was unmoved.

"She is Mademoiselle Violet," he declared.

The coupe drew up before the great block of buildings in which was Wingrave's flat. The footman threw open the door.

"Come in with me," Wingrave said. "I have something

E. Phillips Oppenheim

more to say to you."

"I would rather not," the young man muttered, and would have slouched off, but Wingrave caught him by the arm.

"Come!" he said firmly, and the youth obeyed.

Wingrave led the way into his sitting room and dismissed his servant who was setting out a tray upon the sideboard.

"Sit down," he ordered, and his strange guest again obeyed. Wingrave looked at him critically.

"It seems to me," he said deliberately, "that you are another of those poor fools who chuck away their life and happiness and go to the dogs because a woman had chosen to make a little use of them. You're out of work, I suppose?"

"Yes!"

"Hungry?"

"I suppose so."

Wingrave brought a plate of sandwiches from the sideboard, and mixed a whisky and soda. He set them down in front of his guest, and turned away with the evening paper in his hand.

"I am going into the next room for some cigarettes," he remarked.

He was gone scarcely two minutes. When he returned,

the room was in darkness. He moved suddenly towards the electric lights, but was pushed back by an unseen hand. A man's hot breath fell upon his cheek, a hoarse, rasping voice spoke to him out of the black shadows.

"Don't touch the lights! Don't touch the lights, I say!"

"What folly is this?" Wingrave asked angrily. "Are you mad?"

"Not now," came the quick answer. "I have been. It has come to me here, in the darkness. I know why she is angry, I know why she will not speak to me. It is - because I failed."

Wingrave laughed, and moved towards the lights.

"We have had enough of this tomfoolery," he said scornfully. "If you won't listen to reason -"

He never finished his sentence. He had stumbled suddenly against a soft body, he had a momentary impression of a white, vicious face, of eyes blazing with insane fury. Quick to act, he struck - but before his hand descended, he had felt the tearing of his shirt, the sharp, keen pain in his chest, the swimming of his senses. Yet even then he struck again with passionate anger, and his assailant went down amongst the chairs with a dull, sickening crash!

Then there was silence in the room. Wingrave made an effort to drag himself a yard or two towards the bell, but collapsed hopelessly. Richardson, in a few moments, staggered to his feet.

He groped his way to the side of the wall, and found

the knobs of the electric lights. He turned two on and looked around him. Wingrave was lying a few yards off, with a small red stain upon his shirt front. His face was ghastly pale, and he was breathing thickly. The young man looked at him for several moments, and then made his way to the side table where the sandwiches were. One by one he took them from the dish, and ate deliberately. When he had finished, he made his way once more towards where Wingrave lay. But before he reached the spot, he stopped short. Something on the wall had attracted his attention. He put his hand to his head and thought for a moment. It was an idea - a glorious idea.

. . . .

Lady Ruth's maid stepped back and surveyed her mistress ecstatically.

"Milady," she declared, "has never, no never, appeared more charming. The gown, it is divine - and the coiffure! Milady will have no rivals."

Lady Ruth looked at herself long and earnestly in the glass. Her face reflected none of the pleased interest with which her maid was still regarding her. The latter grew a little anxious.

"Milady thinks herself a trifle pale, perhaps - a little more color?"

Lady Ruth set down the glass.

"No, thank you, Annette," she answered. "I shall do very well, I suppose. Certainly, I won't have any rouge."

"Milady knows very well what becomes her," the woman answered discreetly. "The pallor, it is the more distinguished. Milady cannot fail to have all the success she desires!"

Lady Ruth smiled a little wearily. And at that moment, there came a knock at the door. A servant entered.

"Someone wishes to speak to your ladyship on the telephone," the girl announced.

"On the telephone, at this time of night?" Lady Ruth exclaimed. "Ridiculous! They must send a message, whoever they are!"

"Parkins told them so, your ladyship," the girl answered; "but they insisted that the matter was important. They would give no name, but said that they were speaking from Mr. Wingrave's rooms."

Lady Ruth raised her eyebrows.

"It is very extraordinary," she said coldly, "but I will come to the telephone."

"IT WAS AN ACCIDENT"

Lady Ruth took up the receiver. Some instinct seemed to have prompted her to close the door of the study.

"Who is there?" she asked. "Who is it that wants me?"

A thin, unfamiliar voice answered her.

"Is that Lady Ruth Barrington?"

"Yes!"

"Is it - Mademoiselle Violet?"

The receiver nearly dropped from her hand.

"I don't understand you," she answered, "I am Lady Ruth Barrington! Who are you?"

"You are Mademoiselle Violet," was the answer, "and you know who I am! Listen, I am in Mr. Wingrave's rooms."

She would have liked to have rung off and gone away, but it seemed a sheer impossibility for her to move! And all the time her knees were shaking, and the fear of evil things was in her heart.

"What are you doing there?" she asked.

"He brought me in himself," the thin voice answered. "Can you hear me? I don't want to speak any louder for fear anyone else should be listening."

"Yes, I can hear," she answered. "But how dared you ring me up? Say what you desire to quickly! I am going away."

"Wait, please," the voice answered. "I know why you have been angry with me. I know why you have kept away from me, why you have been so cruel! It was because I failed. Was it not, dear Mademoiselle Violet?"

She had not the breath or the courage to answer him. In a moment or two he continued, and there was a note of suppressed exultation in his tone.

"Listen! This time - I have not failed!"

She nearly screamed. The receiver in her hand burned like a live thing. Her eyes were set in a fixed and awful stare as though she were trying to see for herself outside the walls of the little room where she stood into the larger chamber from which the voice - that awful voice - came! Her own words were hysterical and uncertain, but she managed to falter them out at last.

"What do you mean? Where is Mr. Wingrave? Tell me at once!"

The voice, without being raised, seemed to take to itself a note of triumph.

"He is dying - on the floor - just here! Listen hard! Perhaps you can hear him groan! Now will you believe that I am not a coward?"

Her shriek drowned his words. She flung the receiver from her with a crash and rushed from the room into the hall. She brushed past her maid with a wild gesture.

"Never mind my wraps. Open the door, Parkins! Is the carriage waiting?"

"Yes, Milady! Shall -"

But she was past him and down the steps.

"No. 18, Grosvenor Mansions," she cried to the man. "Drive fast."

The man obeyed. The servants, who had come to the door, stood there a little frightened group. She ignored them and everything else completely. The carriage had scarcely stopped when she sprang out and crossed the pavement in a few hasty steps. The tall commissionaire looked in amazement at her. She wore an opera cloak - she was a bewildering vision of white satin and diamonds, and her eyes were terrible with the fear which was in her heart.

She clutched him by the arm.

"Come up with me to Mr. Wingrave's rooms," she exclaimed. "Something terrible has happened. I heard through the telephone."

The man dashed up the stairs by her side. Wingrave's suite was on the first floor, and they did not wait for the lift. The commissionaire put his finger on the bell of the outside door. She leaned forward, listening breathlessly. Inside all was silence except for the shrill clamor of the bell.

"Go on ringing," she said breathlessly. "Don't leave off!"

The man looked at her curiously. "Mr. Wingrave came in about an hour ago with a young man, madam," he said.

"Yes, yes!" she cried. "Listen! There's someone coming."

They heard a hesitating step inside. The door was cautiously opened. It was Richardson, pale, disheveled, but triumphant, who peered out.

"Mademoiselle - Mademoiselle Violet," he cried. "You have come to see for yourself. This way!"

She raised her arm and struck him across the face so that, with a little moan, he staggered back against the wall. Then she hastened forward into the room towards which he had pointed and the door of which stood open. The commissionaire followed her. The servants were beginning to appear.

The room was in darkness save for one electric light. A groan, however, directed them. She fell on her knees by Wingrave's prostrate figure and raised his head slightly. His servant, too, was hurrying forward. She looked up.

"Get me some brandy," she ordered. "Send someone

E. Phillips Oppenheim

for a doctor. Don't let that young man escape. The brandy, quick!"

She forced some between his lips. There was already a spot of blood upon the gown which, a few minutes ago, had seemed so immaculate. One of the ornaments fell from her hair. It lay unnoticed by her side. Suddenly Wingrave opened his eyes. She saw at once that he was conscious and that he recognized her.

"Don't move, please," she begged. "It will be better for you not to speak. The doctor will be here directly."

He nodded.

"I don't think that I am much hurt," he said slowly. "Your young friend was a born bungler!"

She shuddered, but said nothing.

"How on earth," he asked, "did you get here?"

She whispered in his ear.

"The brute - telephoned. Please don't talk."

The doctor arrived. His examination was over in a few moments.

"Nothing serious," he declared. "The knife was pretty blunt fortunately. How did it happen? It seems like a case for the police."

"It was an accident," Wingrave declared coolly.

The doctor shrugged his shoulders. He was busy

making bandages. Lady Ruth rose to her feet. She was white and giddy. The commissionaire and Morrison were talking together at the door. The latter turned to Lady Ruth.

"Do you think that we had better send for the police, your ladyship?" he asked. "It was the young man who came in with Mr. Wingrave who must have done this! I thought he was a very wild-looking sort of person."

"You heard what Mr. Wingrave said," she answered. "I don't think that I should disobey him, if I were you. The doctor says that, after all, it is not very serious."

"He can't have got far," the hall porter remarked. "He only slipped out as we came in."

"I should let him go for the present," Lady Ruth said. "If Mr. Wingrave wishes to prosecute afterwards, it will be easy for him to do so."

She stepped back to where Wingrave lay. He was in a recumbent position now and, although a little pale, he was obviously not seriously hurt.

"If there is nothing else that I can do," she said, "I will go now!"

"By all means," Wingrave answered. "I am exceedingly obliged to you for your kindness," he added a little stiffly. "Morrison, show Lady Barrington to her carriage!"

She spoke a few conventional words of farewell and departed. Outside on the pavement she stood for a moment, looking carefully around. There was no sign of Richardson anywhere! She stepped into the carriage and leaned back in the corner.

AYNESWORTH PLANS A LOVE STORY

Wingrave disappeared suddenly from London. Aynesworth alone knew where he was gone, and he was pledged to secrecy. Two people received letters from him. Lady Ruth was one of them.

"This," she remarked quietly, handing it over to her husband, "may interest you."

He adjusted his eye glasses and read it aloud: -

"Dear Lady Ruth, - I am leaving London today for several weeks. With the usual inconsistency of the person to whom life is by no means a valuable asset, I am obeying the orders of my physician. I regret, therefore, that I cannot have the pleasure of entertaining your husband and yourself during Cowes week. The yacht, however, is entirely at your disposal, and I have written Captain Masterton to that effect. Pray extend your cruise, if you feel inclined to. - I remain, yours sincerely, W."

Mr. Barrington looked at his wife inquiringly.

"That seems to me entirely satisfactory, Ruth," he said. "I think that he might have added a word or two of acknowledgment for what you did for him. There is no doubt that, but for your promptness, things might have gone much worse."

"Yes," Lady Ruth said slowly, "I think that he might have added a few words."

Her husband regarded her critically.

"I am afraid, dear," he said, "that all this anxiety has knocked you up a little. You are not looking well."

"I am tired," she answered calmly. "It has been a long season. I should like to do what Wingrave has done - go away somewhere and rest."

Barrington laid his hand upon hers affectionately. It seemed to him that the rings hung a little loosely upon the thin, white fingers. She was pale, too, and her eyes were weary. He did not notice that, as soon as she could, she drew her hand away.

"Pon my word," he said, "I wish we could go off somewhere by ourselves. But with Wingrave's yacht to entertain on, we must do something for a few of the people. I don't suppose he minds whom we ask, or how many."

"No!" she answered, "I do not suppose he cares."

"It is most opportune," Barrington declared. "I wanted particularly to do something for the Hendersons. He seems very well disposed, and his influence means everything just now. Really, Ruth, I believe we are going to pull through after all."

She smiled a little wearily.

"Do you think so, Lumley?"

"I am sure of it, Ruth," he answered. "I only wish I could see you a little more cheerful. Surely you can't still - be afraid of Wingrave," he added, glancing uneasily across the table.

She looked him in the eyes.

"That is exactly what I am," she answered. "I am afraid of him. I have always been afraid. Nothing has happened to change him. He came back to have his revenge. He will have it."

Lumley Barrington, for once, felt himself superior to his clever wife. He smiled upon her reassuringly.

"My dear Ruth," he said, "if only you would reflect for a few moments, I feel sure you would realize the absurdity of such fancies. We did Wingrave a service in introducing him to society here, and I am sure that he appreciated it. If he wished for our ruin, why did he lend us eight thousand pounds on no security? Why does he lend us his yacht to entertain our friends? Why did he give me that information which enabled me to make the only money I ever did make on the Stock Exchange?"

She smiled contemptuously.

"You do not understand a man like Wingrave," she declared. "Nothing that he has done is inconsistent with my point of view. He gave you a safe tip, knowing very well that when you had won a little, you would try again on your own account and lose - which you did. He lent us the money to become our creditor;

and he lends us the yacht to give another handle to the people who are saying already that he occupies the position in our family which is more fully recognized on the other side of the Channel!"

"You are talking rubbish," he declared vehemently. "No one would dare to say such a thing of you - of my wife!"

She laughed unmercifully.

"If you were not my husband," she said cruelly, "you would have heard it before now. I have been careful all my life - more careful than most women, but I can hear the whisperings already. There are more ways to ruin than one, Lumley."

"We will refuse the yacht," Barrington said sullenly, "and I will go to the Jews for that eight thousand pounds."

"We will do nothing of the sort," Lady Ruth answered. "I am not going to be a laughing stock for Emily and her friends if I can help it. We'll play the game through now! Only - it is best for you to know the risks . . ."

Wingrave's second letter was to Juliet. She found it on her table one afternoon when she came back from her painting class. She tore it open eagerly enough, but her face clouded over as she read.

"Dear Juliet, - I am sorry that I am unable to carry out my promise to come and see you, but I have been slightly indisposed for some days, and am leaving London, for the present, almost at once. I trust that you are still interested in your work, and will enjoy your trip to Normandy.

"I received your letter, asking for my help towards re-establishing in life a poor family in whom you are interested. I regret that I cannot accede to your request. It is wholly against my principles to give money away to people of this class. I look upon all charity as a mischievous attempt to tamper with natural laws, and I am convinced that if everyone shared my views, society would long ago have been re-established on a sounder and more logical basis. To be quite frank with you, also, I might add that the gift of sympathy has been denied to me. I am quite indifferent whether the family you allude to starve or prosper.

"So far as you yourself are concerned, however, the matter is entirely different. If it gives you pleasure to assist in pauperizing any number of your fellow creatures, pray do so. I enclose a check for L100. It is a present to you. Use it entirely as you please - only, if you use it for the purpose suggested in your letter to me, remember that the responsibility is yours, and yours alone. - I remain, sincerely yours, Wingrave Seton."

Juliet walked straight to her writing table. Her cheeks were flushed, and her eyes were wet with tears. She drew out a sheet of note paper and wrote rapidly: -

"My dear guardian, - I return you the check. I cannot accept such presents after all your goodness to me. I am sorry that you feel as you do about giving money away. You are so much older and wiser than I am that I dare not attempt to argue with you. Only it seems to me that life would be a cruelly selfish thing if we who are so much more fortunate than many of our fellow creatures did not sometimes try to help them a little through their misery. Perhaps I feel this a little more keenly because I wonder sometimes what might not have become of me but for your goodness.

"I am sorry that you are going away without coming to see me again. You are not displeased with me, I hope, for asking you this, or for any other reason? I am foolish enough to feel a little lonely sometimes. Will you take me out again when you come back? - Your affectionate ward, Juliet."

Juliet went out and posted her letter. On the way back she met Aynesworth.

"Come and sit in the Park for a few minutes," he begged.

She turned and walked by his side willingly enough.

"Have you been in to see me?" she asked.

"Yes!" he answered. "I have some tickets for the Haymarket for tonight. Do you think we could persuade Mrs. Tresfarwin to come?"

"I'm sure we could," she answered, laughing. "Hannah never wants any persuading. How nice of you to think of us!"

"I am afraid," he answered, "that I think of you a good deal."

"Then I think that that also is very nice of you!" she declared.

"You like to be thought of?"

"Who doesn't? What is the play tonight?"

"I'll tell you about it afterwards," he said. "There is something else I want to say to you first."

She nodded. She scarcely showed so much interest as he would have liked.

"It is about Berneval," he said, keeping his eyes fixed upon her face. "I saw Mr. Pleydell today, and he told me that you were all going there. He suggested that I should come too!"

"How delightful!" she exclaimed. "Can you really get off?"

"Yes. Sir Wingrave is going away, and doesn't want me. I must go somewhere, and I thought that I might go over and take rooms near you all. Would you care to have me?"

"Of course I would," she answered frankly. "Oh!" she exclaimed suddenly, her face clouding over - "I forgot!"

"Well?"

"I am not sure," she said, "that I am going."

"Not going?" he repeated incredulously. "Mr. Pleydell told me that it was all arranged."

"It was - until today," she said. "I am a little uncertain now."

He looked at her perplexed.

"May I know why?" he asked.

She raised her eyebrows slightly.

"You are rather an inquisitive person," she remarked. "The fact is, I may need the money I have saved for Berneval for somewhere else."

"Of course," he said slowly, "if you don't go - I don't. But you can't stay in London all through the hot weather!"

"Miss Pengarth has asked me to go down there," she said.

He laid his hand suddenly upon hers.

"Juliet," he said.

She shook her head.

"Miss Lundy, please!"

"Well, Miss Lundy then! May I talk to you seriously?"

"I prefer you frivolous," she murmured. "I like to be amused."

"I'll be frivolous enough later on this evening. I've been wondering if you'd think it impertinent if I asked you to tell me about your guardian."

"What do you want to know?" she asked.

"Just who he is, and why he is content to let you live with only an old woman to look after you. It isn't the best thing in the world for you, is it? I should like to know him, Juliet."

She shook her head.

"I am sorry," she said, "I cannot tell you anything."

There was a short silence. Aynesworth was disappointed, and showed it.

"It isn't exactly ordinary curiosity," he continued. "Don't think that! Only I feel that you need someone who has the right to advise you and look after you. I should like to be your guardian, Juliet!"

She laughed merrily.

"Good!" she declared. "I like you so much better frivolous. Well, you shall have your wish. You shall be my guardian for the evening. I have one cutlet for dinner, and I am sure it will be spoilt. Will you come and share it?"

She rose to her feet and stood looking down upon him. He was struck, for the first time, by something different in her appearance. The smooth, delicate girlishness of her young face was, as yet, untroubled. Her eyes laughed frankly into his, and all the grace of natural childhood seemed still to linger about her. And yet - there was a change! Understanding was there; understanding, with sorrow in its wake. Aynesworth was suddenly anxious. Had anything happened of which he was ignorant? He rose up slowly. He was sure of himself now! Was he sure of her?

A DEED OF GIFT

Wingrave threw the paper aside with an impatient exclamation. A small notice in an obscure corner had attracted his attention; the young man, Richardson, had been fished out of the river half drowned, and in view of his tearful and abject penitence, had been allowed to go his way by a lenient magistrate. He had been ill, he pleaded, and disappointed. His former employer, in an Islington emporium, gave him a good character, and offered to take him back. So that was an end of Mr. Richardson, and the romance of his days!

A worm like that to have brought him - the strong man, low! Wingrave thought with sullen anger as he leaned back in his chair with half-closed eyes. Here was an undignified hiatus, if not a finale, to all his schemes, to the even tenor of his self-restrained, purposeful life! The west wind was rippling through the orchards which bordered the garden. The muffled roar of the Atlantic was in his ears, a strange everlasting background to all the slighter summer sounds, the murmuring of insects, the calling of birds, the melodious swish of the whirling knives in the distant hayfield. Wingrave was alone with his thoughts, and he hated them!

Even Mr. Pengarth was welcome, Mr. Pengarth very warm from his ride, carrying his hat and a small black bag in his hand. As he drew nearer, he became hotter and was obliged to rest his bag upon the path and mop his forehead. He was more afraid of his client than of anything else in the world.

"Good afternoon, Sir Wingrave," he said. "I trust that you are feeling better today."

Wingrave eyed him coldly. He did not reply to the inquiry as to his health.

"You have brought the deed?" he asked.

"Certainly, Sir Wingrave."

The lawyer produced a roll of parchment from his bag. In response to Wingrave's gesture, he seated himself on the extreme edge of an adjacent seat.

"I do not propose to read all that stuff through," Wingrave remarked. "I take it for granted that the deed is made out according to my instructions."

"Certainly, Sir Wingrave!"

"Then we will go into the house, and I will sign it."

Mr. Pengarth mopped his forehead once more. It was a terrible thing to have a conscience.

"Sir Wingrave," he said, "I apologize most humbly for what I am about to say, but as the agent of your estates in this county and your - er - legal adviser with regard to them, I am forced to ask you whether you are quite determined upon this - most unexampled piece of generosity. Tredowen has been in your mother's family for a great many years, and although I must say that I have a great affection for this young lady, I have also an old fashioned dislike to seeing - er - family property pass into the hands of strangers. You might, forgive me - marry!"

Wingrave smiled very faintly, otherwise his face was inscrutable.

"I might," he admitted calmly, "but I shall not. Do you consider me, Mr. Pengarth, to be a person in possession of his usual faculties?"

"Oh, most certainly - most certainly," the lawyer declared emphatically.

"Then please do not question my instructions any further. So far as regards the pecuniary part of it, I am a richer man than you have any idea of, Mr. Pengarth, and for the rest - sentiment unfortunately does not appeal to me. I choose to give the Tredowen estates away, to disappoint my next of kin. That is how you may regard the transaction. We will go into the house and complete this deed."

Wingrave rose slowly and walked with some difficulty up the gravel path. He ignored, however, his companion's timid offer of help, and led the way to the library. In a few minutes the document was signed and witnessed.

"I have ordered tea in the garden," Wingrave said, as the two servants left the room; "that is, unless you prefer any other sort of refreshment. I don't know much about the cellars, but there is some cabinet hock, I believe -"

Mr. Pengarth interposed.

"I am very much obliged," he said, "but I will not intrude upon you further. If you will allow me, I will ring the bell for my trap."

"You will do nothing of the sort," Wingrave answered testily. "You will stay here and talk to me."

"I will stay with pleasure if you desire it," the lawyer answered. "I had an idea that you preferred solitude."

"Then you were wrong," Wingrave answered. "I hate being alone."

They moved out together towards the garden. Tea was set out in a shady corner of the lawn.

"If you will forgive my remarking it," Mr. Pengarth said, "this seems rather an extraordinary place for you to come to if you really dislike solitude."

"I come to escape from an intolerable situation, and because I was ill," Wingrave said.

"You might have brought friends," the lawyer suggested.

"I have no friends," Wingrave answered.

"Some of the people in the neighborhood would be very glad -" Mr. Pengarth began.

"I do not wish to see them," Wingrave answered.

Mr. Pengarth took a peach, and held his tongue.

E. Phillips Oppenheim

Wingrave broke the silence which followed a little abruptly.

"Tell me, Mr. Pengarth," he said, "do I look like a man likely to fail in anything he sets out to accomplish?"

The lawyer shook his head vigorously.

"You do not," he declared.

"Nor do I feel like one," Wingrave said, "and yet my record since I commenced, shall I call it my second life, is one of complete failure! Nothing that I planned have I been able to accomplish. I look back through the months and through the years, and I see not a single purpose carried out, not a single scheme successful.

"Not quite so bad as that, I trust, Sir Wingrave," the lawyer protested.

"It is the precise truth," Wingrave affirmed drily. "I am losing confidence in myself."

"At least," the lawyer declared, "you have been the salvation of our dear Miss Juliet, if I may call her so. But for you, her life would have been ruined."

"Precisely," Wingrave agreed. "But I forgot! You don't understand! I have saved her from heaven knows what! I am going to give her the home she loves! Benevolence, isn't it? And yet, if I had only the pluck, I might succeed even now - so far as she is concerned."

The lawyer took off his spectacles and rubbed them with his handkerchief. He was thoroughly bewildered.

"I might succeed," Wingrave repeated, leaning back in his chair, "if only -"

His face darkened. It seemed to Mr. Pengarth as he sipped his tea under the cool cedars, drawing in all their wonderful perfume with every puff of breeze, that he saw two men in the low invalid's chair before him. He saw the breath and desire of evil things struggling with some wonderful dream vainly seeking to realize itself.

"Some of us," the lawyer said timidly, "build our ideals too high up in the clouds, so that to reach them is very difficult. Nevertheless, the effort counts."

Wingrave laughed mockingly.

"It is not like that with me," he declared. "My plans were made down in hell."

"God bless my soul!" the lawyer murmured. "But you are not serious, Sir Wingrave?"

"Ay! I'm serious enough," Wingrave answered. "Do you suppose a man, with the best pages of his life rooted out, is likely to look out upon his fellows from the point of view of a philanthropist? Do you suppose that the man, into whose soul the irons of bitterness have gnawed and eaten their way, is likely to come out with a smirk and look around him for the opportunity of doing good? Rubbish! My aim is to encourage suffering wherever I see it, to create it where I can, to make sinners and thieves of honest people."

"God bless my soul!" the lawyer gasped again. "I don't think you can be - as bad as you think you are. What

E. Phillips Oppenheim

about Juliet Lundy?"

Fire flashed in Wingrave's eyes. Again, at the mention of her name, he seemed almost to lose control of himself. It was several moments before he spoke. He looked Mr. Pengarth in the face, and his tone was unusually deliberate.

"Gifts," he said, "are not always given in friendship. Life may easily become a more complicated affair for that child with the Tredowen estates hanging round her neck. And anyhow, I disappoint my next of kin."

Morrison, smooth-footed and silent, appeared upon the lawn. He addressed Wingrave.

"A lady has arrived in a cab from Truro, sir," he announced. "She wishes to see you as soon as convenient."

A sudden light flashed across Wingrave's face, dying out again almost immediately.

"Who is she, Morrison?" he asked.

The man glanced at Mr. Pengarth.

"She did not give her name, sir."

Mr. Pengarth and Wingrave both rose. The former at once made his adieux and took a short cut to the stables. Wingrave, who leaned heavily upon his stick, clutched Morrison by the arm.

"Who is it, Morrison?" he demanded.

"It is Lady Ruth Barrington, sir," the man answered.

"Alone?"

"Quite alone, sir."

E. Phillips Oppenheim

FOR PITY'S SAKE

The library at Tredowen was a room of irregular shape, full of angles and recesses lined with bookcases. It was in one of these, standing motionless before a small marble statue of some forgotten Greek poet, that Wingrave found his visitor. She wore a plain serge traveling dress, and the pallor of her face, from which she had just lifted a voluminous veil, matched almost in color the gleaming white marble upon which she was gazing. But when she saw Wingrave, leaning upon his stick, and regarding her with stern surprise, strange lights seemed to flash in her eyes. There was no longer any resemblance between the pallor of her cheeks and the pallor of the statue.

"Lady Ruth," Wingrave said quietly, "I do not understand what has procured for me the pleasure of this unexpected visit."

She swayed a little towards him. Her head was thrown back, all the silent passion of the inexpressible, the hidden secondary forces of nature, was blazing out of her eyes, pleading with him in the broken music of her tone.

"You do not understand," she repeated. "Ah, no! But can I make you understand? Will you listen to me for once as a human being? Will you remember that you are a man, and I a woman pleading for a little mercy - a little kindness?"

Wingrave moved a step further back.

"Permit me," he said, "to offer you a chair."

She sank into it - speechless for a moment. Wingrave stood over her, leaning slightly against the corner of the bookcase.

"I trust," he said, "that you will explain what all this means. If it is my help which you require -"

Her hands flashed out towards him - a gesture almost of horror.

"Don't," she begged, "you know that it is not that! You know very well that it is not. Why do you torture me?"

"I can only ask you," he said, "to explain."

She commenced talking quickly. Her sentences came in little gasps.

"You wanted revenge - not in the ordinary way. You had brooded over it too long. You understood too well. Once it was I who sought to revenge myself on you because you would not listen to me! You hurt my pride. Everything that was evil in me rebelled -"

"Is this necessary?" he interrupted coldly. "I have never reproached you. You chose the path of safety for yourself. Many another woman in your place would doubtless have done the same thing! What I desire to know is why you are here in Cornwall. What has happened to make this journey seem necessary to you?"

"Listen!" she continued. "I want you to know how thoroughly you have succeeded. Before you came, Lumley and I were living together decently enough, and, as hundreds of others live, with outside interests for our chief distraction. You came, a friend! You were very subtle, very skillful! You never spoke a word of affection to me, but you managed things so that - people talked. You encouraged Lumley to speculate - not in actual words, perhaps, but by suggestion. Then you lent me money. Lumley, my husband, let me borrow from you. Everyone knew that we were ruined; everyone knew where the money came from that set us right. So misery has been piled upon misery. Lumley has lost his self respect, he is losing his ambition, he is deteriorating every day. I - how can I do anything else but despise him? He let me, his wife, come to your rooms to borrow money from you. Do you think I can ever forget that? Do you think that he can? Don't you know that the memory of it is dragging us apart, must keep us apart always - always?"

Wingrave leaned a little forward. His hands were clasped upon the handle of his stick.

"All that you tell me," he remarked coldly, "might equally well have been said in London! I do not wish to seem inhospitable, but I am still waiting to know why you have taken an eight hours' journey to recite a few fairly obvious truths. Your relations with your husband, frankly, do not interest me. The deductions which society may have drawn concerning our friendship need scarcely trouble you, under the circumstances."

Then again the light was blazing in her eyes.

"Under the circumstances!" she repeated. "I know what you mean. It is true that you have asked for nothing. It is true that all this time you have never spoken a single word which all the world might not hear, you have never even touched my fingers, except as a matter of formality. Once I was the woman you loved - and I - well you know! Is this part of your scheme of torture, to play with me as though we were marionettes, you and I, with sawdust in our veins, dull, lifeless puppets! Well, it is finished - your vengeance! You may reap the harvest when you will! Publish my letters, prove yourself an injured man. Take a whip in your hand if you like, and I will never flinch. But, for heaven's sake, remember that I am a woman! I am willing to be your slave, nurse you, wait upon you, follow you about! What more can your vengeance need? You have made me despise my husband, you have made me hate my life with him! You have forced me into a remembrance of what I have never really forgotten - and oh! Wingrave," she added, opening her arms to him with a little sob, "if you send me away, I think that I shall kill myself. Wingrave!"

There was a note of despair in her last cry. Her arms fell to her side. Wingrave was on his way to the further end of the room. He rang the bell and turned towards her.

"Listen," he said calmly, "you will return to London tonight. If ever I require you, I shall send for you - and you will come. At present I do not. You will return to your husband. Understand!"

"Yes," she gasped, "but -"

He held out his hand. Morrison was at the door.

"Morrison," he said, "you will order the motor to be round in half an hour to take Lady Ruth to Truro, She has to catch the London express. You will go with her yourself, and see that she has a reserved carriage. If, by any chance, you should miss the train, order a special."

"Very good, sir."

"And tell the cook to send in tea and wine, and some sandwiches, in ten minutes."

Once more they were alone. Lady Ruth rose slowly to her feet and, trembling in every limb, she walked down the room and fell on her knees before Wingrave.

"Wingrave," she said, "I will go away. I will do all that you tell me; I will wear my chains bravely, and hold my peace. But before I go, for heaven's sake, say a kind word, look at me kindly, kiss me, hold my hands; anything, anything, anything to prove to me that you are not a dead man. I could bear unkindness, reproaches, abuse. I can bear anything but this deadly coldness. It is becoming a horror to me! Do, Wingrave - do!"

She clasped his hand - he drew it calmly away.

"Lady Ruth," he said, "you have spoken the truth. I am a dead man. I have no affections; I care neither for you nor for any living being. All that goes to the glory and joy of life perished in that uncountable roll of days, when the sun went out, and inch by inch the wall rose which will divide me forever from you and all the world. Frankly, it was not I who once loved you. It was the man who died in prison. His flesh and bones may have survived - nothing else!"

She rose slowly to her feet. Her eyes seemed to be dilating.

"There is another woman!" she exclaimed softly. Her voice was like velvet, but the agony in her face was unmistakable.

"There is no other woman," he answered.

She stood quite still.

"She is here with you now," she cried. "Who is it, Wingrave? Tell me the truth!"

"The truth is already told," he answered. "Except my cook and her assistants, there is not a woman in the house!"

Again she listened. She gave a little hoarse cry, and Wingrave started. Out in the hall a girl's clear laugh rang like a note of music to their ears.

"You lie!" she cried fiercely. "You lie! I will know who she is."

Suddenly the door was thrown open! Juliet stood there, her hands full of roses, her face flushed and brilliant with smiles.

"How delightful to find you here!" she exclaimed, coming swiftly across to Wingrave. "I do hope you won't mind my coming. Normandy is off, and I have nowhere else to go."

She saw Lady Ruth and stopped.

"Oh! I beg your pardon!" she exclaimed. "I did not know."

"This is Lady Ruth Barrington," Wingrave said; "my ward, Miss Juliet Lundy."

"Your - ward?" Lady Ruth said, gazing at her intently.

Juliet nodded.

"Sir Wingrave has been very kind to me since I was a child," she said softly. "He has let me live here with Mrs. Tresfarwin, and I am afraid I sometimes forget that it is not really my home. Am I in the way?" she asked, looking wistfully towards Wingrave.

"By no means!" he exclaimed. "Lady Ruth is just going. Will you see that she has some tea or something?"

Lady Ruth laughed quietly.

"I think," she said, "that it is I who am in the way! I should love some tea, if there is time, but whatever happens, I must not miss that train."

A DREAM OF PARADISE

It seemed to Wingrave that the days which followed formed a sort of hiatus in his life - an interlude during which some other man in his place, and in his image, played the game of life to a long-forgotten tune. He moved through the hours as a man in a maze, unrecognizable to himself, half unconscious, half heedless of the fact that the garments of his carefully cultivated antagonism to the world and to his fellows had slipped very easily from his unresisting shoulders. The glory of a perfect English midsummer lay like a golden spell upon the land. The moors were purple with heather, touched here and there with the fire of the flaming gorse, the wind blew always from the west, the gardens were ablaze with slowly bursting rhododendrons. Every gleam of coloring, every breath of perfume, seemed to carry him unresistingly back to the days of his boyhood. He fished once more in the trout streams; he threw away his stick, and tramped or rode with Juliet across the moors. At night time she sang or played with the windows open, Wingrave himself out of sight under the cedar trees, whose perfume filled with aromatic sweetness the still night air. Piles of letters came every day, which he left unopened upon his study table. Telegrams followed, which he threw into the wastepaper basket. Juliet watched the accumulating heap with amazement.

E. Phillips Oppenheim

"Whatever do people write to you so much for?" she asked one morning, watching the stream of letters flow out of the post bag.

Wingrave was silent for a moment. Her question brought a sudden and sharp sting of remembrance. Juliet knew him only as Sir Wingrave Seton. She knew nothing of Mr. Wingrave, millionaire.

"Advertisements, a good many of them," he said. "I must send for Aynesworth some day to go through them all."

"What fun!" she exclaimed. "Do send for him! He thinks that I am staying with Miss Pengarth, and I haven't written once since I got here!"

To Wingrave, it seemed that a chill had somehow stolen into the hot summer morning. His feet were very nearly upon the earth again.

"I forgot," he said, "that Aynesworth was - a friend of yours. He came and saw you often in London?"

She smiled reflectively.

"He has been very, very kind," she answered. "He was always that, from the first time I saw you both. Do you remember? It was down in the lower gardens."

"Yes!" he answered, "I remember quite well."

"He was very kind to me then," she continued, "and you - well, I was frightened of you." She stopped for a moment and laughed. Her eyes were full of amazed reminiscence. "You were so cold and severe! I never could have dreamed that, after all, it was you who were going to be the dearest, most generous friend I could ever have had! Do you know, Walter - I mean Mr. Aynesworth - isn't very pleased with me just now?"

"Why not?"

"He cannot understand why I will not tell him my guardian's name. I think it worries him."

"You would like to tell him?" Wingrave asked.

She nodded.

"I think so," she answered.

Wingrave said no more, but after breakfast he went to his study alone. Juliet found him there an hour later, sitting idly in front of his table. His great pile of correspondence was still untouched. She came and sat on the edge of the table.

"What are we going to do this morning, please?" she asked.

Wingrave glanced towards his letters.

"I am afraid," he said, "that I must spend the day here!"

She looked at him blankly.

"Not really!" she exclaimed. "I thought that we were going to walk to Hanging Tor?"

Wingrave took up a handful of letters and let them fall through his fingers. He had all the sensations of a man who is awakened from a dream of Paradise to face the dull tortures of a dreary and eventless life. His eyes were set in a fixed state. An undernote of despair was in his tone.

"You know we arranged it yesterday," she continued eagerly, "and if you are going to send for Mr. Aynesworth, you needn't bother about these letters yourself, need you?"

He turned and regarded her deliberately. Her forehead was wrinkled a little with disappointment, her brown eyes were filled with the soft light of confident appeal. Tall and elegantly slim, there was yet something in the graceful lines of her figure which reminded him forcibly that the days of her womanhood had indeed arrived.

She wore a plain white cambric dress and a simple, but much beflowered hat; the smaller details of her toilet all indicated the correct taste and instinctive coquetry of her French descent. And she was beautiful! Wingrave regarded her critically and realized, perhaps for the first time, how beautiful. Her eyes were large and clear, and her eyebrows delicately defined. Her mouth, with its slightly humorous curl, was a little large, but wholly delightful. The sun of the last few weeks had given to her skin a faint, but most becoming, duskiness. Under his close scrutiny, a flush of color stole into her cheeks. She laughed not altogether naturally.

"You look at me," she said, "as though I were someone strange!"

"I was looking," he answered, "for the child, the little

black-frocked child, you know, with the hair down her back, and the tearful eyes. I don't think I realized that she had vanished so completely."

"Not more completely," she declared gaily, "than the gloomy gentleman who frowned upon my existence and resented even my gratitude. Although," she added, leaning a little towards him, "I am very much afraid that I see some signs of a relapse today. Don't bother about those horrid letters. Let me tell Mrs. Tresfarwin to pack us up some lunch, and take me to Hanging Tor, please!"

Wingrave laughed a little unsteadily as he rose to his feet. One day more, then! Why not? The end would be soon enough! . . .

Sooner, perhaps, than even he imagined, for that night Aynesworth came, pale and travel-stained, with all the volcanic evidences of a great passion blazing in his eyes, quivering in his tone. The day had passed to Wingrave as a dream, more beautiful even than any in the roll of its predecessors. They sat together on low chairs upon the moonlit lawn, in their ears the murmur of the sea; upon their faces, gathering strength with the darkness, the night wind, salt and fragrant with all the sweetness of dying flowers. Wingrave had never realized more completely what still seemed to him this wonderful gap in his life. Behind it all, he had a subconsciousness that he was but taking a part in some mystical play; yet with an abandon which, when he stopped to think of it, astonished him, he gave himself up without effort or scruple to this most amazing interlude. All day he had talked more than ever before; the flush on his cheeks was like the flush of wine or the sun which had fired his blood. As he had talked the more, so had she grown the more silent. She was sitting now with her hands clasped and her head thrown back, looking up at the stars with unseeing eyes.

"You do not regret Normandy, then?" he asked.

"No!" she murmured. "I have been happy here. I have been happier than I could ever have been in Normandy."

He turned and looked at her with curious intentness.

"My experience," he said thoughtfully, "of young ladies of your age is somewhat limited. But I should have thought that you would have found it - lonely."

"Perhaps I am different, then," she murmured. "I have never been lonely here - all my life!"

"Except," he reminded her, "when I knew you first."

"Ah! But that was different," she protested. "I had no home in those days, and I was afraid of being sent away."

It was in his mind then to tell her of the envelope with her name upon it in his study, but a sudden rush of confusing thoughts kept him silent. It was while he was laboring in the web of this tangled dream of wild but beautiful emotions that Aynesworth came. A pale, tragic figure in his travel-stained clothes, and face furrowed with anxiety, he stood over them almost before they were aware of his presence.

"Walter ! " she cried, and sprang to her feet with

extended hands. Wingrave's face darkened, and the shadow of evil crept into his suddenly altered expression. It was an abrupt awakening this, and he hated the man who had brought it about.

Aynesworth held the girl's hands for a moment, but his manner was sufficient evidence of the spirit in which he had come. He drew a little breath, and he looked from one to the other anxiously.

"Is this - your mysterious guardian, Juliet?" he asked hoarsely.

She glanced at Wingrave questioningly. His expression was ominous, and the light faded from her own face. While she hesitated, Wingrave spoke.

"I imagine," he said, "that the fact is fairly obvious. What have you to say about it?"

"A good deal," Aynesworth answered passionately. "Juliet, please go away. I must speak to your guardian - alone!"

Again she looked at Wingrave. He pointed to the house.

"I think," he said, "that you had better go."

She hesitated. Something of the impending storm was already manifest. Aynesworth turned suddenly towards her.

"You shall not enter that house again, Juliet," he declared. "Stay in the gardens there, and presently you shall know why."

THE AWAKENING

Wingrave had risen to his feet. He was perfectly calm, but there was a look on his face which Juliet had never seen there before. Instinctively she drew a little away, and Aynesworth took his place between them.

"Are you mad, Aynesworth?" Wingrave asked coolly.

"Not now," Aynesworth answered. "I have been mad to stay with you for four years, to look on, however passively, at all the evil you have done. I've had enough of it now, and of you! I came here to tell you so."

"A letter," Wingrave answered, "would have been equally efficacious. However, since you have told me -"

"I'll go when I'm ready," Aynesworth answered, "and I've more to say. When I first entered your service and you told me what your outlook upon life was, I never dreamed but that the years would make a man of you again, I never believed that you could be such a brute as to carry out your threats. I saw you do your best to corrupt a poor, silly little woman, who only escaped ruin by a miracle; I saw you deal out what might have been irretrievable disaster to a young man just starting in life. Since your return to London, you have done as little good, and as much harm, with your millions as any man could."

Wingrave was beginning to look bored.

"This is getting," he remarked, "a little like melodrama. I have no objection to being abused, even in my own garden, but there are limits to my patience. Come to the point, if you have one."

"Willingly," Aynesworth answered. "I want you to understand this. I have never tried to interfere in any of your malicious schemes, although I am ashamed to think I have watched them without protest. But this one is different. If you have harmed, if you should ever dare to harm this child, as sure as there is a God above us, I will kill you!"

"What is she to you?" Wingrave asked calmly.

"She - I love her," Aynesworth answered. "I mean her to be my wife."

"And she?"

"She looks upon me as her greatest friend, her natural protector, and protect her I will - even against you."

Wingrave shrugged his shoulders.

"It seems to me," he said, "that the young lady is very well off as she is. She has lived in my house, and been taken care of by my servants. She has been relieved of all the material cares of life, and she has been her own mistress. I scarcely see how you, my young friend, could do better for her."

Aynesworth moved a step nearer to him. The veins on his forehead were swollen. His voice was hoarse with passion.

"Why have you done this for her?" he demanded, "secretly, too, you a man to whom a good action is a matter for a sneer, who have deliberately proclaimed yourself an evil-doer by choice and destiny? Why have you constituted yourself her guardian? Not from kindness for you don't know what it is; not from good nature for you haven't any. Why, then?"

Wingrave shrugged his shoulders.

"I admit," he remarked coolly, "that it does seem rather a problem; we all do unaccountable things at times, though."

"For your own sake," Aynesworth said fiercely, "I trust that this is one of the unaccountable things. For the rest, you shall have no other chance. I shall take her to Truro tonight."

"Are you sure that she will go?"

"I shall tell her the truth."

"And if she does not believe you?"

"She will! If you interfere, I shall take her by force."

"I interfere!" Wingrave remarked. "You need not be afraid of that. The affair as it stands is far too interesting. Call her, and make your appeal."

"I shall tell her the truth," Aynesworth declared.

"By all means! I shall remain and listen to my indictment. Quite a novel sensation! Call the young lady, by all means, and don't spare me."

Aynesworth moved a few steps up the path. He called to her softly, and she came through the little iron gates from the rose gardens. She was very pale, and there was a gleam in her eyes which was like fear. Aynesworth took her by the hand and led her forward.

"You must be brave, dear," he whispered. "I am compelled to say some disagreeable things. It is for your good. It is because I care for you so much."

She looked towards Wingrave. He was sitting upon the garden seat, and his face was absolutely expressionless. He spoke to her, and his cold, precise tone betrayed not the slightest sign of any emotion.

"Aynesworth," he remarked, "is going to tell you some interesting facts about myself. Please listen attentively as afterwards you will be called upon to make a somewhat important decision."

She looked at him a little wistfully and sighed. There was no trace any longer of her companion of the last few weeks. It was the stern and gloomy stranger of her earlier recollections who sat there with folded arms.

"Is it really necessary?" she asked.

"Absolutely," Aynesworth answered hurriedly. "It won't take long, but there are things which you must know."

"Very well," she answered, "I am listening."

E. Phillips Oppenheim

Aynesworth inclined his head towards the place where Wingrave sat.

"I will admit," he said, "that the man there, whom I have served for the last four years and more, never deceived me as to his real character and intentions. He had been badly treated by a woman, and he told me plainly that he entered into life again at war with his fellows. Where he could see an opportunity of doing evil, he meant to do it; where he could bring misery and suffering upon anyone with whom he came into contact, he meant to grasp the opportunity. I listened to him, but I never believed. I told myself that it would be interesting to watch his life, and to see the gradual, inevitable humanizing of the man. So I entered his service, and have remained in it until today."

He turned more directly towards Juliet. She was listening breathlessly to every word.

"Juliet," he said, "he has kept his word. I have been by his side, and I speak of the things I know. He has sought no one's friendship who has not suffered for it, there is not a man or woman living who owes him the acknowledgment of a single act of kindness. I have seen him deliberately scheme to bring about the ruin of a harmless little woman. I have seen him exact his pound of flesh, even at the cost of ruin, from a boy. I tell you, Juliet, of my own knowledge, that he has neither heart nor conscience, and that he glories in the evil that his hand finds to do. Even you must know something of his reputation - have heard something of his doings, under the name he is best known by in London - Mr. Wingrave, millionaire."

She started back as though in terror. Then she turned to

Wingrave, who sat stonily silent.

"It isn't true," she cried. "You are not - that man?"

He raised his eyes and looked at her. It seemed to her that there was something almost satanic in the smile which alone disturbed the serenity of his face.

"Certainly I am," he answered; "when I returned from America, it suited me to change my identity. You must not doubt anything that Mr. Aynesworth says. I can assure you that he is a most truthful and conscientious young man. I shall be able to give him a testimonial with a perfectly clear conscience."

Juliet shuddered as she turned away. All the joy of life seemed to have gone from her face.

"You are Mr. Wingrave - the Mr. Wingrave. Oh! I can't believe it," she broke off suddenly. "No one could have been so kind, so generous, as you have been to me."

She looked from one to the other of the two men. Both were silent, but whereas Aynesworth had turned his head away, Wingrave's position and attitude were unchanged. She moved suddenly over towards him. One hand fell almost caressingly upon his shoulder. She looked eagerly into his face.

"Tell me - that it isn't all true," she begged. "Tell me that your kindness to me, at least, was real - that you did not mean it to be for my unhappiness afterwards. Please tell me that. I think if you asked me, if you cared to ask me, that I could forgive everything else."

"Every vice, save one," Wingrave murmured, "Nature has lavished upon me. I am a poor liar. It is perfectly true that my object in life has been exactly as Aynesworth has stated it. I may have been more or less successful - Aynesworth can tell you that, too. As regards yourself -"

"Yes?" she exclaimed.

"I congratulate you upon your escape," Wingrave said. "Aynesworth is right. Association of any sort with me is for your evil!"

She covered her face with her hands. Even his tone was different. She felt that this man was a stranger, and a stranger to be feared. Aynesworth came over to her side and drew her away.

"I have a cart outside," he said. "I am going to take you to Truro -"

Wingrave heard the gate close after them - he heard the rumble of the cart in the road growing fainter and fainter. He was alone now in the garden, and the darkness was closing around him. He staggered to his feet. His face was back in its old set lines. He was once more at war with the world.

REVENGE IS - BITTER

At no time during his career did Wingrave appear before the public more prominently than during the next few months. As London began to fill up again, during the early part of October, he gave many and magnificent entertainments, his name figured in all the great social events, he bought a mansion in Park Lane which had been built for Royalty, and the account of the treasures with which he filled it read like a chapter from some modern Arabian Nights. In the city, he was more hated and dreaded than ever. His transactions, huge and carefully thought out, were for his own aggrandizement only, and left always in their wake ruin and disaster for the less fortunate and weaker speculators. He played for his own hand only, the camaraderie of finance he ignored altogether. In one other respect, too, he occupied a unique position amongst the financial magnates of the moment. All appeals on behalf of charity he steadily ignored. He gave nothing away. His name never figured amongst the hospital lists; suffering and disaster, which drew their humble contributions from the struggling poor and middle classes, left him unmoved and his check book unopened. In an age when huge gifts on behalf of charity was the fashionable road to the peerage, his attitude was all the more noticeable. He would give a thousand pounds for a piece of Sevres china which took his fancy; he would not give a thousand farthings

E. Phillips Oppenheim

to ease the sufferings of his fellows. Yet there were few found to criticize him. He was called original, a crank; there were even some who professed to see merit in his attitude. To both criticism and praise he was alike indifferent. With a cynicism with seemed only to become more bitter he pursued his undeviating and deliberate way.

One morning he met Lady Ruth on the pavement in Bond Street. She pointed to the vacant seat in her landau.

"Get in, please, for a few minutes," she said. "I want to talk to you. I will take you where you like."

They drove off in silence.

"You were not at the Wavertons' last night," he remarked.

"No!" she answered quietly. "I was not asked."

He glanced at her questioningly.

"I thought that you were so friendly," he said.

"I was," she answered. "Lady Waverton scarcely knows me now! It is the beginning of the end, I suppose."

"You are a little enigmatical this morning," he declared.

"Oh, no! You understand me very well," she answered. "Everybody knows that it is you who keep us going. Lumley has not got quite used to taking your money.

He has lost nearly all his ambition. Soon his day will have gone by. People shrug their shoulders when they speak of us. Two years ago the Wavertons were delighted to know me. Society seems big, but it isn't. There are no end of little sets, one inside the other. Two years ago, I was in the innermost, today I'm getting towards the outside edge. Look at me! Do you see any change?"

He scrutinized her mercilessly in the cold morning light.

"You look older," he said, "and you have begun to use rouge, which is a pity."

She laughed hardly.

"You think so? Well, I don't want Emily to see my hollow cheeks - or you! Are you satisfied, Wingrave?"

"I am afraid I don't understand -" he began.

"Don't lie," she interrupted curtly. "You do understand. This is your vengeance - very subtle and very crafty. Everything has turned out exactly as you planned. You have broken us, Wingrave! I thought myself a clever woman, but I might as well have tried to gamble with the angels. Why don't you finish it off now - make me run away with you?"

"It would bore us both," he answered calmly. "Besides, you wouldn't come!"

"I should, and you know that I would," she answered. "Everyone expects it of us. I think myself that it would be more decent."

He looked at her thoughtfully.

"You are a strange woman," he said. "I find it hard sometimes to understand you."

"Then you are a fool," she declared in a fierce little whisper. "You know what is underneath all my suffering, all my broken pride! You know that I was fool enough to keep the flame flickering - that I have cared always and for no one else!"

He stopped the carriage.

"You are the most original woman I ever met," he said quietly. "I neither wish to care nor be cared for by anyone. Go home to your husband, and tell him to buy Treadwells up to six."

That same afternoon Wingrave met Aynesworth and cut him dead. Something in the younger man's appearance, though, perplexed him. Aynesworth certainly had not the air of a successful man. He was pale, carelessly dressed, and apparently in ill health. Wingrave, after an amount of hesitation, which was rare with him, turned his car towards Battersea, and found himself, a few minutes later, mounting the five flights of stone steps. Juliet herself opened the door to him. She gave a little gasp when she saw who it was, and did not immediately invite him to enter.

"I am sorry," Wingrave said coldly, "to inflict this visit upon you. If you are alone, and afraid to ask me in, we can talk here."

Her cheeks became as flushed as a moment before they had been pale. She looked at him reproachfully, and, standing on one side to let him pass, closed the door behind him. Then she led the way into her sitting room.

"I am glad that you have come to see me," she said. "Won't you sit down?"

He ignored her invitation, and stood looking around him. There was a noticeable change in the little room. There were no flowers, some of the ornaments and the silver trifles from her table were missing. The place seemed to have been swept bare of everything, except the necessary furniture. Then he looked at her. She was perceptibly thinner, and there were black rings under her eyes.

"Where is Mrs. Tresfarwin?" he asked.

"In Cornwall," she answered.

"Why?"

"I could not afford to keep her here any longer."

"What are you doing for a living - painting still?"

She shook her head a little piteously.

"They can't sell any more of my pictures," she said. "I am trying to get a situation as governess or companion or - anything."

"When did you have anything to eat last?" he asked.

"Yesterday," she answered, and he was just in time to catch her. She had fainted.

He laid her upon the sofa, poured some water over her face, and fanned her with a newspaper. His expression of cold indifference remained unmoved. It was there in his face when she opened her eyes.

"Are you well enough to walk?" he asked.

"Quite, thank you," she answered. "I am so sorry!"

"Put on your hat," he ordered.

She disappeared for a few minutes, and returned dressed for the street. He drove her to a restaurant and ordered some dinner. He made her drink some wine, and while they waited he buried himself in a newspaper. They ate their meal almost in silence. Afterwards, Wingrave asked her a question.

"Where is Aynesworth?"

"Looking for work, I think," she answered.

"Why did you not stay down in Cornwall?"

"Miss Pengarth was away - and I preferred to return to London," she told him quietly.

"When are you going to marry Aynesworth?" he asked.

She looked down into her glass and was silent. He leaned a little towards her.

"Perhaps," he remarked quietly, "you are already married?"

Still she was silent. He saw the tears forced back from

her eyes. He heard the sob break in her throat. Yet he said nothing. He only waited. At last she spoke.

"Nothing is settled yet," she said, still without looking at him.

"I see no reason," he said calmly, "why, until that time, you should refuse to accept your allowance from Mr. Pengarth."

"I cannot take any more of your money," she answered. "It was a mistake from the first, but I was foolish. I did not understand."

His lip curled with scorn.

"You are one of those," he said, "who, as a child, were wise, but as a young woman with a little knowledge, become - a prig. What harm is my money likely to do you? I may be the Devil himself, but my gold is not tainted. For the rest, granted that I am at war with the world, I do not number children amongst my enemies."

She raised her eyes then, and looked him in the face.

"I am not afraid of you," she declared. "It is not that; but I have been dependent long enough. I will keep myself - or starve."

He shrugged his shoulders and paid the bill.

"My man," he said, "will take you wherever you like. I have a call to make close here."

They stood upon the pavement. She held out her hand a little timidly. Her eyes were soft and wistful.

"Goodbye, guardian," she said. "Thank you very much for my lunch."

"Ah!" he said gravely, "if you would let me always call myself that!"

She got into the car without a word. Wingrave walked straight back to his own house. Several people were waiting in the entrance hall, and the visitors' book was open upon the porter's desk. He walked through, looking neither to the right nor the left, crossed the great library, with its curved roof, its floor of cedar wood, and its wonderful stained-glass windows, and entered a smaller room beyond - his absolute and impenetrable sanctum. He rang the bell for his servant.

"Morrison," he said, "if you allow me to be disturbed by any living person, on any pretense whatever, until I ring, you lose your place. Do you understand?"

"Perfectly, sir."

Wingrave locked the door. The next hour belonged to himself alone . . .

When at last he rang the bell, he gave Morrison a note.

"This is to be delivered at once," he said.

The man bowed and withdrew. Wingrave, with his hands behind him, strolled out into the library. In a remote corner, a small spectacled person was busy writing at a table. Wingrave crossed the room and stood before him.

"Are you my librarian?" he asked.

The man rose at once.

"Certainly, sir," he answered. "My name is Woodall. You may have forgotten it. I am at work now upon a new catalogue."

Wingrave nodded.

"I have a quarto Shakespeare, I think," he said, "that I marked at Sotheby's, also a manuscript Thomas a Kempis, and a first edition of Herrick. I should like to see them."

"By all means," the man answered, hurrying to the shelves. "You have, also, a wonderful rare collection of manuscripts, purchased from the Abbey St. Jouvain, and a unique Horace. If you will permit me."

Wingrave spent half an hour examining his treasures, leaving his attendant astonished.

"A millionaire who understands!" he exclaimed softly as he resumed his seat. "Miraculous!"

Wingrave passed into the hall, and summoned his major domo.

"Show me the ballroom," he ordered, "and the winter garden."

The little man in quiet black clothes - Wingrave abhorred liveries - led him respectfully through rooms probably unequaled for magnificence in England. He spoke of the exquisite work of French and Italian artists; with a gesture almost of reverence he pointed out the carving in the wonderful white ballroom.

E. Phillips Oppenheim

Wingrave listened and watched with immovable face. Just as they had completed their tour, Morrison approached.

"Mr. Lumley and Lady Ruth Barrington are in the library, sir," he announced.

Wingrave nodded.

"I am coming at once," he said.

THE WAY OF PEACE

They awaited his coming in varying moods. Barrington was irritable and restless, Lady Ruth gave no signs of any emotion whatever. She had the air of a woman who had no longer fear or hope. Only her eyes were a little weary.

Barrington was walking up and down the room, his hands in his pockets, his eyes fixed upon his wife. Every now and then he glanced nervously towards her.

"Of course," he said, "if he wants a settlement - well, there's an end of all things. And I don't see why he shouldn't. He hasn't lent money out of friendship. He hates me - always has done, and sometimes I wonder whether he doesn't hate you too!"

Lady Ruth shivered a little. Her husband's words came to her with peculiar brutality. It was as though he were blaming her for not having proved more attractive to the man who held them in the hollow of his hand.

"Doesn't it strike you," she murmured, "that a discussion like this is scarcely in the best possible taste? We cannot surmise what he wants - what he is going to do. Let us wait!"

The door opened and Wingrave entered. To

E. Phillips Oppenheim

Barrington, who greeted him with nervous cordiality, he presented the same cold, impenetrable appearance; Lady Ruth, with quicker perceptions, noticed at once the change. She sat up in her chair eagerly. It was what she had prayed for, this - but was it for good or evil? Her eyes sought his eagerly. So much depended upon his first few words.

Wingrave closed the door behind him. His greetings were laconic as usual. He addressed Lady Ruth.

"I find myself obliged," he said, "to take a journey which may possibly be a somewhat protracted one. I wished, before I left, to see you and your husband. I sent for you together, but I wish to speak to you separately - to your husband first. You have often expressed a desire to see over my house, Lady Ruth. My major domo is outside. Will you forgive me if I send you away for a few minutes?"

Lady Ruth rose slowly to her feet.

"How long do you wish me to keep away?" she asked calmly.

"A few minutes only," he answered. "You will find me here when Parkinson has shown you round."

He held the door open and she passed out, with a single upward and wondering glance. Wingrave closed the door, and seated himself close to where Barrington was standing.

"Barrington," he said, "twenty years ago we were friends. Since then we have been enemies. Today, so far as I am concerned, we are neither."

Barrington started a little. His lips twitched nervously. He did not quite understand.

"I am sure, Wingrave -" he began.

Wingrave interrupted him ruthlessly.

"I give you credit," he continued, "for understanding that my attitude towards you since I - er - reappeared, has been inimical. I intended you to speculate, and you did speculate. I meant you to lose, and you have lost. The money I lent to your wife was meant to remain a rope around your neck. The fact that I lent it to her was intended to humiliate you, the attentions which I purposely paid to her in public were intended to convey a false impression to society - and in this, too, I fancy that I have been successful."

Barrington drew a thick breath - the dull color was mounting to his cheeks.

Wingrave continued calmly -

"I had possibly in my mind, at one time," he said, "the idea of drawing things on to a climax - of witnessing the final disappearance of yourself and your wife from the world - such as we know it. I have, however, ceased to derive amusement or satisfaction from pursuing what we may call my vengeance. Consequently, it is finished."

The light of hope leaped into Barrington's dull eyes, but he recognized Wingrave's desire for silence.

"A few feet to your left, upon my writing table," Wingrave continued, "you will find an envelope addressed to yourself. It contains a discharge, in full, for the money I have lent you. I have also ventured to place to your credit, at your own bank, a sum sufficient to give you a fresh start. When you return to Cadogan Square, or, at least, this evening, you will receive a communication from the Prime Minister, inviting you to become one of the International Board of Arbitration on the Alaskan question. The position, as you know, is a distinguished one, and if you should be successful, your future career should be assured."

Barrington broke down. He covered his face with his hands. Great sobs shook him. Wingrave waited for a few minutes, and then rose to his feet.

"Barrington," he said, "there is one thing more! What the world may say or think counts for very little. Society reverses its own judgments and eats its own words every day. A little success will bring it to your feet like a whipped dog. It is for yourself I say this, for yourself alone. There is no reason why you should hesitate to accept any service I may be able to render you. You understand me?"

Barrington's face was like the face of a young man. All the cloud of suspicion and doubts and fears was suddenly lifted. He looked through new eyes on to a new world.

"Thank God!" he exclaimed. "Not that I ever doubted it, Wingrave, but - thank God!" . . .

Barrington left the house radiant, - Lady Ruth and Wingrave were alone. She watched him close the door and turn towards her, with a new timidity. The color came and went in her pale cheeks, her eyes were no longer tired. When he turned towards her, she leaned to him with a little seductive movement of her body. Her hands stole out towards him.

"Wingrave!" she murmured.

His first action seemed to crush all the desperate joy which was rising fast in her heart. He took one hand, and he led her to a chair.

"Ruth," he said, "I have been talking to your husband. There are only a few words I want to say to you."

"There are only three I want to hear from you," she murmured, and her eyes were pleading with him passionately all the time. "It seems to me that I have been waiting to hear them all my life. Wingrave, I am so tired - and I am losing - I want to leave it all!"

"Exactly," he answered cheerfully, "what you are going to do. You are going to America with your husband."

"What do you mean?" she asked sharply.

He shrugged his shoulders.

"I am rather tired of the game," he said, "that is all. I am like the child who likes to build up again the house of bricks which he has thrown down. I have procured for your husband a seat on the Alaskan Board. It is a very distinguished position, and you will find that it will entail considerable social obligations in America. When you return, he will be able to claim a judgeship, or a place in the Government. You will find things go smoothly enough then."

"But you!" she cried; "I want you!"

He looked at her gravely.

"Dear Lady Ruth," he said, "you may think so at this moment, but you are very much mistaken. What you really desire is a complete reconciliation with your husband and a place in the great world which no one shall be able to question. These things are arranged for you; also - these."

He handed her a little packet. She dropped it idly into her lap. She was looking steadfastly away from them.

"You are free from me now," he continued. "You will find life run quite smoothly, and I do not think that you will be troubled with me when you come back from America. I have other plans."

"There was a slave," she murmured, "who grew to love her gaoler, and when they came to set her free and take her back to her own people - she prayed only to be left in her cell! Freedom for her meant a broken heart!"

"But that was fiction," he answered. "For you, freedom will mean other things. There is work for you to do, honorable work. You must fan the flame of your husband's ambition, you must see that he does justice to his great opportunities. You have your own battle to fight with society, but you have the winning cards for, before you go, you and your husband will be received as guests - well, by the one person whose decision is absolute."

She looked at him in amazement.

"My word of honor," he said quietly, "was enough for Lord Marendon. You will find things go smoothly with you."

"You are wonderful," she gasped, "but - you - you spoke of going away."

"I am going to travel," he said quietly, "rather a long journey. I have lived three lives, I am going to try a fourth!"

"Alone?" she asked.

"Quite alone," he answered.

"Tell me where you are going?" she begged.

"I cannot do that," he answered. "It is my secret."

She rose to her feet. She was very pale. She stood in front of him, and she laid her hands upon his shoulders.

"Wingrave," she said, "I will obey. I will live the life you have shown me, and I will live it successfully. But I will know this. Who is it that has succeeded where I have failed?"

"I do not understand you," he answered.

"You do!" she declared, "and I will know. For years you have been a man with a shell upon your heart. Every good impulse, every kind thought seemed withered up. You were absolutely cold, absolutely passionless! I have worn myself out trying to call you back to your own, to set the blood flowing once more in your veins, to break for one moment the barriers which you had set up against Nature herself. Some day, I felt that it must come - and it has! Who has done it, Wingrave? It is not - Emily?"

"Emily!" he exclaimed. "I have not seen her for months. She has no interest for me - she never had."

"Then tell me who it is!"

"Nature unaided," he answered carelessly. "Human intervention was not necessary. It was the swing of the pendulum, Ruth, the eternal law which mocks our craving for content. I had no sooner succeeded in my new capacity - than the old man crept out."

"But Nature has her weapons always," she protested. "Wingrave, was it the child?"

He touched the electric bell. Taking her hands, he bent down and kissed them.

"Dear lady," he said, "goodbye - good fortune! Conquer new worlds, and remember - white is your color, and Paquin your one modiste. Morrison, Lady Barrington's carriage."

"LOVE SHALL MAKE ALL THINGS NEW"

Mr. Pengarth was loth to depart. He felt that all pretext for lingering was gone, that he had outstayed his welcome. Yet he found himself desperately striving for some excuse to prolong an interview which was to all effects and purposes concluded.

"I will do my best, Sir Wingrave," he said, reverting to the subject of their interview, "to study Miss Lundy's interests in every way. I will also see that she has the letter you have left for her within eight days from now. But if you could see you way to leave some sort of address so that I should have a chance of communicating with you, if necessary, I should assume my responsibilities with a lighter heart."

Wingrave gave vent to a little gesture of annoyance.

"My dear sir," he said, "surely I have been explicit enough. I have told you that, within a week from now, I shall be practically dead. I shall never return to England - you will never see me again. I have given life here a fair trial, and found it a failure. I am going to make a new experiment - and it is going to be in an unexplored country. You could not reach me there through the post. You, I think, would scarcely care to follow me. Let it go at that."

E. Phillips Oppenheim

Mr. Pengarth took up his bag with a sigh.

"Sir Wingrave," he said, "I am a simple man, and life with me has always been a very simple affair. I recognize the fact, of course, that I am not in a position to judge or to understand the mental attitude of one who, like yourself, has suffered and passed through great crises. But I cannot help wishing that you could find it possible to try, for a time, the quiet life of a countryman in this beautiful home of yours."

Wingrave shrugged his shoulders.

"Mr. Pengarth," he said, "no two men are born alike into this world. Some are blessed with a contented mind, some are wanderers by destiny. You will forgive me if I do not discuss the matter with you more fully. My journey, wherever and whatever it is, is inevitable."

Mr. Pengarth was braver than he had ever been in his life.

"Sir Wingrave," he said, "there is one journey which we must all take in God's good time. But the man who starts before he is called finds no welcome at the end. The greatest in life are those who are content to wait!"

"I am not in the least disposed to doubt it, Mr. Pengarth," Wingrave said calmly. "Now I must really send you away."

So Mr. Pengarth went, but Wingrave was not long destined to remain in solitude. There was a sound of voices in the hall, Morrison's protesting, another insistent. Then the door opened, and Wingrave looked up with darkening face, which did not lighten when he recognized the intruder.

"Aynesworth!" he exclaimed, "what are you doing here? What do you want with me?"

"Five minutes," Aynesworth answered, "and I mean to have it. You may as well tell your man to take his hand off my shoulder."

Wingrave nodded to Morrison.

"You can go," he said. "Come back when I ring."

They were alone! Aynesworth threw down his hat and crossed the room until he was within a few feet of Wingrave.

"Well, sir?"

Aynesworth laughed a little unnaturally.

"I had to come," he said. "It is humiliating, but the discipline is good for me! I was determined to come and see once more the man who has made an utter and complete fool of me."

Wingrave eyed him coldly.

"If you would be good enough to explain," he began.

"Oh, yes, I'll explain," Aynesworth answered. "I engaged myself to you as secretary, didn't I, and I told you the reason at the time? I wanted to make a study of you. I wanted to trace the effect of your long period of isolation upon your subsequent actions. I entered upon

E. Phillips Oppenheim

my duties - how you must have smiled at me behind my back! Never was a man more completely and absolutely deceived. I lived with you, was always by your side, I was there professedly to study your actions and the method of them. And yet you found it a perfectly simple matter to hoodwink me whenever you chose!"

"In what respect?" Wingrave asked calmly.

"Every respect!" Aynesworth answered. "Let me tell you two things which happened to me yesterday. I met a young New York stockbroker, named Nesbitt, in London, and in common with all London, I suppose, by this time, I learnt the secret of all those anonymous contributions to the hospitals and other charitable causes during the last year."

"Go on," Wingrave said.

"I have come here on purpose to tell you what I think you are," Aynesworth said. "You are the greatest hypocrite unhanged. You affect to hate your fellows and to love evil-doers. You deceived the whole world, and you deceived me. I know you now for what you are. You conceived your evil plans, but when the time came for carrying them out, you funked it every time. You had that silly little woman on the steamer in your power, and you yourself, behind your own back, released her with that Marconigram to her husband, sent by yourself. You brought the boy Nesbitt face to face with ruin, and to his face you offered him no mercy. Behind his back you employ a lawyer to advance him your own money to pay your own debt. You decline to give a single penny away in charity and, as stealthily as possible, you give away in one year greater sums than any other man has ever parted with. You decline to help the poor little orphan child of the village organist, and secretly you have her brought up in your own home, and stop the sale of your pictures for the sake of the child whom you had only once contemptuously addressed. Can you deny any one of these things?"

"No!" Wingrave answered quietly, "I cannot."

"And I thought you a strong man," Aynesworth continued, aggrieved and contemptuous. "I nearly went mad with fear when I heard that it was you who were the self-appointed guardian of Juliet Lundy. I looked upon this as one more, the most diabolical of all your schemes!"

Wingrave rose to his feet, still and grave.

"Aynesworth," he said, "this interview does not interest me. Let us bring it to an end. I admit that I have made a great failure of my life. I admit that I have failed in realizing the ambitions I once confided to you. I came out from prison with precisely those intentions, and I was conscious of nothing in myself or my nature to prevent my carrying them out. It seems that I was mistaken. I admit all this, but I do not admit your right to force yourself into my presence and taunt me with my failure. You served me well enough, but you were easily hoodwinked, and our connection is at an end. I have only one thing to say to you. I am leaving this part of the world altogether. I shall not return. That child has some foolish scruples about taking any more of my money. That arises through your confounded interference. She is poor, almost in want. If you should fail her now -"

Aynesworth interrupted with a hoarse little laugh.

"Wingrave," he said, "are you playing the simpleton? If Juliet will not take your money, why should she take mine?"

Wingrave came out from his place. He was standing now between Aynesworth and the door.

"Aynesworth," he said, "do I understand that you are not going to marry the child?"

"I? Certainly not!" Aynesworth answered.

Wingrave remained quite calm, but there was a terrible light in his eyes.

"Now, for the first time, Aynesworth," he said, "I am glad that you are here. We are going to have a complete understanding before you leave this room. Juliet Lundy, as my ward, was, I believe, contented and happy. It suited you to disturb our relations, and your excuse for doing so was that you loved her. You took her away from me, and now you say that you do not intend to marry her. Be so good as to tell me what the devil you do mean!"

Aynesworth laughed a little bitterly.

"You must excuse me," he said, "but a sense of humor was always my undoing, and this reversal of our positions is a little odd, isn't it? I am not going to marry Juliet Lundy because she happens not to care for me in that way at all. My appearance is scarcely that of a joyous lover, is it?"

Wingrave eyed him more closely. Aynesworth had certainly fallen away from the trim and carefully turned out young man of a few months back. He was paler, too, and looked older.

"I do not understand this," Wingrave said.

"I do!" Aynesworth answered bitterly. "There is someone else?"

"Someone whom I do not know about?" Wingrave said, frowning heavily. "Who is he, Aynesworth?"

Aynesworth shrugged his shoulders. He said nothing. Wingrave came a step nearer to him.

"You may as well tell me." he said quietly, "for I shall postpone my journey until I know the whole truth."

"It is not my secret," Aynesworth answered. "Ask her yourself!"

"Very well," Wingrave declared, "I will. I shall return to London tonight."

"It is not necessary," Aynesworth remarked.

Wingrave started.

"You mean that she is here?" he exclaimed.

Aynesworth drew him towards the window.

"Come," he said, "you shall ask her now."

Wingrave hesitated for a moment. An odd nervousness

seemed to have taken possession of him.

"I do not understand this, Aynesworth," he said. "Why is she here?"

"Go and ask her your question," Aynesworth said. "Perhaps you will understand then."

Wingrave went down the path which led to the walled garden and the sea. The tall hollyhocks brushed against his knees; the air, as mild as springtime, was fragrant with the perfume of late roses. Wingrave took no note of these things. Once more he seemed to see coming up the path the little black-frocked child, with the pale face and the great sad eyes; it was she indeed who rose so swiftly from the hidden seat. Then Wingrave stopped short for he felt stirring within him all the long repressed madness of his unlived manhood. It was the weakness against which he had fought so long and so wearily, triumphant now, so that his heart beat like a boy's, and the color flamed into his cheeks. And all the time she was coming nearer, and he saw that the child had become a woman, and it seemed to him that all the joy of life was alight in her face, and the one mysterious and wonderful secret of her sex was shining softly out of her eager eyes. So that, after all, when they met, Wingrave asked her no questions. She came into his arms with all the graceful and perfect naturalness of a child who has wandered a little away from home . . . .

"I am too old for you, dear," he said presently, as they wandered about the garden, "much too old."

"Age," she answered softly, "what is that? What have we to do with the years that are past? It is the years to come only which we need consider, and to think of them makes me almost tremble with happiness. You are much too rich and too wonderful a personage for a homeless orphan like me; but," she added, tucking her arm through his with a contented little sigh, "I have you, and I shall not let you go!"

E. Phillips Oppenheim